What They Don't Tell You About Failing

By J.K. Weyant

This is a work of fiction. Names, characters, organizations, events, and incidents are either products of the author's imagination or are used fictitiously.

Table of Contents

Prologue
Chapter One: The Move Back
Chapter Two: Exposing Oneself to New Things
Chapter Three: Monica the Criminal
Chapter Four: The Rescue Rex
Chapter Five: Throwing a Shit Fit
Chapter Six: One Point for Chris, Zero for Monica
Chapter Seven: Birds of a Feather
Chapter Eight: The Almost Kiss
Chapter Nine: Road Trip to my Feelings
Chapter Ten: I've Already Seen Your Boobs
Chapter Eleven: What We Don't Know Will Hurt Us
Chapter Twelve: You're Infuriating
Chapter Thirteen: A Rescheduled Date
Chapter Fourteen: A Kiss Worth Waiting Eight Years For
Chapter Fifteen: You Should Have Told Me
Chapter Sixteen: Temporary House Guest
Chapter Seventeen: Stay Tonight
Chapter Eighteen: Yes, We're Together
Chapter Nineteen: Satan Needs Earmuffs
Chapter Twenty: Girls Night In
Chapter Twenty-One: I'm Not Wearing Panties
Chapter Twenty-Two: Homecoming
Chapter Twenty-Three: Once a Failure, Always a Failure
Chapter Twenty-Four: Past Secrets
Chapter Twenty-Five: Is Hell a Dry or Humid Heat?
Chapter Twenty-Six: The Make Up
Epilogue
Trigger Warnings
Author's Note
Acknowledgements
About the Author

Dedication

This book is for all the people who work at animal rescues and sacrifice their time, money, and their hearts.

Also, to our "first baby", Tango. You were the best boy.

Trigger Warning list will be at the end of the book due to spoilers. Please review before reading if you have any concerns.

Prologue

You know that saying, if you keep falling, get back on that horse? Or maybe if you fall seven times, get up eight? Yeah, the people who said that were the biggest assholes. No one said I'd *actually* be falling off a horse. I thought it would be a metaphorical horse, not a real one.

My body slammed to the ground, dust floating around me. I puffed out a breath I didn't even know I had left in my body. I think at some point I'd popped a lung.

Was that possible? It felt like it.

I groaned and I sat up on my elbows just in time to see the brown horse galloping off towards the edge of the pen, his ears back. I slowly stood up and glared at him as I brushed the dust off my already raggedy clothes. My black jeans officially had rips in the knees, and though I didn't spend hundreds of dollars on them, twenty dollars at a country store was still twenty dollars.

"Chicken shit!" I yelled towards the horse in the late evening light.

Just like everything else in my life, I was failing. To Sam, that wasn't a big surprise and to the people of Cold Spring, it was normal. To me, I was pissed. I failed at my relationships, my job, my family…even at horse training, which I shouldn't have been doing in the first place. Had Grandma still been around, she would have been standing beside me and encouraging me to not give up.

"Stop your complaining. No one is going to help you back up when you fall. You have to do it yourself. So do it."

Grandma was right, no one had ever helped me up when I fell, and no one was about to now. It was my job to do it.

Monica Locklear stops failing as of today.

I walked over and grabbed the reins of the devil horse. "We are going to work together if it's the last thing I do. You will not be another failure for me, got it? You and I are going to be successful."

He shook his head and neighed. I took that as a good sign as I put my hands onto the horn of the saddle and pulled myself up. He paused, as if we had a breakthrough. As if this was finally him realizing I wasn't here to hurt him but to help him.

Yes! This was it. I did it!

Before I could celebrate any more, I felt him buck and of course I went flying.

My back hit the ground again but this time I lay there and stared up at the fading blue sky in the evening light.

Okay, so maybe today is another failure day. There's always tomorrow.

Chapter One

The Move Back

"You're fired," my boss Charlotte said. Her tone was nonchalant, as if I hadn't just handed her the usual soy latte with two pumps of vanilla that was always just the right temperature.

"What?" I asked in surprise, the papers in my hands still warm from the copier.

Charlotte sat back in her chair. She was my mother's age, but we'd connected when I started working with her as an intern after college. We were similar in our drive and spirit, and I thought I would spend most of my career working for her.

She sighed and adjusted the pen that held her gray hair in a bun. "I'm sorry, kid. We got bought out. They are laying most of us off. Your position was first on the chopping block. I wish it weren't true, but I had no say in this," she explained with some remorse. I could hear it in her voice, but she was blunt and factual, and I had always admired that about her. Up until now.

Could you do a little sugar coating?

I sat down heavily in the chair across from her, the papers in my hand almost falling to the floor. "Laid off?"

She shrugged. "Your position is being eliminated, Monica. You know I'm not good at adjusting words to fit everyone. You know what I mean."

My mouth opened and I looked down at my black pumps with the red soles. They cost nearly two paychecks when I was an intern. I'd saved for months to buy them so I would be respected here in San Diego. Yes, it had definitely gotten me more attention. I was already five foot ten, so with the added heels, I was over six feet tall. People often mistook me for a model with my slim build and long black hair.

"I don't understand. I have rent…San Diego isn't cheap–"

"I'm well aware of that, but I can't stop this. It's effective immediately. You can clean out your desk and leave. I'll write a reference for your next job." She looked back to her computer screen and was silent for a second before looking back up as if shocked to see me still sitting there. "Oh, and Monica..." This was definitely forced, and her smile was even more fake, but I couldn't even blame her. It wasn't like Charlotte to easily give compliments or sympathy. "I know you'll do great someplace else."

"Thanks," I mumbled.

I placed the papers on her desk then went back to my cubicle where I stared at my computer screen. It was a picture of a beautiful beach scene. I had been saving up to go on vacation with my boyfriend, but I'd broken up with him the previous year and never got to go. After attending my brother's rehearsal and wedding without a guy, I had realized how much I wanted to find someone. And not someone like Jay–someone real and genuine. Jay was a male model and was more concerned about his looks than his girlfriend of two years. He wasn't the first guy I'd dated who was more into his appearance than he was into me, but I vowed, he'd be the last.

I'd grown up in California. When I was in eighth grade and my grandmother got sick, my father decided to move us to Cold Spring to be closer to her. A lot of my cousins and family were there along with the Native American tribe my father grew up in. They always had something going on and my parents were involved most of the time. So was my big brother, Sam. I enjoyed going to the events sometimes, but I craved my life back in California.

As soon as I graduated, I left for college in San Diego. I lived out my dreams by getting the best life I could have in California. Little did I know that that life would come to a screeching halt.

An email popped up on my computer from Charlotte that contained severance package information and a sad face next to it.

Was this my sign to move back to Cold Spring? Sam had married Emma the previous year and during the time they were engaged, Emma and I got close. She felt more like a sister than a sister-in-law. A few months after their wedding, she called me to tell me they were pregnant. My niece, Savannah, had been born earlier this year and I'd only gotten to meet her once in person. I wanted to be a part of her life and not be the long-distance aunt who only visited for holidays. Maybe it was time to move back and start fresh.

Two weeks later, I packed all my belongings and had them shipped to Cold Spring. I ended my month-to-month lease and flew back to New York. The severance package from my job was decent, thanks to Charlotte. The money was already collecting interest in my account before I even got on the plane. It was comforting to know I had that cushion so I could take my time finding a new job.

As soon as I got to Cold Spring, I rented a car and got a room at a local hotel. My first step was getting my own place. It didn't take long, and I easily found a two-bedroom apartment above the bagel shop in town. Billy, my landlord, informed me I could only have small pets in the place with a fee, I could park along the street except when they did street cleaning, and I could get free bagels on Fridays. I let him know there was no way I'd ever have an animal so no issues with that, no problem about parking along the street, and the free bagels on Friday was definitely something I would take advantage of.

The apartment was modern with high ceilings and an updated kitchen and living space. It even had a walk-in closet and a nice place for the shoe collection that I'd brought with me. It didn't take long to unpack and settle in. It was perfect! It was as if everything was falling into place.

I might have failed at being in San Diego, but I vowed I wouldn't fail here, and this was proof that my luck was back! Well, did I ever really have any luck?

Sam, Emma, and my parents didn't know I'd moved back but thought I was just visiting. After I settled down in my new place, I texted them to meet me at the coffee shop down the street. I'd become good at poop sandwiches since my parents were notoriously known to shame me for failing at anything. I figured I could tell them I got fired from my job, moved back to Cold Spring, and I was planning to be the best daughter, sister, and sister-in-law to all of them and the coolest aunt to Savannah. That's a pretty good poop sandwich if you asked me.

I hadn't come back from California often, except on holidays and special events like Emma's bachelorette party and their wedding. I knew my parents had wanted me home more, but they were proud that I had gone to college and gotten a good job. I was sure they wouldn't be thrilled about being fired. They would see it as a failure, even if my company had been sold, and my job eliminated. They'd see it as if I'd done a shit job and the company let me go. Maybe if I kept telling myself that, I'd be prepared for the critical blow from them.

I arrived early at the coffee shop, with my laptop in hand, to look for jobs in town. It was a warm June day in New York, so I wore a short black dress and my favorite pair of name brand sandals that had gold and jewels on the top. The sandals cost me a whopping three hundred dollars, but I loved looking at them. Most of my clothing had been switched out for designer brands when I moved to San Diego. I learned quickly that to be taken seriously, I needed an expensive, tasteful wardrobe.

I'd visited Spring Awake once when I was home for Emma and Sam's wedding. As I walked in a few people looked up at me while sipping their coffee or eating a pastry or sandwich, and I realized I recognized some of them.

Great. People from high school.

I looked straight ahead and found a small table that had the perfect view out a window. I booted up my laptop then glanced at the menu displayed on the wall behind the counter. I decided to order something while my laptop came on.

"Can I get you something to drink?" a female voice asked as I walked up to the counter.

I blinked and looked at her, then realized she was familiar.

Erin Jones.

She'd been in the band, and I'd teased her about her braces several times.

She didn't have braces now though. She was thin and beautiful with rich brown hair and green eyes. She wasn't the chunky girl I'd known from high school. I vaguely remembered hearing she'd opened Spring Awake a few years ago but hadn't paid much attention.

"Hi, Erin," I said with a genuine smile. "It's been a few years."

She looked surprised I'd remembered her, but her gaze narrowed slightly. "Do I know you?"

I knew she knew me. She wasn't stupid. She was trying to make me feel small. Yikes…I guess she hadn't gotten over my teasing about her braces.

"Monica Locklear."

"Ah, yes. What would you like to drink?"

Well, I guess small talk wasn't going to happen. I ordered something off the menu and a pastry from the glass case. She grabbed it out and placed it on a plate then handed it over the counter.

"I'll bring your coffee," she said stiffly and turned her back before I could say thank you.

I rolled my eyes then went over to my laptop and took a big bite of the chocolate brownie.

I really hoped she wouldn't spit in my coffee for what I'd done to her years earlier. That'd really make my life worse than it already was. If only Erin knew my fall from grace would put me below her. At least she had a job.

Maybe it wasn't such a good idea to have moved home. Maybe I should have just moved to New York City.

Yeah right. The cost of living there was just as bad as San Diego.

"Monica?" The squeal was from a high-pitched voice and one I remembered all too well. I turned in my seat and saw my high school friend, Sophie. She was still the petite, bleach blonde girl that all of us had envied. Except instead of pom-poms in her hands, she had a baby on her hip.

"Sophie! Oh wow!" I stood up and we embraced as much as we could with the little blonde-haired girl clinging to her.

By the time I got to high school, I was a part of the popular crowd with a few close girlfriends. Natalie, Sophie, and I had all been on the cheerleading squad together. Our last two years, Sophie and I had become co-captains. The three of us were inseparable. We were invited to all the parties, and everyone wanted to be friends with us.

"It's good to see you! Are you here visiting your parents? Natalie and I thought maybe we'd see you in town for Sam's wedding, but we didn't seem to catch you," she said with a smile. I realized she'd gotten lip injections.

I'd spent eight years in California and somehow had skipped that trend.

"I was only able to fly in for the rehearsal and wedding. I flew back out Sunday morning. I had to get back to San Diego for work on Monday," I explained.

Her eyes glittered with what I knew was envy. "You're still living in San Diego? That sounds so exciting! It's been eight years! It'd be easier to keep in contact if you posted on social media more!" she scolded.

I was very particular about what I posted. It had to be photos of me living my best life or none at all. I had an image to uphold, especially in San Diego. But now...what was my image? A photo in a coffee shop in the town where I spent my high school years? The town I'd been so quick to leave as soon as I graduated high school. I hated every minute of living in Cold Spring, and everyone knew it. The only people I hadn't hated were my grandma and...*him.*

"Any hot boyfriend back in Callie?"

Should I tell her? Just do it, Monica. Rip it off like waxing your legs.

"I actually moved back to Cold Spring this week. San Diego just wasn't working out for me anymore. I'm looking for a new adventure," I finally said.

She seemed stunned. "You're moving back here for good? I'm surprised. Natalie and I both thought you'd never come back to live in Cold Spring again after being in San Diego."

I raised an eyebrow at the judgment I heard from her. "San Diego just isn't for me anymore."

"But you had the perfect life, Monica. Why would you throw it away to come back here?"

I reeled back in surprise. "My life wasn't that great, so I didn't throw anything away, Sophie. If you feel that way about Cold Spring, why didn't you leave?"

She pressed her lips together and looked at her daughter. "I probably need to go. Good to see you." She took off to the register where she picked up her to-go order and flew past me without a second glance.

Erin came by with a large round cup of coffee with a leaf pattern poured into it.

"Thank you," I mumbled, taking a sip. I was rewarded with a very nice flavor, one that would beat even the most popular coffee shops in San Diego. Erin didn't leave my table and placed her hands on her hips looking at me.

"What pissed off Sophie?"

I put the cup down and looked at her. "My life choices. Care to add your opinion on my move back to Cold Spring?"

Erin's lip twitched with amusement. "No. Just as long as you don't voice yours on my life."

"Deal. This is a great cup of coffee," I murmured while taking another sip.

I searched for jobs for an hour and found none in Cold Spring. I'd found a few in New York City and Albany but I'd have to commute to them, and I wasn't about to try to do that in my tiny rental car. I looked around the room at the small coffee shop and even during lunch hour there wasn't a large lunch rush.

Did Erin market her business? Did she have a team? A social media page?

I looked her up online. She'd opened *Spring Awake* five years ago, but her website was "still under construction." It seemed like she had a lot of local customers, but she was in the perfect spot to bring in tourists, too.

Maybe I could do work for small businesses? Maybe build my own company and do it on the side? Would that generate enough money?

Emma! She was always posting on social media for her store, Feather Blue, but even she and her best friend, Brynn, couldn't always keep up. Especially since Brynn was managing the store a lot more now that Emma had Savannah. Brynn was still technically a newlywed too. She and Luke had gotten married last fall in Niagara Falls then had a big reception at their house. She probably wanted to spend more time with her husband, and I couldn't blame her. Luke was every girl's wet dream with sweet eyes, tall frame, big hands, and abs for days. If he'd been single during Sam and

Emma's engagement party, I would have put on the "Monica Charm" and wooed him right into my bed.

Feather Blue had become one of the most popular stores in Cold Spring since they'd found the diamonds in the old register that belonged to the previous jewelry store owners. Maybe I could convince Emma to let me do some marketing for her, for free at first, to see if I could get her more clicks, more business, more interest.

I shut the laptop and finished off my second coffee with a grin.

That's exactly what I was going to do! I had a plan!

The doorbell dinged and Emma and Sam came in together. Savannah was now three months and strapped to the front of Emma's chest. I only could see the patch of black hair sticking out. I waved to them and Emma gave me an awkward hug around Savannah. My sister-in-law was glowing with happiness and being a mother truly fit her well. She was a few years older than me, closer to Sam's age, and she had been in her senior year of high school when we'd moved here. We had barely even spoken until Sam started dating her. When I came to their rehearsal dinner and watched my big brother with her, I knew their love was true. It was probably what got me really thinking about Jay. He looked at himself the way Sam looked at Emma, but would he ever look at me that way? I realized quickly that was a hard no. I'd broken up with him a week after getting back to San Diego. I'd rather be alone than with someone who wasn't really interested in me.

"It's so good to see you!" Emma gushed and then Sam leaned in to give me a hug.

I glanced down at Savannah, who blinked a few times as she looked at me. She had dark blue eyes, a cute button nose, and darker skin that reminded me of Sam.

"She's even more beautiful than I remember," I whispered softly.

"Do you want to hold her?" Emma asked.

I'd come back about a month after Savannah was born and did hold her then, but she seemed so...breakable. I'd kept her for only a second before handing her over to my mother.

"No, it's okay. She looks rather comfortable on you," I said quickly, which made Emma laugh.

We sat down and Sam put his arm around Emma, and she leaned against him. It was sweet and made me happy for my big brother, but also envious.

"Where are you staying? You should come stay at our house! You shouldn't have to pay for a hotel!" Emma said.

I smiled. "Don't worry, I'm fine." I wasn't ready to tell them yet, not until Mom and Dad were here, but I also wasn't about to live with a new baby either. Weren't they little criers? "How are you guys? How's the store?"

Emma talked about the increase in sales that seemed to keep getting better and better every year. Brynn had covered for Emma while she was on maternity leave for twelve weeks. Mackayla, their full-time associate, had also helped out in her absence.

"Do you think you may need more marketing?" I inquired stealthily.

She thought for a moment. "Possibly. Brynn has been so busy with her photography and of course I'm busy with Savannah, we haven't had time to post on social media."

"There's our girl!"

I looked up to see my mother flowing into the coffee shop with her long hair clipped into a turquoise barrette. She was tall and lean with beautiful features. My father, always the stoic kind, had frown lines between his thick black eyebrows as he pulled two chairs over to the table. I hugged my mother tightly and smelled her familiar rose scent that reminded me of being a child. Then I hugged my dad, who patted me on the back; he wasn't a hugger.

When we all sat down, my father leaned his big frame back in the chair, crossed his arms and looked at all of us. He had always been a bit intimidating and not very approachable. Because I took after him in the looks department, I learned early on that if I didn't smile, I also gave that same vibe. It worked for me when I didn't want to talk to guys but trying to make friends, well, that kind of sucked.

Mom asked to hold baby Savannah and Emma gladly pulled her from the carrier to hand her over.

This was great. Savannah was going to be my buffer for the news! This was perfect.

"How long will you be in town?" my mother asked, as she cooed at the baby.

"Well," I started, looking at everyone. "That's why I wanted to talk to you all today. I moved back to Cold Spring!"

Everyone's jaws seemed to drop at the news.

"That's great!" Emma said first.

Dad and Sam frowned but Mom was the first to speak. "That's great, Mon! I'm a little surprised, as I'm sure everyone else is."

"What happened?" my dad asked. His deep voice reminded me of all the times he'd caught me sneaking out of my room to go to a party. I'd gotten a lot better at bullshitting my way out of things, but my dad always seemed to see right through me.

"I wanted a new start. I'm sick of San Diego and wanted to be around family. I already moved into an apartment, it's above the bagel shop a few doors down," I said, hopeful my father would stop there.

In Locklear fashion, he did not, and Sam joined in.

"Mon, you loved San Diego and your job and your life out there. Are you sure nothing happened?" Sam's prodding made my back stiffen but I looked at the curious eyes around me and caved.

"I was let go from my job. The company was sold, and my position was eliminated."

Mom's gasp was loud enough for everyone to hear.

"What about Jay?" Emma asked.

"I broke up with Jay a week after I came back from your wedding. It wasn't working out," I explained. I hadn't told them I'd been single for a while now. What had it been? A year now? God this dry spell sucked.

"Let go from your job?" Dad only heard that, and I knew it. A job was an important factor for the Locklears. They prided themselves on it and expected everyone to have a successful career.

Hello failure in the family, my name is Monica.

"Yes." I didn't add anything else even as my dad stared me down. I shifted under his gaze.

"What do you expect to do now?" Sam asked, his tone like my father's.

I saw my mother lay a hand on Sam's arm as if to tell him to slow his roll. Mom had always been less hard on me than Dad and Sam, but she didn't always outwardly tell them to chill.

"I got a severance package that will help for a while, and I have money saved up. Rent is cheaper here so I'm saving money there. I have a job lead idea...but I have to do a bit more research before I can pursue it."

Mom nodded, liking that I had a plan.

"A job should be your number one priority, Monica. You do not have a partner to take care of you and your mother and I won't either. You knew when you moved out to San Diego you had to survive on your own. The same goes for now," my father said with that commanding voice.

Emma flinched and I saw her give me an "I'm sorry" look. At least she was understanding.

"I'll be fine. I don't need help," I said through gritted teeth.

I needed a lot of help, and I wasn't sure money was going to do that.

Chapter Two

Exposing Oneself to New Things

I parked in front of my apartment building that evening and went upstairs to my place. I changed into my small bike shorts and a large white shirt. It had been washed tons of times and was thin as paper, but it was the comfiest shirt I owned. I settled down on the big black sofa I'd brought from California. It had cost me a decent amount of money to bring everything back but there was no way I was going to leave it or anything else behind. I began to look through the list of all the small businesses of Cold Spring.

Feather Blue

Spring Awake

BP Photography

I thought maybe I could help Brynn at some point with her small business, as long as she could forget the night of Emma's bachelorette party. On our way home from Albany, we'd gotten a flat tire and from what I remember, I got yelled at and shoved into a car with Mackayla, their co-worker from Feather Blue, who proceeded to throw up beside me. I had to keep myself from puking after smelling hers, which was no easy feat. I shivered, remembering the awful hangover from that night. It took Emma, Mackayla, and me days to fully recover. I promised myself I'd never drink tequila again.

I was sure I could convince Brynn, or even have Emma talk to her. They were close, like sister close, which made me a little envious. I never had someone like that before in my life. Even Sophie, Natalie, and I hadn't been like that. They would have thrown me under the bus if they needed to.

I had one friend from San Diego, Phoebe, who I'd met at college. We tried to keep in contact, but I hadn't even told her I'd moved back to Cold Springs. I guess I was a bad friend. It had taken me months to tell her I'd broken up with Jay because it had happened so suddenly. I had no feelings for Jay after we broke up. We'd been together because we 'looked' like the perfect couple. There was no love there. Was it so hard to find someone that looks at me the way I look at a cupcake behind the case at Spring Awake? Apparently, it was.

I sighed and ran my hand through my long hair. I hadn't had a successful relationship ever in my life. The men in San Diego had six packs, Lamborghinis, and mansions but those relationships were shallow and meaningless. I didn't feel loved even when they bought me expensive gifts like purses and dresses and shoes. It made me feel like a trophy girlfriend. Especially with Jay.

I rolled onto my back to stare at the high ceilings. The wood fan moved slowly to help circulate the air, but it was still hot. Even though I liked it a warm 74 degrees, being in an apartment above a bagel shop made my house even warmer. I'd cranked up the AC as much as I could to help keep the apartment cool.

I was single and jobless, but I had a place to live. I had my things, my shoes, and I had a plan. No failure here. At least not today.

This was the beginning of something good, I told myself. *You've got this.*

"Two hundred dollars!" I yelled as I read my first electric bill. "I've been here barely two weeks!" There was no one here to hear my rant of course. I'd gotten my mail delivered in the early morning by one of the employees from the bagel shop who'd accidentally gotten a few of my letters.

I crumpled up the bill and threw it across the room then stalked over to my thermostat and looked at the temperature.

68 degrees. The AC was roaring heavily, as if it was half killing it being on all day.

Okay, well I could survive with it being warmer. I looked down at my shirt and sweatpants. I could live naked here if I had to. It wasn't like anyone would see me. I hadn't even had any visitors.

I turned up the thermostat and heard the AC kick off. I ripped off my socks and changed into my favorite thin t-shirt and a pair of short shorts.

No more expensive electric bills.

I heard a beeping sound and went to look out my front window. There was a tow truck loading up– "My car!" I screeched.

I ran out the door in bare feet, practically jumping down the flight of stairs and ripped open the front door. I ran to the tow truck driver, my breath coming in gasps.

I'd stopped going to the gym a while ago and that was my first problem. I needed to join one ASAP.

"That's," big breath. "my," another breath, "car!"

The tow truck driver glared at me. "No street parking on cleaning days. Move it."

"I will, just don't tow it, please. It's a rental," I finally rasped.

He nodded then gave me a quirky smile as his gaze went down to my chest. I ignored his expression as a surge of joy radiated from me at his agreement not to ruin my day.

"Thank you! I owe you!"

He kept smiling and went back to his truck as I turned around and heard laughing. There on the sidewalk were two teenage boys who looked about fourteen years old. They had their phones up and pointed at me.

I frowned. Did they think my car getting towed was funny? Because it wasn't!

Then I looked down at myself and realized what they were looking at....my white shirt was literally see through...and it was a crisp June morning.

I gasped and crossed my arms over my chest.

Shit! No, no, no!

I glared at the two boys. "You perverts! Delete that now!"

They didn't listen and I ran down the sidewalk after them. They scurried away laughing, and I knew I had no chance of catching up to them. Especially since I'd just run down the stairs and was out of breath. I finally gave up, leaning forward to put my hands on my knees and catch my breath to calm down.

I looked over my shoulder and saw the tow truck driver staring at my ass now, smiling.

I straightened up, realizing my short shorts probably looked like underwear.

"Shit!" I ran inside, up the stairs and leaned heavily against the closed door.

I once again looked down at my chest, saw my perky nipples, and squeezed my eyes shut.

Had I gone outside of my house in San Diego like this, it would have been modest compared to some, but not in Cold Spring.

Focus. Go move your rental car before it gets towed. I couldn't afford that bill on top of the electric bill.

I reached for my keys and was about to go back out when I stopped myself.

"Get some damn clothes on!" I yelled at myself and tore into the other room to put on more clothes than was necessary.

I called Emma after moving my car and asked if I could stop by the store to talk to her. She told me she opened at ten, and I could stop by any time after that.

I had a plan to show her some of my ideas, and I was looking forward to that. The morning was forgotten, and I wanted to keep it that way as I packed up my laptop and slipped out the door.

I got in my car that was now safely parked behind the bagel shop and headed down the road. I badly needed a second cup of coffee, and I quickly got in line at the drive-thru at Spring Awake. I planned to take in some pastries to woo the girls at Feather Blue.

There were a few cars ahead of me as I pulled in behind a red pickup truck. It was bright and had mud caked on the sides and back of it. On the bumper was a sticker that was worn down and the only words you could read were "Animal Rescue."

My phone vibrated as we moved towards the speaker. It was Phoebe. We'd taken an English class together in college when she was going for a fashion design degree. She worked at a few different brand name stores throughout our friendship and always got me the best discounts. Now she was working for a magazine in San Diego. She was the perfect best friend because she knew fashion and men better than anyone.

Phoebe: *How dare you not tell me you moved OUT OF THE STATE??*

I flinched at the text. She had been traveling for the last month and I hadn't told her I was moving. She must have found out from a mutual friend which was the worst way for her to find out that news.

Me: *Is sorry going to cut it or do I need to do a lot more sucking up?*

Phoebe: *A LOT more sucking up. Tell me I'm pretty and you're on your knees begging for my forgiveness.*

Me: *You are beautiful *currently on knees**

Phoebe: *Almost forgiven. Did you get settled in you little traitor?*

Me: *Yes, I did. There's a whole room for you when you come to visit.*

Phoebe: *You better have a room for me. It needs some cotton sheets too. I miss you already!*

I chuckled and glanced up to see the line had moved. I inched forward and gave my order through the speaker. My phone vibrated again, and I expected it to be Phoebe, but it wasn't. Someone had tagged me in something on social media. I clicked the notification and when it popped up, it was a picture.

Of *me.*

My heart stopped in my chest, and I stared unblinkingly at the photo. It was of me standing on the sidewalk, wearing my long white t-shirt, my breasts clearly visible and cold through the fabric. My hair was messy, and my shirt was so long and my shorts so short that it looked like I was only wearing panties. The look on my face was of pure confusion.

The caption read "Are there prostitutes in Cold Spring?"

To say the least, it was a rather unattractive picture of my face. My body, not so bad though.

And low and behold the person who tagged me was Sophie.

"Monica, is that you??"

A car horn beeped behind me, scaring me and I dropped my phone between the seat and the console.

"No, no, no," I panicked, and I tried to use my hand to find the missing phone.

I had to untag myself and report the photo! My foot lifted off the brake as my fingers touched the edge of the phone.

Yes!

No sooner did I look up, than my car lurched forward, and I rear-ended the truck in front of me. My head jerked and I felt stunned for a moment. I slowly looked up over the front of my car to see the damage.

Oh god.

The front of my rental was stuck under the bumper of the red truck. The driver got out of the vehicle and came into view. He was an extremely tall man, at least six foot three with dark blonde hair and tan skin. He looked like a farm guy with dirty jeans and a black t-shirt that hugged every muscle. He didn't even glance my way as he slammed his door shut and came to the back of his truck to look at the bumper.

I stared through the windshield until he finally looked toward me through the windshield. He had sunglasses on, but I could tell he was not happy about this situation.

I gulped.

I scrambled out of the car, my hands shaking. "I-I'm so sorry–I didn't–"

"What the hell were you doing in there?" he demanded without a pause. "This bumper is going to have to be replaced!"

His voice was deep and demanding and I flinched. It almost sounded familiar.

The horns started beeping behind us. "Get out of line! We have places to be!" the guy in the car behind me yelled.

The guy whose truck I hit turned his temper towards them. "Mike, I swear to god, I'll put you through a door if you don't shut up!" He pointed a strong finger towards Mike who hurriedly rolled up his window behind us.

He looked back at me, and something flashed across his gaze. "I know you," he sneered. "Monica Locklear."

I stared at him, my hands moving to my hips. "And you are?"

He scoffed. "Of course you don't remember who I am. Because the San Diego girl never remembers anyone from Cold Spring."

I wanted to say that I couldn't forget a hot piece of pie like him but decided that was not the appropriate answer, at least not at the moment.

He pulled off his sunglasses then crossed his arms and stared at me with that long straight nose, the brown stubble across his square jaw and those eyes...brown with flecks of gold. Recognition flickered inside me like an ember catching flame again.

It's him

"Chris," I breathed. The bumper sticker...

Chris Rhodes. Long Rhodes Ahead Animal Rescue.

He had been one of the guys in school who had liked me but hadn't gotten the nerve to ask me out until graduation. The one who I'd had feelings for and did my best to stop thinking of through all these years but who never actually left the back of my mind.

"Hurry up!" someone else shouted from behind Mike who had surprisingly kept quiet.

We both turned to look and saw the line had stretched out to the main road.

"Park there, now," he said pointing to the right.

The feminist in me wanted to object and tell him not to tell me what to do but the logical part of my brain said don't even sass him.

When he pulled away, I heard metal scraping and crunching. I flinched at the noise then drew up next to him in the parking lot. He was out of the truck in seconds and knelt down to check the damage to the bumper. I heard him wince as he shifted his position.

There was a dent in the truck, like a gigantic dent.

I looked at the front of my rental and saw that the right light was bashed in and dented as well.

Shit. I put a hand on my head. *Could this day get any worse?*

Shit. Shit. Shit! The photo I was tagged in!

I got back in my car and scrambled for the phone. When I found it, something occurred to me: I didn't have car insurance. It had been expensive to add to the rental package and I'd told them I had personal insurance that covered a rental instead of buying theirs because at the time, I did. When I got rid of my apartment, I cut everything, including car insurance. I was a safe driver, and I figured I wouldn't get into any accidents. Boy was I wrong.

"Listen, we can exchange information and–"

I turned around to face Chris and saw him pulling out his phone.

"I don't have..." I trailed off as he looked up at me and squinted. He had kept his sunglasses off and I noticed the small crow's feet on either side of his eyes. He looked handsome. Rugged. Chris had definitely grown up since I'd last seen him. He honestly hadn't changed a lot, other than filling out more, growing a beard, and becoming more intimidating. He'd been very approachable back then and easy to hang out with but now? Now he was pure fire and radiated sexy masculinity that made me want to take a bite—

I blinked as I saw his look of exasperation. "Are you trying to say you don't have car insurance?"

I had half a mind to get back in my car and speed off, but Sam would be the one to come pick up my ass and it wouldn't be good. Especially since it wouldn't have been the first time.

"Yes, I mean no. I don't have insurance right now. I just moved back from San Diego—"

"You've got to be kidding me," he growled, looking up towards the sky and slamming a hand down onto his truck.

"I'll pay you back, I promise. Or just give me a day to get insurance!" I snapped, angrily. "This is a rental. You think I have the money to pay for this outright? No! I don't!"

He looked surprised by my outburst but didn't flinch away. I realized his eyes looked more golden brown now with the sun reflecting into them. They'd always been warm and sweet when he used to look at me in high school. It'd made butterflies in my stomach then, now it just made me squirm.

"I have to be at a meeting in ten minutes, and I don't have time to deal with your shit," he growled. "I'm not done with you." If he'd said that in a different tone, it might have been a turn on. But now, standing next to his dented truck that I'd just hit while trying to look at a picture some sick fourteen-year-old posted of my boobs headlighting everyone online, it wasn't the least bit sexy.

"I don't need your asshole-ness today, Chris!" I finally snapped and jumped into my car. I backed up and barely missed the corner of his truck as he yelled something at me. I ignored him and sped out of the parking lot towards Feather Blue.

Ugh! That asshole! That condescending asshole!

I parked in front of the store and pulled out my phone yet again. When I clicked on the tagged photo, it was gone and said that it had "violated their terms and conditions."

Oh, thank god! It pissed me off because Sophie knew exactly what she was doing when she tagged me. She had it out for me since our last conversation, but I wasn't going to let her ruin my day.

I got out of the car and walked into Feather Blue and tried to smile and seem okay after the horrible morning I'd just had.

Emma and Brynn were at the register and Mackayla was fixing something on a mannequin.

"Monica! Good to see you!" Emma came out from around the register to hug me and Brynn gave a wave.

Mackayla squealed and ran over and threw her arms around me. I hugged her back, surprised by how excited she was.

"I heard you moved back!" she said, pulling away. Her hair was nicely done, and her nails were bright pink.

"I did. I have an apartment above the bagel shop."

"We should hang out! I can bring over some tequila and we can watch a movie," she offered.

I threw up slightly in my mouth thinking of the tequila. "How about wine instead?" I suggested.

She howled laughing, knowing why I suggested wine. Emma's bachelorette party and alcohol had done a number on me. We were still in a love/hate relationship at this point.

"Deal! You still have my number, right? Just text me when you want to get together."

I nodded and she went to the fitting rooms to help a customer. I smiled, despite my terrible morning, because maybe I actually had someone to hang out with here in town. Obviously reminiscing with Sophie wasn't going to be happening since I'd apparently made her my enemy.

I looked at Emma and Brynn. "I thought I could speak to both of you if you wouldn't mind?"

We went to the back room where they had a small office set up and they pulled a chair out for me. I opened up my laptop and displayed a presentation I'd put together for the store.

"When I was in California, I was an assistant marketing director. My job was to help companies with social media campaigns and advertising to bring in more business. I'm looking to do some freelance work and wanted to see if you'd let me do it for the store. It would be free of course until you start seeing profits," I shared.

"I haven't been doing as much since you've been out on maternity leave," Brynn admitted to Emma.

She waved a hand. "I know, and that's totally okay. The shop comes first, marketing second. But with Monica's help, it may get a little easier."

"You both would have more free time if I worked for you. First thing we could try is getting influencers to shop at the store. There are a few in New York. You could partner with them, give them a few products to try out then have them post a review about them. It would reach a lot of people. It might even make it worthwhile to open an online store." Emma looked surprised by that notion. I continued, "I would be willing to be the first person to do that for you too. I have a decent following on most of my platforms and could do a post about Feather Blue and add a few pictures of your summer favorites. It would get a buzz going!" I felt like I was on fire and back where I needed to be.

Brynn and Emma exchanged a look. "Do you think we could have an online store?"

I shut my laptop and smiled. "I think with the right marketing and customer base, it's possible."

Brynn shrugged. "I think we should consider, Em. We'd have to see results before moving further into it though."

Emma nodded and looked at me. "We'll discuss everything and let you know. Is that okay, Mon?"

"Absolutely! Take your time. You know where to find me. Before I go, I'm going to shop around a bit." It'd been way too long since I'd had some retail therapy and even though they didn't have name brands, their products were adorable and more in my price range.

I stood up and went back out onto the sales floor. Mackayla was busy helping a few ladies in the dressing rooms and I browsed the earring rack as I looked at a few feather earrings.

An older lady squeezed past me, her shoulder bumping into mine. I looked at her just as she glared and muttered, "Hussy."

I rolled my eyes. Screw her and screw the fourteen-year-old boys and screw Chris! My positive energy was coming back.

The next day Emma called me to say that they would gladly take my help. After hearing that, I was overjoyed. I spent the week at Spring Awake working on some posts for the store and getting a plan mapped out. Erin seemed mildly curious as to why I was hanging out there, but she never asked. I watched a lot of her customers and saw they were regulars. I knew with some marketing, she could do better. So, I went home one night and made up a presentation like the one I did for Feature Blue.

The following morning, I was getting it finished up when I heard a knock at the door. When I opened it, Sam was standing in the hall with papers in his hands and his expression was one I was all too familiar with.

Disappointment.

It looked like he'd just come from work because he was in uniform, wearing his utility belt with his gun and taser still attached.

"What?" I asked automatically, crossing my arms.

He came into my apartment without even asking so I rolled my eyes and shut the door behind me.

"Monica, I don't even know where to begin," Sam said, his tone exasperated.

I laughed without humor. "Maybe the part where you explain why you're here at my apartment?"

He turned towards me and slapped the papers down onto the kitchen counter. "This isn't a joke, Monica. These papers are a summons to court, for *you*."

"For *me*?" I questioned.

"For indecent exposure to a minor, Monica! Ring a bell? When did this even happen?" Sam barked. "You've haven't even been in Cold Spring a month!"

"What?" I whispered in shock, my heart hammering. I ran to the documents and saw the write-up was for the morning my rental car was being towed. "No, no, no, no," I repeated over and over again as I read through.

I was being summoned to court…. next week!

"What the hell! This has got to be a joke!" I expressed with panic. Sam's arms were crossed as he looked at me with our father's expression.

"What happened, Monica? And why am I hearing about this at work?" he demanded. "The big-mouthed secretary couldn't wait to spread the gossip."

I growled and threw the papers back onto the counter, my hands shaking in anger.

"I don't need you to berate me right now, Sam." I ran my hand over my forehead, wishing this was a fever dream but it wasn't. "I had a shirt on! I had a freaking shirt on! And those damn fourteen-year-old boys took a picture of me! A *picture*! Without my consent! Then they posted it on social media! It wasn't my fault! I was trying to stop my car from being towed!" It came out like word vomit and Sam looked surprised.

"Your car was being towed?"

"They were trying! I parked on the day they were doing street cleaning and didn't realize it." I sat down on my couch with a huff and put my head in my hands. "I can't believe this. What am I going to do?"

I looked up at my brother who was frowning at me with the police expression I knew too well.

"I think I know someone who can help."

"If you say Mom or Dad, I'm going to tell them about that time you snuck into Libby's room when we were teenagers!"

It wasn't Mom and Dad, thank god. Surprisingly, it was Brynn Price.

Brynn, Sam, and Emma met at my apartment. They brought along Savannah, who happily cooed as we all sat down in my living room. I bit my thumb nail, still feeling panicked about the situation.

"It isn't illegal for a woman to show her breasts in the state of New York. That was overruled years ago. I think you could easily fight it," Brynn said, much to my relief.

"Oh, thank god!" I cried. "Would there still be implications?"

Brynn sucked a breath between her teeth and scrunched up her nose. "You want to hear the sugar-coated version or the truth?"

"Rip it off like a band aid," I said, my stomach filling with knots.

"Worst case scenario is a misdemeanor on your record and community service. Best case is that we give them push back on this and you only get a $250 fine," Brynn said.

I nodded, my brain going a mile a minute. "I can do this. I can stand in front of everyone there and tell my side."

Chapter Three

Monica the Criminal

One week later

I can't do it, I can't do it!

Especially as the judge stared down at me from the bench. His eyes narrowed as if I'd kicked puppies for a living.

I wore my best and luckiest of shoes, the red bottom ones of course, with a full suit from an expensive brand. Even as I stood tall and unwavering I felt like a palm tree during a hurricane.

"Miss Locklear, you were summoned to the Court of Cold Spring due to your indecent exposure to minors incident on June 10th at 9:35am. Are you aware of when this occurred?"

"Yes, sir, but there is more to it than that," I admitted, praying it didn't piss off the old man who looked like he would be disappointed in all his children. "There is more to the story than what is being shown."

The judge steepled his fingers and pressed his lips together. "Oh?"

I explained the situation, but he didn't look convinced. "I'll give you an option," he started. "Plead guilty and I'll only give you the indecent exposure fine of $250 and apologize to the boys who were present during the occurrence."

I paused before it struck me what the judge had said. "Are you kidding me?" I demanded, before I could stop myself.

"Shit," I heard Sam mutter behind me.

"Apologize to two perverted boys who took *my* picture without *my* consent, then posted it on social media? Hell. No."

"I don't think this was part of the plan," Brynn whispered but I ignored her.

The judge's face grew a little purple as I stood up for myself. There was no way I was going to apologize to anyone!

"Miss Locklear, watch the way you speak to me in my courtroom," he uttered with a tight lip. "Do you think that just because you're Sam Locklear's sister you can get away with that attitude? That's not how it is here in Cold Spring. Whether you're from San Diego or New York City, you're abiding by my rules. I sentence you to one hundred hours of community service, the $250 fine and *you will* apologize to those boys."

I clenched my jaw. "No."

"Monica!" I heard Sam whisper-yell behind me.

The judge's eyes seethed with anger. "Two hundred hours! That's final!" The slam of the gavel hit the bench, and I flinched.

Everyone stood up and Sam grabbed my arm. "Are you kidding me, Monica! You should have taken the guilty plea!"

Brynn and Emma looked everywhere but at me and Sam. "I'm not apologizing to those little shit heads. They didn't have to take the picture, but they did," I snapped.

I looked up just as the two boys and their mother were standing in the aisle to go out the door. She glared me and the boys just grinned.

Before I knew what I was doing, I threw up both my middle fingers to them. The boys looked shocked as the mother gasped and pulled them out of the room.

"What the hell, Monica!" Sam said in exasperation.

I ground my teeth together but then it hit me. *Two hundred hours of community service.* I didn't have time to do two hundred hours of community service! That was like twenty-five days if I did eight hours each day! That's a job that doesn't pay. I *can't* afford that!

Sam was running a hand over his jaw, his eyes looking around as if to find the answer in the walls.

"I can fight him, right? This isn't it!" I asked looking at Brynn.

I saw the answer to my question in her gaze as she looked at me with pity. "It would take more money and time to fight it. The good thing is he didn't give you a misdemeanor or jail time. It's just community service and you can work it around your schedule," she said, trying to make me feel better.

I swallowed. *How was I going to tell my parents?* We had successfully kept this from them for the week, but I didn't want to enlighten them now. What happens when I can't work, and I run out of money? When I can't afford to live in my apartment because I was too busy doing community service?

As if Emma knew what I was thinking, she came up to me and touched my hand. "We'll help you with whatever we can, Monica. You know that."

I hated how I felt at that moment. For the first time since I was in high school, I felt like a child. I felt incapable of helping myself and needed someone to help me. My parents had always taught us not to lean on anyone. To be successful and never ask for anything. They'd set those expectations high so when I did fail, it felt like I'd never get over it.

"What do I have to do next to get this shit started?" I asked, trying not to let my emotions out. Locklears didn't do that. Not for anyone, not even family.

Sam saw the resolve in my expression, and he opened his mouth then closed it. "Follow me, we'll get you registered for community service, and they will give you a few options as to where to work your hours."

I looked down at my shoes and frowned. They weren't lucky anymore.

Emma and Brynn went home while Sam took me to the secretary who eyed me up as if I was the new juicy gossip. And if I knew Cold Spring like I did, I was exactly that.

"Fill out this paperwork. You'll have to have the facility sign off every day you put in your hours. My suggestion is to keep it with Gemma, and she'll make sure it's filled out," the secretary said, pulling out the papers and paperclipping them together.

I paused. "Gemma?"

Oh no. I knew who that was. I knew that name.

The secretary smiled. "Gemma Rhodes of course. She's the only place in the area that is a part of our community service program. You'll be doing your two hundred hours with Long Rhodes Ahead Animal Rescue."

"Long Rhodes Ahead...?" I asked, slowly, as if it was taking me time to process what she was saying, but I knew exactly what she was saying. I just wasn't letting my brain fully take it in.

She nodded, tilting her head to the side. "You look a bit pale. Are you alright?"

Sam looked at me and frowned.

No. "Yes."

Gemma Rhodes, as in the mother of Christopher Rhodes. As in the man I had hit with my car and still hadn't gotten insurance for. And the same man who'd had a crush on me and finally asked me on a date, but.... I stood up because I'd left for college early. The man who currently hated my guts.

"I should have stayed in San Diego," I breathed.

I didn't want to go. I hated even the thought of going and spending my days with animals. We'd only had one dog growing up and when he got old, my parents told us they "took him to a good place." I knew they'd put him down, but we never got another animal afterwards. I lived a life of staying out late and traveling so I didn't have time for an animal.

How hard would it be though? I could walk a few dogs, play with them, even groom them. I could get over them being smelly and drooly just for a little while.

My biggest concern was seeing Chris again. And not just because of hitting his truck and never calling him, but because of the history we had. My thoughts almost wandered to our past, but I pushed them away.

The next day I put on some nice jeans, my favorite pair of black boots that cost several pretty pennies–totally worth it–and a lace up tank top. It was chilly out in the morning, but I knew by afternoon it was going to be warm.

I headed towards the animal rescue with resolve. I would work my hours and be done. I would do as much as I could while still trying to work on my business. Who knew if Chris was even still involved with it? Maybe he'd moved on and had a family already and would be nowhere in sight. I tried not to let that bug me, but it did, which annoyed me even more.

I drove down the long driveway and saw the large sign that said *Long Rhodes Ahead Animal Rescue* and was shocked to see fenced areas filled with horses and cows.

As I came up to the house, there was a large red barn off to the left and several other barns and buildings around the property. To the right was a small log rancher set back towards the tree line. The main house was beautiful with black shutters and a big porch with several chairs on it.

I'd never come out here before when I was in high school. Chris never hosted parties, but he'd gone to all of them.

The door to the house was open as I pulled up and parked beside a truck. I got out of the car holding my papers for community service and turned to see a few workers brushing the horses outside the biggest barn. There were dogs barking close by and I realized it was coming from the main house and from another outbuilding. Several men who were wearing plaid shirts, jeans, and cowboy boots stopped to stare at me. I pushed my sunglasses up on my head, so my hair was away from my face as I looked over the men.

I almost grinned to myself. I was glad I wore something nice today. It was going to be easy to walk some dogs and look cute for these New York cowboys.

I went up the steps to the house and knocked on the screen door. Five dogs came running from somewhere and proceeded to bark at me behind the screen. One was on a set of large wheels to support its back legs. Another had only one eye and that one eye was looking at me as if I was a snack. I flinched back. They were all different sizes but most of them looked mean.

I backed away from the door. "It's okay, p-puppies," I stammered.

"Guys! Knock it off!" a woman's voice yelled from inside. She came over towards the door and blinked several times at me. "Oh! Hi!"

"Hi," I muttered and gave a wave, recognizing her easily.

She opened the door and the dogs ran out, sniffing and growling at me.

"Whoa! Back off!" I warned and put my hands up as the dogs circled me.

"They're harmless!" she said, stepping out onto the porch. "Leave her be."

They listened surprisingly well except for the little white dog who continued to bark and growl at me. Disgusted, I almost kicked it away but thought that wouldn't look good for me starting my community service hours... at an animal rescue.

Chris's mom, Gemma, was beautiful with graying blonde hair and blue-gray eyes. She wore a baseball cap with the name of the rescue on it along with dirty jeans, boots, a tank top and an open button-down shirt that looked like it had seen better days. She looked much the same as she did eight years ago.

She was shorter than me of course by several inches but she stood confident and strong. Seeing her brought back memories from high school. She cheered for Chris along the sidelines of the football field every Friday night with her husband, Keith.

The night was cool, and the lights were bright against the dark sky. The music from the band was loud and I could barely hear our cheer as we shook our pom-poms and shouted about teamwork. We ended with a shout and the crowd roared. Sophie and Natalie were whispering about a few of the football players, but my eyes focused on a woman standing not far from me. She was leaning on the fence, her blonde hair pulled pack in a ponytail, and wearing a sweatshirt with the high school's mascot on it.

She seemed very friendly as she watched the game intently, her eyes alight and a smile on her lips.

"Who are you cheering for tonight?" I asked, as I walked over to her.

The woman looked at me. "Chris Rhodes, do you know him?"

I leaned my back against the fence beside her and looked out across the lit green field. I spotted Chris right away. He was taller than all the others and was a good player. I'd met him a few weeks ago at the beginning of the school year at the local diner. I'd felt an instant connection with him, and we'd been talking and hanging out since.

"Yes, I know Chris. He's been doing really well this season. I'm Monica Locklear, by the way," I added.

Her eyes lit up. "Are you Clayton Locklear's daughter?"

"Yes, I am." Shit, she knew my dad.

"Chris's dad works with him sometimes with the horses for the tribal meetings. He's a great guy."

"Sure is," I said trying hard not to sound disrespectful. "You have the animal rescue? Long Rhodes Ahead?"

"That's us." She looked at me a little while longer. "Chris should bring you by sometime," she offered.

I smiled as an older-looking Chris came up behind her with nachos in his hands. He smiled at me. "Who's this?"

"Monica Locklear, Clayton's daughter," Chris's mom said.

"Oh, good man. Want a nacho?" he asked.

I laughed and took advantage and ate one. "Thanks!"

"My name is Gemma, and this is my husband, Keith," she said.

They'd always been a part of Chris's life and had been supportive of him. I'd liked them from the moment I met them. Just like Chris.

"Can I help you?" Gemma asked as I came out of my thoughts.

"I'm here to start my community service." I handed her my papers, and she continued to look at me without glancing down.

"You look familiar, what's your name?" she asked.

I shifted onto my other foot. "Monica."

Her expression changed and she smiled largely. "Monica Locklear! Look at you! You have grown up so much since the last time I saw you! Give me a hug!" She reached for me before I could say something and hugged me tightly.

Surprised by her reaction, I didn't hug her back for a second. "Oh…you remember me?"

She pulled back. "Of course I do! Come on in." She waved me into the house and to the right was an office with several dog beds lying on the floor around it. She went behind the desk and sat down and put on little reading glasses then gestured towards the seat in front.

I hesitantly sat down as the dogs rushed in to smell me more and demand attention. The one on the wheels ran over my foot and after I moved it, another dog dropped a wad of slobber over my expensive black boots. I grimaced and prayed that his slobber wouldn't stain.

"What's wrong with him?" I asked, pointing to the dog on wheels who ran into the corner of the wall.

"That's Wheely. He had an accident a few years ago and can't use his back legs. He's...still getting used to his cart."

I stared as the dog's tongue lulled out happily. The one-eyed dog and the larger black one sat beside me and panted their hot breath across my arm. I moved before they could lick or bite me.

"So, community service. I'll say I'm surprised," Gemma said, squinting at the paperwork. "I thought you'd get this when you were young, not..." she glanced up at me. "How old are you now? You and Chris are the same age, right?"

I flinched at his name. "I'm twenty-six," I answered.

She nodded. "Sounds right." She whistled then laid the papers down. "Two hundred hours is a lot. You must have pissed off Judge Lowell."

I groaned. "He's insufferable and old-fashioned."

She laughed. "Can't say that's the first time I've heard that. Anyhow, I know you can get that time here," she said. "It's not going to be easy though."

I stiffened. "Not easy? What all are you expecting me to do?"

She glanced at the dog who was wagging his tail beside me, staring at me with obvious attention-seeking eyes. I avoided that gaze and put my hands together in my lap. How many times would I have to wash my hands if I touched that…animal?

"You'll have to be around them for one. Cleaning their kennels, feeding, filling water bowls, and fixing beds."

I could do that. Even cleaning their kennels didn't seem too bad. "I don't really have a choice, do I?"

She chuckled. "According to this note from the judge, I'd say no." She put it down and leaned forward with a soft expression. "I won't let you get stuck working with animals you're not comfortable with. Even if it's the larger dogs, I don't mind working with you on this."

Relief filled me. "Thank you, Gemma. I wasn't–"

"Mom, who's car is out–" The male voice jarred me in my seat, and I looked over my shoulder to see a man walking in the front door, a brown lab on his heels.

Chris.

He wore a similar outfit to the one I'd seen him in at Spring Awake, but this time he wore a baseball cap that had the rescue's name on it. His dark blonde hair was peeking out from under his cap close to his ears, making it look like he needed a haircut. He looked even more like a working man than the day I'd hit his truck. I hated that I felt that warmth pull in my stomach.

When his brown eyes landed on me, shock filtered over his face, followed by anger.

God, he was an open book. Did he even know how to hide his expressions?

"What the hell are you doing here?" he demanded, stepping further into the room.

"None of your business," I snapped back.

Gemma sighed. "She is here to serve her community service, Chris. I'd appreciate you not speaking like that."

He raised an eyebrow. "Community service?" he repeated.

I felt my face flush.

"For what?" he asked, his tone still demanding.

"Again, none of your business," I gritted out.

I looked back at Gemma who seemed amused by the whole situation and our interaction. Maybe I didn't like her as much as I remembered.

"Anyhow, you were saying?" I decided ignoring Chris was my best bet right now.

Gemma tried to hide her smile, but she continued. "You can start today. My suggestion is four hours a day until you're done. We'll sign off at the end of each day for you. Do you have a probation officer?"

"No. My…crime didn't warrant one," I mumbled, hoping that Chris's silence was because he'd left the room, but I had an inkling he was still there staring at me. My neck prickled with awareness, so I knew he was still there.

"I'll need you to sign a waiver first since you'll be working around all sorts of animals. Did you bring along clothes to change into?" Gemma asked as she reached for an accordion folder.

I looked down at myself with a frown. "No, this is what I'm wearing."

Her eyes wandered to my nice black boots with the gold branding and she tsked. "You're going to get pretty dirty, but I'll let you find that out. Chris, are you just going to stand there or actually be useful?" Gemma sighed with annoyance.

I looked over my shoulder to see him leaning up against the doorframe with his arms crossed. He had a smug look on his face, and I hated it.

"I can show her around and get her started whenever you're finished," Chris said with that snarky tone.

"No way!" I snapped. "Not going to happen."

Gemma almost winced and leaned towards me. “Hate to break this to you Monica, but he’s my lead for the rescue. He’ll be the one you report to for the next few months. Chris will sign off on your hours.”

I felt my whole body deflate and it took everything not to throw a pen at Chris’s head. Wait…she’d said months, not weeks, but *months*. Plural.

Chris came over beside me and I glared at him even as his grin made my heart stutter in response.

“Well baby, the day is wasting away, let’s get started,” he mused.

The *baby* comment made me glare harder.

“Give her a tour first, Christopher. I want her to be familiar with the rescue,” Gemma explained, giving him a look.

He waved her off with a hand as I stood up and followed him outside.

It was a warm day, and I was already starting to sweat.

I followed Chris to the biggest barn where several of the workers were still taking care of the horses. One man had a large brown and white horse out and it shifted on its feet as we both stared at each another. It was huge. Forget worrying about the dogs, the horses were even scarier.

"Dale, this is Monica. She'll be putting in her community service time with us for the next few months," Chris introduced.

"Weeks," I corrected him with my lips pressed tightly together. If I had to do ten-hour workdays to get these hours in, I would. Several months was not an option.

Dale looked me up and down, mostly just staring at the expensive boots.

"You ever been around horses before?" he asked.

"Not at all. Which is why I won't be working with them," I said matter-of-factly.

Chris chuckled beside me. "You won't be working with them *right now*, Locklear. But eventually, you will be."

I whipped my head towards him. *Just shut up, Monica. Let him believe what he wants, but that won't happen.*

"Are you going to finish the tour?" I snapped.

Dale whistled. "First one to talk back, huh, Chris?"

Chris didn't look at Dale he stared bullets at me. "Let's go." He turned his back and walked towards the next barn.

I followed with my head held high that I'd won that argument…but I was losing the war.

I was inside but the air conditioning barely kept me from sweating, especially since I had been shoveling dog poop out of the kennels for hours. To make matters worse, Chris sat on a metal bench in the hall watching me as the dogs' barking echoed under the tin roof. I pushed back my hair with my forearm and grumbled when I stepped in a rather wet poop pile.

Why did I wear these boots? They cost me over eight hundred dollars!

"So, what got you the community service?" Chris asked from behind me. I felt his eyes on my butt the entire time I worked.

"Don't you have anything better to do right now?" I demanded.

"Nah, this is way better."

I looked over my shoulder as I caught his gaze traveling over my body then finally up to my face as I glared at him.

He gave me a wicked grin that made me feel all tingly and I hated it. "Just go away, Chris! Isn't this enough torture?"

He stood up gracefully and came over as I leaned against the cold wall. It felt good as sweat dripped down my back.

"What got you the community service?" he asked again.

I growled. "Can you please leave me alone?"

He crossed his muscular arms and braced his feet apart. "I will if you tell me."

"You can't laugh," I warned. I couldn't believe I was considering telling him.

He gave a nod.

I leaned the shovel up against the door and tried not to touch my face with the gross gloves I was wearing. "My rental car was getting towed early one morning and I ran out to stop it. I happened to be wearing a very old, very see-through white t-shirt and short shorts. Two fourteen-year-old boys happened to be standing by and took pictures of me and posted them online."

Chris just stared then blinked twice before he erupted into laughter. I ground my teeth together as he continued until he had to sit back down on the metal bench.

"You promised not to laugh," I snapped.

Chris caught his breath and wiped a tear from his eyes. "I'll pay for my own damn truck now that I found out what you've been through. God, this is going to be the best few months of my life." Chris stood back up and I stared in shock at him.

"What do you mean?"

He was starting to leave the barn but stopped and turned to me.

"I mean, what better revenge for you hitting my truck than seeing you clean up dog shit for showing your tits to kids. Even Karma herself couldn't come up with that," Chris explained, grinning again. "That was all you, Monica Locklear." I opened my mouth to call him something colorful when he continued. "I'll be back in an hour. When you're finished with the kennels, we'll feed the dogs."

He was stupid! He was an asshole! I hated him. I should never have told him about why I was here. Unfortunately, he would've found out anyway, the way this stupid town's rumor mill spins.

He did leave me alone though and I finished cleaning out the kennels. I was exhausted and my back was killing me. I was ready to leave but he came back in right as I sat down on the bench to catch my breath. I ripped off my gloves and pushed my hair back from my face.

"Get up, we aren't done yet," Chris said.

"What is this? Bootcamp? Give me a few minutes to catch my breath," I fought back.

He went over to a switch on the wall and hit a button. All the kennel doors opened, and the dogs ran in from outside, sniffing their beds and water dishes, looking for food. The dog barking intensified, and I knew what Chris had done: he'd made them more obnoxious than himself so I couldn't just sit there.

"Alright, alright!" I stood up and glared at him, his lips twitching into a grin. "What's next?"

"Grab a bag of dog food and a handful of bowls. Fill them up halfway and slide them under each kennel door," he instructed. Chris leaned down closer to me, and I was too shocked to move.

"And don't let your fingers get too close. Some of them can get a little... excited."

I didn't mean to, but I definitely gulped loudly.

I filled up a bowl, almost over filling, trying to handle the heavy bag of food. With shaky hands I slid the dish under the first door. The dog happily started eating.

Okay, that wasn't so bad.

I did three more as Chris stood back and watched, he was on his phone a few times, texting or making a call.

I came up to a large German Shepherd who had dark eyes and watched me with an intensity I didn't like. I filled up the food bowl and as I went to slide it underneath, he charged me, snapping through the gate. I squealed and jumped, knocking over the bag of food.

The dog scarfed down the food as if it hadn't just tried to eat me. Chris laughed behind me.

"That's Rex. He's overprotective of his food," he said with a smugness that made me glare at him.

"You asshole!" I stood up and almost did a cartoon split, slipping on the food, as I ran up to get in his face. "I've had enough of you and your dumb hellhounds!"

He went toe to toe with me, his arms crossed and hitting my chest. He was still taller than me, even in my expensive–now ruined–boots. It was then I saw his left hand had no ring on it, not even a tan line for where a ring might have been.

"You can't do anything about it. You're stuck here with me."

There was a pause, my anger simmering a bit. I felt an energy that made my belly quake at his expression, his presence, and it made me even more mad.

I didn't like these feelings coming back after eight years. I didn't like *him*. I should absolutely not care about a ring on his finger. I should care that he's a jerk making my life more miserable than it already was.

I growled and stormed off toward the main house. I slammed the screen door behind me, getting Gemma's attention where she sat at her desk.

"I can't do this! Your son is infuriating!"

Gemma looked up from her paperwork, three dogs sitting beside her. They sat up and trotted over to me, but I growled and pushed them back with my foot. I didn't like them getting that close to me.

She sighed and took off her reading glasses. "I'm sorry, Monica. Here, take a seat." She gestured to the chair where I'd been earlier that day. I sat down and felt the tiredness over run my body. "Chris is…. I don't even want to get into it. He's like his father. He holds grudges but the best way to handle him is to ignore him. He'll come around and get over the grudge. It just takes time."

I closed my eyes and leaned my head back on the chair. "I don't want to be here. I don't care for animals, especially not giant ones looking to bite off my arm while trying to give them food," I muttered.

"Oh, Rex? He's a good dog. He just needs training, that's all."

I opened my eyes and looked at her and I could see her understanding. I'd forgotten how much I had liked her.

I heard a noise and looked out the screen door and saw a sparrow sitting on the railing of the porch. Its small head tilted back and forth, looking inside at me. I swallowed, memories flooding my mind.

"When you come back, get that thick skin I know you have and don't let him get under it," Gemma said, pulling my attention to her.

"Thanks, Gemma," I mumbled.

I stood, my legs shaking, and walked out to my car. The bird had flown away but seeing it caused all sorts of emotions to start churning in my soul, just as I knew it would.

I slipped on my sunglasses and saw Chris and the horse handlers over by the barn. They paused to watch me.

"See you next time!" Chris called with a smug wave.

I turned my back to get in my car and smelled dog poop.

Shit. My boots. My expensive boots had dog shit on them. I growled and turned around to face Chris again. They were still watching of course. "Screw off!" I yelled before getting into my car and driving off.

Chapter Four

The Rescue Rex

I slept like I did in college after a full semester or a busy night of drinking. Maybe I wouldn't have to go back to the gym if I kept this up to get my hours in. At this rate, I had no energy left for the gym or much of anything else.

A week passed and I worked at the rescue several more days which took a decent chunk out of my two hundred hours. At least it felt that way until I looked at my actual accrued hours and saw that I'd only completed thirty.

I took Sunday off and slept most of the day. In the evening, I ran to the store to buy work boots, jeans, and t-shirts. Emma had texted earlier in the week about working for them, but I hadn't had a lot of time. I didn't even have time to work on the presentation for Erin. I told myself it was temporary until I could get my hours done and out of the way.

When Monday came, I reluctantly went back to the rescue, feeling more rested and ready, including wearing my new work clothes. My poor designer boots had faded to a light black, almost gray color and still smelled of poop, so I'd purchased duck boots instead to wear and ruin. They weren't stylish and Phoebe would have been mortified but there was no way I was going to destroy another pair of shoes that I'd spent too much of my hard-earned money on.

On the drive to the rescue, I had to psych myself up to get ready to deal with Chris. The dogs weren't a problem anymore since I was growing used to them and getting to know their personalities. They weren't all that bad, even Rex. We'd come to an understanding that as long as I pulled my hand back in enough time, he wouldn't try to bite it off.

I could handle Rex… but Chris was the type of dog who you knew would bite you; you just didn't know when. He was constantly on my back, making me reclean stuff or just standing around to watch me work. It was annoying and frustrating. It had been a week, and I wondered if he was done gloating yet. I just needed to get this shit over with, do my time, and get out. I was never going to come back again and that meant I'd never have to see him again.

When I arrived, I parked in the same spot, and I was happy to find that Chris's truck wasn't there. I walked towards the house and found Gemma in the exact same place I left her on Friday. I noticed the two empty coffee cups beside her as she looked up in surprise.

"It's morning already?" she asked, her voice sounding tired.

"Have you slept at all this weekend, Gemma?"

She rubbed a hand over her eyes. "A little bit. We got a call at eleven last night for a rescue in Pennsylvania. Chris and I left and didn't get back until 4am." She looked into one of the empty cups and sighed when she realized it was exactly that, empty. "I had to fill out some paperwork and I guess I lost track of time."

"Is there anything I can do?" I'd do anything to get out of going to deal with the dogs and Chris. Plus, she seemed overworked, and I felt bad for her.

Gemma smiled at me. "No, but thank you. Chris is probably asleep. Do you think you can get this morning's chores done without him?"

All too excited about not having to work with him, I nodded eagerly. "Yes!"

I put in my ear buds and cranked up my music then walked to the dog kennels. They were loud this morning, even with my music blaring through the headphones. I hit the button so all the barking dogs were let out to the yard then I hit the button to shut the doors and open the inside ones so I could start cleaning the kennels. I got to the fourth kennel and as I opened it, I saw something move.

I jumped and stood extremely still.

Rex was in the kennel, sitting on his haunches, staring at me. His brown eyes looked dark, and I felt my palms sweat. I reached for the kennel door, but I had to move back out of the room to shut it.

Could I do that in enough time? Why hadn't he gone outside?

He laid down, not putting any weight on his right paw and tucked it under himself a bit. Then he started licking it, not taking his eyes off me.

"You're hurt," I said quietly.

He didn't look like the regular Rex I'd seen the past week. He looked sad and I heard him whimper.

I felt a sudden urge to touch him. His coat looked soft with a pretty mixture of browns and blacks and tans, but I put that thought aside because I was nuts if I thought Rex was touchable. Also…dogs were kind of gross.

I slowly backed out and shut the door without even a move from Rex. Something was definitely wrong with him. What if his paw was broken? Or maybe he had stepped on something? There wasn't any blood…but maybe it was broken. I locked his kennel and ran out towards the main house. Gemma wasn't in her office.

Shit, she probably finally went to sleep.

I went to the barn where I saw Dale and a few other men were and they all paused to look at me.

"Dale, is there a vet on the property?"

He looked at me strangely. "Why? Is something wrong?"

"I think Rex hurt his foot. He's not going out into the yard," I explained, the panic evident in my voice.

Dale looked surprised but nodded his head to follow him. We went further into the barn and stopped at a stall that Chris was in. Beside him was a beautiful woman. Her blonde hair was in a brown clip, and she wore a white coat covered in blood and mud that protected her clothing. She was petite with a small nose and heart-shaped face. She held several vials in her gloved hands.

"Chris, just hold his leg up further," she instructed. Chris was holding up the horse's foot, but his forearms strained as the horse tried to pull away.

He looked like a mess. His hat was off, and his thick hair was mussed, as if he had run his hands through it multiple times. He had dark shadows under his eyes and his pants were bloodstained. The horse they were dealing with had sores all over it and its hoof looked in rough shape.

"Boss, she thinks there is something wrong with Rex. Can we get the doc to go check on him afterwards?" Dale asked.

Chris looked up and frowned as his eyes landed on me. "Rex?"

The female vet finally glanced at me after using the syringe of whatever and shooting it into the horse. "Isn't that the German Shepherd ya'll rescued last year?" the vet asked, barely even giving me a second look. She had a slight accent that made her even more likeable.

"Yeah," Chris said. "I know you've been here for a while, but can you check him before you leave?"

Chris's look at her made my stomach knot for some reason. His words were gentle and mixed with gratefulness.

"Of course." Her smile back made me wonder with disappointment if they were together.

Dale tapped my shoulder and nudged me to leave. I followed him out of the barn. "They've been with the new rescue since early this morning. I'm sure she's tired but she'll go look at him. Did Rex let you in his kennel?" Dale asked me.

"Yes, but only because he's injured. Normally, he's not that friendly," I mumbled, concern filling me.

"Alright, just go finish the kennels and Doc will be out later."

I cleaned the rest of the kennels then when I finished, I went back to Rex. He was sitting on his bed curled up, his food and water untouched.

I frowned, staring down at him.

Wasn't that a sign that an animal was sick if they didn't eat? I shouldn't care though. I was done with my work; I should get home and finish that presentation for Spring Awake so I could show it to Erin this week. But I couldn't leave. I looked towards the entrance of the kennel and didn't see anyone. How long until the vet came?

It should only be a little while, maybe half an hour until she came, right? I looked at the floor and made a disgusted face but before I could talk myself out of it, I sat down by the kennel door. Rex's head went up to stare at me.

"Why don't you eat a little bit, Rex?" I tried to coax. I put my hand through the door and moved the bowl. He didn't even stir but his tail did wag slightly.

I sighed and put my head against the cold wall. "Listen, I may not like you and you may not like me, but this isn't how you're going to die," I told him. "You are going to try to bite my arm off at least a dozen more times."

The German Shepherd just huffed again and closed his eyes. I swallowed hard at the sadness that swarmed me. It was silly to feel this way about a dog but part of me...part of me liked Rex.

I can't believe I'm admitting that.

His brown eyes looked at me and it melted my heart a little.

"I think he'll be okay. Just give him time to acclimate," a female voice said as Chris and the vet walked into the kennels

"I know, he just wasn't in a good environment, I'm worried..." Chris trailed off as he saw me sitting by Rex's gate and he frowned.

"What are you still doing here?" His voice changed from kind to sharp.

The vet heard this and looked between us. "Chris, she's obviously worried about the dog. You don't have to be so mean."

Alright, I liked her. No matter how involved she was with Chris, I was going to enjoy being around her.

She looked at me as I stood and wiped my hands on my pants. "I'm Skyler, by the way," she introduced.

"Monica Locklear."

She smiled at me. "Sam Locklear's sister?"

I flinched. "Yep."

"He's a great guy."

"So I've been told."

"He's helped me a few times with animal abuse situations. How nice you're here volunteering! Gemma and Chris always need help."

Chris's face turned wicked, and we both spoke at the same time.

"Thank you."

"She's not volunteering."

I glared at him, and she looked between us again, probably trying to figure out our relationship.

"It's a long story," I muttered. "It's for community service."

She made an *O* with her mouth but didn't ask any more questions. Skyler walked over next to me by the kennel and looked in at Rex.

"What's going on with him?" She kneeled, trying to get a better view of the dog. Chris stood with his arms crossed, his amused expression changed to a more serious one now.

"This morning, he wouldn't go out into the yard and he hasn't eaten or drank all day. When I was here Friday, he was fine. I don't know what could have happened but he's favoring his right front paw," I explained.

The vet nodded. "Could be a sprain. German Shepherds are high energy. He might have stepped on it wrong."

"So, he'll be okay?"

She stood up and smiled at me and I realized how small and petite she was compared to my five-foot-nine. She was probably Chris's type. Cute, little, and kind. She definitely hadn't been the mean girl in high school who'd bullied some people like I had.

Chris and I had become friends our senior year and had gotten to know each other. When I was around him, I felt like he could see the real me. My parents were adamant about not dating since I planned to go to college, and they thought it would be a barrier between me and having a career. It didn't stop me from hanging out with guys, but it was different with Chris. We'd had a friendship, and it had felt...good to be with him. Obviously, times had changed.

"Yes, I'm sure he'll be okay." She looked past me to Chris. "He needs a muzzle, can you grab one?"

Chris disappeared into one of the storage closets and came out with a black muzzle.

"What are you going to do?" I asked quietly, feeling a little nervous for Rex.

She smiled softly at me. "It's only for my protection so he doesn't harm me. I promise it won't hurt him," she said.

"You can go now. Your hours are up," Chris said tightly.

"I'd like to–"

"No," he cut me off. "Just go home, Monica."

I gritted my teeth as we stared each other down. He was so different than I remembered. He had become hard and mean.

I didn't say anything more to him as I walked out of the barn.

He was right. I needed to go home anyhow. I didn't care about Rex. I had way more important things to focus on today.

That evening, I worked on my proposal for Erin. My presentation would show her how to use marketing tools like creating a social presence, making a theme for her coffee shop, and getting a few influencers to stop in and post their experience, to improve her customer base. I smiled when I finished it and closed my laptop. I grabbed my wine glass and took a few sips.

I was feeling pretty good about myself.

Then my mother called.

"Hey Mom, what's up?"

"Monica, your father and I haven't heard from you in a while. I wanted to see how you're doing. Were you able to find a job?"

I took a longer sip of my wine before answering. "Yes, I did," I lied. "I'm working on marketing for Erin at Spring Awake and for Emma. It'll be more freelance, but it will bring in some money."

My mom was quiet for a moment. "Honey, freelance? Is that going to give you a steady income?"

I tried not to let her words affect me, but it was hard. "I've been a successful businesswoman for years. I can do this, Mom."

"Okay…well if you need to, I'm sure I can convince Dad to let you stay with us," Mom started, as if she hadn't heard what I just said.

"I'm not moving back in with you guys!" I said with exasperation. "I have my own place and I'm going to pay for it on my own."

She sighed. "I'm just giving an option, Monica."

"I have to go. Love you, bye."

I hung up after she said goodbye and stared at the phone.

Failure is never an option. Not in the Locklear family.

What would they say if they found out what had happened in court? One child working in law enforcement and the other a criminal.

If Sam hadn't already been the favorite child, his place in the family would now be set in stone for the rest of our lives.

It was hard living up to the same standard as my big brother. He'd moved back with us to Cold Spring but had immediately gotten his own place and went into the police academy. On the day he graduated from the academy, I watched one single tear run down my father's cheek. That was the first and only time I'd ever seen him 'cry.' Our father was an expressionless man who led his family and set the expectations high. Unfortunately, I'd barely been able to meet them.

My parents had encouraged me to go to an Ivy League College and get a degree in the medical field. Or even go into the military. Something that would make my parents and my country proud. Being uprooted from San Diego at the age of fourteen right as I was starting high school had ruined my life, or at least it felt that way. I was so angry at them for making me move to Cold Spring that when the time came, I'd only applied to colleges in San Diego and had always planned to move back. The week after I graduated from high school, I'd gotten into a big fight with them and left early for college. I hadn't told anyone I'd booked a one-way flight until I left town the following morning. My original plan had looked a lot different. One that had made my parents upset. The only person I'd ever told that plan to was Chris.

I stood up and went to the kitchen to pour more wine into my glass. I picked up the mail and opened the water bill. I almost choked on my wine. The price was more than I thought it would be. Does that mean no more showers? I can't do that! Not when I work at an animal rescue.

I threw the letter down in disgust and drained the wine. I went into my bedroom and to the walk-in closet and looked at my shoes lining the wall. They were gorgeous colors and styles, lined up perfectly from boots to wedges to heels to flats. Then there were my newly cleaned designer boots that still smelled of dog poop. On the right side of the wall were the purses. Italian designer brands in pretty blacks and florals. I went over and touched one and I saw how grungy my fingernails looked against the expensive leather.

God, if my old boss would've seen them, she would have sent me home.

I grabbed a pretty black bag that had a gold strap and sighed. "I'm sorry, I'm sorry, I'm sorry," I chanted as I snapped a picture of it then put it back on the shelf. "I promise I will find you a good home. Someplace where you won't just sit in the closet and smell dog shit from your matching boots."

I felt a little sad but uploaded the photos of the purse and other items to an online website that sold designer clothes and within minutes, I had a buyer.

The money rolling into my bank account to pay my bills was bittersweet. Mostly bitter.

I got up early the next morning and drove to the rescue. I kept thinking about Rex the whole night, wondering if he was okay and if they'd figured out what was wrong. The dogs barked loudly as I stepped into the kennels and flipped on the lights. I walked down to Rex's kennel and saw it was open, and the floor was clean but no aggressive shepherd was inside.

My heart dropped. *Where was he?*

I searched the other kennels, but Rex was not there. I ran back to the stables and found Dale.

"Dale," I said out of breath. The other horse handlers and volunteers looked at me. "Where is Rex? Did the vet take him?"

Dale frowned. "I don't know to be honest. Check with the boss lady, she might know."

I took off towards the house, my stomach dropping the closer I got.

What if they had put him down? I hadn't been nice to him. I'd called him some colorful words. We were just getting to know each other.

I knocked on the front door and it took a few seconds before someone answered. *Chris.* He had a cup of coffee in his hands, and his shirt was untucked and his hair looked slightly wet. He was surprised to see me this early but before he could say anything snarky, I cut him off. "Where's Rex?"

He searched my face, his forehead showing lines before he backed up from the door and looked at the cage sitting in the living room. Rex lay in a large cage, his right paw wrapped.

"Rex," I breathed, running to the cage and falling to my knees. "Hey buddy."

His tail wagged, smacking the bottom of the crate but he didn't move closer to me.

Chris shut the front door and stood back to watch us.

"What happened?" I kept my eyes on Rex as he finally crawled a little towards me and nudged his nose through the crate to touch my hand.

"Doc said he had a bad sprain. She had to sedate him so she could wrap his leg. He should be fine in a few weeks."

Rex's brown eyes looked up at me and my heart broke a little at his sad expression. "Has he eaten yet?"

"No, he shouldn't for a while."

"Who's here this early?" Gemma asked, coming around the corner wearing a Long Rhodes Ahead Animal Rescue sweatshirt. She saw me and stopped what she was doing. She looked between me and Rex whose tail was still wagging. "My god, he actually looks happy to see someone."

Chris rolled his eyes at his mother, and I looked back at Rex and smiled. I grazed his nose through the cage, and he leaned his head against my hand for more pets.

"It's good to see him so gentle. What'd I tell you, Christopher?" Gemma said, slapping a hand on his shoulder as she walked by him.

He cleared his throat. "Your regular chores are still expected to get done, Locklear. They don't stop because of him."

I stood up feeling lighter and relieved. "You're right."

Without another word, I left the house and headed back to the dog kennels to start the morning routine.

Chapter Five

Throwing a Shit Fit

Chris stopped by after a few hours to lean against the doorframe of the building to watch me. I was filling up the bowls with food since I'd already washed the dog poop out of the kennels.

"Take a picture, it'll last longer," I muttered to him.

I sat the heavy bag of dog food down and put my gloved hands on my hips to glare back at him. His eyes seemed dark under his baseball cap, and it was hard to read his expression.

"Come with me."

It wasn't a suggestion, it was a demand, and it irked me to the point I debated not following him, but I reminded myself that it would be worse if I didn't.

I followed him reluctantly, taking off my gloves as we went into the horse barn. We stopped in front of the first stall that housed a large black and white horse and a large pile of—

"Clean his stall then I'll show you how to take care of the horses," he said calmly.

"No!" I snapped, not getting close to the stall. "Absolutely not! I'm just now getting over my fear of dogs, you are not about to put me with the headless horseman's ride!"

The other workers in the barn stopped what they were doing and leaned out of the stalls they were working in to watch. Dale was among them, and he rested his arm on a shovel as he watched with a coy smile.

Chris's left eye twitched. "Yes, you are. You work for us, not the other way around. Get mucking." Chris pushed the handle of the manure fork into my hands, and I stared in shock and anger as he started to walk away. What even was mucking? He wasn't even going to explain how to do this? There was no way.

"What the hell is your problem? Why are you being such a dick to me?" I yelled, my hands gripping the handle hard.

He stopped his retreat, and I thought maybe he'd continue on, but he turned on his heel and his eyes were sharper and harder.

"You don't remember, do you?" His voice was quiet, and I was sure no one else in the barn heard but me. He scoffed and rolled his eyes when I just looked confused. "You haven't changed a bit, Monica. Still the prissy, self-centered cheerleader I knew in high school. Get to work, *now*."

His words ran over me in a tightening of my spine. My anger fumed to the point I felt a rush of adrenaline spike through my blood.

I was not that person anymore. I was sick of people thinking that's all I was. A self-centered cheerleader. A prissy girl. Okay, so maybe I was still slightly prissy, but I had class! Not when I had tequila in my system, but we wouldn't talk about that.

I couldn't stop myself. As he turned his back towards me, I reached down with my bare hands and grabbed a pile of horse poop from the wheel barrel and chucked it across the barn. It splattered on the back of his head and neck.

My softball coach from middle school would have been proud.

Everything went quiet in the barn except for the sound of some of the poop clumps hitting the floor behind him. My heart beat hard in my chest as I realized what I'd done.

My hand was covered in horse shit and the evidence was still sliding off the back of Chris's head. He wiped his hand across his neck and looked to see it on his fingers. Shock coursed over him as he turned to look at me.

"Did you just throw horse shit at my head?" Chris demanded.

Had I really just thrown horse poop like I was five? Or like a freaking ape in a zoo? Who the hell was I?

The men in the barn erupted in laughter and I straightened my back as I threw the manure fork to the ground and walked over to Chris who stared at me in disbelief.

"Shovel your own shit, Chris," I sneered walking past him. Four workers backed out of my way, trying to hide their smirks and laughs as I stormed past.

I ignored everyone as I went into the house and slammed the front door. Gemma was sitting at her desk. She glanced up, her eyes above her glasses that were sitting low on her nose.

"What's wrong?"

The dogs at her side jumped up and ran to me as I held my right hand in the air away from myself.

"I can't work with him, Gemma. He just tried to make me work with the horses and I don't know anything about them! I'm finally comfortable with the dogs and– he does it right in front of the barn crew!" I paced the room, the dogs following trying to smell my hand. "I tried, Gemma! I tried. He has this vendetta against me for whatever reason! It can't be the bumper incident! For god's sake, the dent should have improved that rust bucket of a truck!"

"Bumper incident?" Gemma asked, confused.

I stopped my pacing. "Yes, I rear ended him in the drive-thru line at Spring Awake. Total accident." I resumed my pacing. "Chris and I were friends in high school and got along really well. So why is he being such an asshole to me?" In the corner of my eye, I saw her flinch and I stopped. "No, no, what was that?"

She gave me a sad expression. "Honey, it isn't my place to share this type of thing. You and he have your own issues you need to work out."

I walked over closer to the desk, still holding my gross hand away from me. It still hadn't hit me yet that I had poop on my hand. "Gemma, *please*. I am stuck here for another 170 hours and have to deal with him. I need to know what his problem is. Please tell me," I begged.

She sighed, taking off her glasses as her warm eyes looked directly into mine. "I'm only able to tell you what I saw, not that I knew what really went on or how he felt," she started. "Chris liked you through high school, honey. Whether you knew that or not he did." The news hit me slightly differently now that I was older. I wasn't sure why but the past tense of *liked* made my chest tighten. It wasn't a shock to find out he'd liked me. We'd hung out at mutual friends' houses, went to the same parties, and had good conversations. He had finally asked me on a date and I'd...

"He finally worked up the nerve to ask you out after graduation and you said yes," she said. I remembered that because he'd been nervous and cute. We'd just thrown our caps, and I was with my two friends when he walked up to ask me out. He said he would pick me up at seven the following Friday...and I had agreed.

Then it struck me; that's why he was so mad. My heart clenched as Gemma continued. "He came by your house to pick you up, but you had left. Your parents said you'd decided to leave a few months early for college in San Diego."

I sat down in the chair across from Gemma with my eyes to the floor. I guess I'd hoped he'd forgotten about that. Maybe I had pushed it so far back in memories and tried to force myself not to remember it. But it was there still and with her mentioning it, it resurfaced quickly. I'd stood him up and never talked to him again. Not a text or a call or…anything.

He had every right to be mad. To him, I was that prissy, self-centered cheerleader that left without saying a word. So much more had happened that pushed me to leave early for college, including a huge fight with my parents. I completely forgot about our date until it was too late.

"I…I didn't do it on purpose. I forgot…." I felt so stupid, so inconsiderate. Of course, he hadn't forgotten about it. Even I hadn't completely. Especially seeing him again, it was bringing up things I didn't want to remember. I glanced out the doorway and looked for the sparrow, but it wasn't there.

Gemma looked sad still. "I'm sure you had your reasons, honey." She then looked at my hand and wrinkled her nose. "Is that horse poop?"

I looked at my hand too and blinked. "Can I use your sink?"

She nodded, frowning as she watched me leave the room to go wash my hands. I scrubbed them well and soaped them up three times before finally drying them off.

I went back out to Gemma who had the small dog on her lap as she reviewed something on her computer.

"Thank you, Gemma," I said, still unsure how I truly felt about the situation.

Gemma smiled kindly and stood up, holding the little dog in her arms. "Like I said, he holds grudges like his dad."

"I can't believe he still remembers that…it's been years. I'm sure he's moved on. Isn't he with Skyler, the vet?" I may have been fishing at this point.

She chuckled. "Everyone can see Skyler likes him, but he hasn't dated in years and unfortunately, he won't date her. He doesn't want to mess up that relationship."

Relief flooded me, which I knew was not fair. "He's been single all these years?"

She nodded. "He's been committed to the rescue, so his time is spent here."

I didn't say anything more, but she patted my arm again. "Take tomorrow off, come back on Wednesday. Things will get better, promise."

I looked over to the empty cage where Rex had been, and she answered before I could ask. "I took him back after you got done with cleaning his cage. He's much better."

Gemma's words followed me out to my car and when I shut the door, I sat there for a few minutes. I glanced over at the ranch house with the front porch light on that I knew was Chris's house. He'd pointed it out on our tour of the rescue.

I wasn't ready to go home yet. Instead, I got out of the car and went back to the kennels. When I knelt by Rex's cage, his tail wagged repeatedly, and I put my fingers through the bars to touch his nose again. He nudged them and I petted the soft hair between his eyes. I looked at his food and saw it was half eaten, which was good.

Chris was angry with me…after eight years he was still upset. When I eventually came home, I never called him or wanted to face him again because I thought he had moved on. I had been a coward. I had put my thoughts and feelings for Chris far away, deep inside me. Now, seeing him again, I felt the wall holding back those feelings and memories quickly eroding.

"I can't wait to get drunk tonight!" Sophie sang as she ripped off the graduation cap.

I laughed and unbuttoned my gown to reveal my black dress with the necklace my grandma had given me to wear. My whole life, I'd never seen her take it off. It was always around her neck, hanging right above her heart. She'd decided to give it to me to wear for graduation since she couldn't attend. She'd been feeling worse as of late and even though I was disappointed she couldn't come, I understood.

Natalie pulled off her gown which revealed a much shorter black dress and a plunging neckline.

"Cute dress!" Sophie said with jealousy in her voice.

"Thanks! Do you think Ricky will notice me?"

"If he doesn't, he must be blind!" I piped in.

"Hey, Monica," a voice called, and I looked over my shoulder.

Chris. He'd taken off his cap too, and his gown was open showing a slightly big plaid shirt and jeans. He was wearing his signature cowboy boots.

We'd gotten close during our senior year. He showed up to all the parties I went to, and he'd almost kissed me one night until Sophie threw up and I had to take care of her.

He was always nice and always smiling, and that smile, it was contagious.

I left Natalie and Sophie to step closer to him. "We were just chatting about the party tonight. Are you coming?"

"No, my parents are having a grad party for me at the rescue with friends and family. Can't sneak out of there," he said, scratching the back of his head nervously.

"Oh, okay. That sucks." I tried not to show my disappointment but I'm sure it was evident.

"Come on, Monica!" Sophie cooed behind me as she and Natalie giggled at us. "We're heading back to Nat's!"

"Looks like I got to go," I said, turning to glance at Chris. "I'll see you around."

"Wait!" Chris took my hand before I could walk off and I turned back to him in surprise. His brown eyes were hopeful as he stared at me. "Do you want to go out next Friday...with me?"

I smiled softly. I'd been hoping he'd get the nerve to ask. Maybe with me staying another year, we could see how things go. Maybe go on a few dates. I'd have to keep it secret from my parents and Sam, but what didn't I keep secret from them?

Chris knew that I was thinking of staying another year since I'd opened up to him about it at the Brown's party a few weeks before. He'd given me his sweatshirt to stay warm and I had it still and loved to sleep in it.

Maybe that night had been his push to finally ask me out.

"I'd love to," I agreed.

His grin was huge and sweet and made butterflies swarm in my stomach. "I'll pick you up at seven then."

He let my hand go and I waved as I went back to meet Natalie and Sophie.

I came out of my memories and looked down at a sleeping Rex. My hand was under his chin, and I softly touched the little black mark on his cheek.

That Friday night date had never happened because of me. Because I'd forgotten about it. The day before had been one of the worst days of my life. I'd been so heartbroken and upset, I'd bought a one-way ticket to San Diego and flew out early the next day. Any thoughts of Cold Spring were forced out of my mind.

How was I going to explain that to him? To him I looked like a selfish person who snubbed him for a date after leading him on our senior year.

I was at a loss at how to make this better.

I went home that night and slept restlessly. I worried about Rex and Chris and even Gemma. She'd obviously known what was causing Chris to treat me so horribly. What did she think of me? Was she happy I'd gotten my karma for ditching him?

I tried to force myself to sleep late the next morning, but I didn't make it past eight. I got up and went to my closet to get out more of my things to sell. Then I reached into one of my dressers and dug deep into the bottom. A worn, black sweatshirt was revealed, and I stared at it. The words *Cold Spring High* were spelled out in white across the front, the letters lightly lifting from the fabric as I ran my fingers across it.

Chris's sweatshirt. I'd kept it all these years because part of me never stopped thinking of him, even though I tried.

I pushed it back in the drawer and returned to snapping photos of my expensive brands to post online.

I reluctantly went to my jewelry box and paused as my hand brushed over the top. When I finally opened it, I saw the beautiful turquoise necklace my grandmother had given me to wear for graduation. Just like Chris's sweatshirt, I hadn't been able to give it back before she died. I kept it without anyone knowing because it was a part of her I was holding on to. I'd taken it off when I got to San Diego and kept it someplace safe, occasionally looking at to remember her.

I lifted it out of the box and brushed my fingertips across the stone. There was a weird noise that sounded in the room. I frowned as I glanced up to my bedroom window and saw a sparrow with a twig in its beak hitting the glass. A lump formed in my throat as the little bird tapped and tapped, turning its head from side to side. My hand wrapped tighter around the necklace as I felt resolve grow inside of me. I slipped it on over my head and tucked it under my shirt.

I needed to apologize to Chris, even if it was eight years too late. *What do I say? Sorry for bailing on you, I had some real heavy shit going on and forgot our date?* It felt stupid, but I knew I had to do something. I owed him that.

It was almost routine to get dressed in my jeans, work boots, and a t-shirt. I threw on a plaid shirt and drove over to the rescue. It was before noon and most of the morning work had been done, and the workers were taking breaks. I pulled up into my regular parking spot and waved to Dale and the barn crew as I got out, but I didn't go chat with them. I went back to check on Rex.

The kennels were cleaned, and new bedding was put down along with bowls filled with food and water. Rex sat up when he saw me and wagged his tail. His food was still only half eaten and worry gnawed at my stomach.

"Hi Rex." I put my fingers through the bars, and he licked them. Surprisingly, it didn't make me feel grossed out. Not after flinging horse shit at someone with my bare hands. Oh, how times had changed. Three months ago, I wouldn't have even handled raw chicken with bare hands, let alone horse poop. Pretty sure some of it was still caked underneath my nails.

Rex went over and lay down on his bed, his brown eyes looking at me.

What if...what if I just went in and sat with him? I looked around the kennels and there was no one around. I mean my car was here so if anything happened to me, they knew I was on the property.

Chris would have a field day if I got eaten by the dog I'd been babying the last week. He'd probably attend my funeral just to gloat and tell my parents that I showed my boobs to minors.

Beyond my better judgment, I opened the kennel door and walked in. Rex lifted his head a little to look at me, but he didn't growl.

"Aren't you hungry, Rex?" I kicked the bowl a little to jar the food, but he put his head down onto the bed. I sat on the cold floor and sighed. He opened his eyes to look at me and popped his head up. As if surprised I'd let myself be vulnerable.

Me too, buddy, me too.

I had a pretty face, the last thing I wanted to do was get it mauled off by a dog.

"Just go right for the jugular, don't let me suffer," I explained darkly.

He slowly got off his bed, tail wagging, and came over to sit beside my outstretched legs. I stared, stunned, as he sighed and rested his head on my lap.

Very slowly, I brushed his ears and his eyes drifted closed. He was warm and my heart soared at his trust.

Gemma was right. He wasn't bad, just misunderstood.

"What the devil?" I heard the voice and jumped. Rex did too and started barking and growling at Dale who was watching the two of us through the kennel gate.

I flinched at the sudden change with Rex but was glad it wasn't towards me.

"Hi."

The older man grinned and put his hands on his hips. "Well, I'll be damned. He can be trained."

I patted Rex on his side, and he turned around and limped back into my lap with a sigh. "He can be. He's a good dog," I said softly.

"Isn't today your day off?"

I shrugged, not looking at him. I was embarrassed by the way I acted yesterday. God…if my parents knew about it, they'd lecture me for three hours. Another thing they would *never* find out about.

"Yes, but I wanted to come check on Rex." And talk to Chris but I hadn't gotten the nerve to do that yet and I wasn't sure if I would.

"Well, I'll let you to it then," he said.

"Dale!" I stopped him. He turned on his heel to look at me. "I'm sorry about yesterday. That wasn't like me at all."

His grin was wide again, and I was surprised how attractive he was at his age. "That's alright, we all get upset sometimes. Throwing shit is just a way we express ourselves." He winked and walked out of the building, his boots clomping on the cement floor.

I sighed and leaned my head back against the cold wall and put a hand on Rex's head. He turned on his back and his tongue lulled out as he stared at me upside down. I scratched his belly and one of his legs started shaking.

I laughed and it echoed in the kennel.

I didn't find the nerve. Instead, I went back to my car a little after noon when I knew the workers and Chris would be having lunch. As I was about to get into my car, Gemma came out of the house holding an empty cage and trying to get it onto the porch. She was struggling so I went to help her.

"Oh! Monica! Is it Wednesday already?"

I laughed. "No, I just stopped in to see how Rex was doing."

She smiled at me, and we worked together to bring the cage out onto the porch. "Do you want adoption papers?"

"What? No! I'm not going to adopt him. I don't even know how to take care of myself, let alone a hundred-pound dog that has a temper," I exclaimed.

She chuckled and brushed her hands off on her jeans. "I'm just offering. It seems like you two are hitting it off, I'd hate to see him get adopted out to someone else."

I shrugged. "He deserves a good home so if one comes along, don't hold back because of me."

She gave me a knowing look but nodded. "Are you headed home then?"

"Yeah," I mumbled, glancing over to Chris's house.

“He’s doing a working lunch from home. You could go talk to him,” she offered, seeing my look.

I swallowed, but that would mean I needed to stop being a little chicken and go talk to him, and I wasn’t sure if I was ready.

I had 170 more hours to go, and I needed this to work. I couldn’t just let it go.

“Yeah, I think I'll stop over.”

She patted my arm. “That’s my girl. Just don’t throw anymore shit please.”

I stopped and turned to give her a horrified look. “You know?”

She smiled with amusement. “Dale doesn’t keep anything from me, and it was the conversation for the rest of the afternoon. I don’t think it’s something my volunteers will easily forget.”

I let out a breath that did nothing to alleviate my stress. “There is no place else I can finish out my community service?”

She laughed again. “Sorry Monica, but no.”

Chapter Six

One Point for Chris, Zero for Monica

I jiggled my keys as I was about to get into my car again but stopped to look across at the little rancher.

Suck it up and face him. You did lots of daring things in San Diego. You faced off with male models and big wigs and even met a few movie stars.

This is just Chris.

Just Chris, who I stood up for one date eight years ago. He hadn't known why, and I wasn't about to explain it all to him, but he did deserve an apology.

I walked over to the house and knocked on the door. I could handle this six-foot-something, wannabe cowboy easily. *Watch me.*

He answered the door, and all of my preplanned words vanished. He looked even more like a cowboy today than any other day with his low-slung jeans, boots, and an open button down shirt with a black t-shirt underneath.

His eyes narrowed as soon as he saw me. "Can you warn me when you throw more shit so I can at least duck?"

I gritted my teeth. "I came to apologize."

"Oh?" He crossed his arms.

I looked off towards the swing on the small porch. “I got frustrated and I shouldn’t have thrown the horse shit.”

His lips twitched at the corner. “And?”

I flipped my attention back to him. “And what? This is your turn to apologize now.”

“*My* turn?”

“Yes, *your* turn! You were being an ass too! I didn’t throw that shit unprovoked, and you know it!” I felt my blood boil with outrage towards him again.

This was not going how I thought it would.

“I gave you a job and you didn’t do it. Anyone else who refuses like that would be fired on the spot,” he said, his eyes sharp.

“Newsflash Chris, I’m not your employee! I’m here because I *have* to be here, not because I want to be,” I snapped. “I have no experience with animals. You know I didn’t grow up with any. Do you really think I’d feel comfortable working with horses?”

“Not yet.” His words sounded soft and foreign considering how we’d been talking to each other for the last few weeks.

I sighed, pressing a finger between my brows. “I just want to get along, Chris. I just want to get my hours in so I can get a full-time job, stop selling my favorite clothes, and be done with it here. Please stop trying to make my life more miserable than it already is.”

He regarded me and I wondered if Gemma had told him about the conversation we'd had yesterday and the fact that he held a grudge against me because of ditching him on our would-be first date.

"Whatever I did in the past was a mistake," I said quietly. "I regret a lot of things from back then and I wish I could take some back, but I can't."

His gaze changed, lines forming between his brows that were somehow adorable in their own way. "Okay," he stated.

I reeled back in surprise. "Okay? Okay what?"

"Okay that we can get along until you're done."

"Great–"

"Under a few conditions."

I glared. "What?"

"If I tell you to do something, you do it," he commanded in a tone that may have caused a tingle to run down my spine.

"Absolutely not!"

"If it's something you're uncomfortable doing, I'll do it with you to start off until you're okay with doing it alone," he explained.

I narrowed my eyes. "Somehow I feel this is going to bite me in the ass."

He just smirked. "Deal?"

"Ugh, fine."

He stuck out his large, calloused hand and I took it. A sharpness went down my arm at the contact, reminding me of the time he'd almost kissed me by the pool. I pulled back quickly, his hand still midair as if he was surprised by the feeling too.

"See you later," I said and left the porch.

I did not even have time to wrap my brain around what just happened.

By the next morning, I felt much better about my situation and how things were going between Chris and me. I happily got to the animal rescue and headed back to the kennels. Much to my delight, Rex was up and moving around a lot more. He seemed to be putting weight on his leg which was great.

I put in my headphones and listened to music as I finished up the kennels then sat in with Rex for a bit.

"Monica?" The voice made me jump since it echoed off the cement walls, but it also made my blood race.

"Yeah?" I called out to Chris.

His footsteps were loud as he walked down to look in the kennel at me.

"What the hell are you doing? He has temperament issues," he said, a tinge of alarm to his voice.

I looked down at Rex who was lying with his head in my lap. "He looks gentle to me."

He rolled his eyes. "You're still on the job, come on."

I got up reluctantly and Rex gave me a sad pathetic look. "Sorry, buddy."

I closed the kennel door and turned towards Chris. "I got the kennels done in three hours. I feel like that's a record."

Chris's lip twitched slightly with amusement. "That's why I came to get you. I've got more work for you." He nodded his head, and I followed him. We were about to walk into the horse barn when I stopped.

"No, no, no! I told you I'm not working with the horses!" I snapped.

He turned towards me and got extremely close, as in kissing distant close and I paused. "Remember what we talked about yesterday?"

What? I couldn't think with him this close to me.

I thought for a moment then remembered: the conditions. *Great. They were biting me in the ass less than a day after I agreed to them.*

"You said you'd do it with me," I gritted quietly.

He smirked. "I'll get the horse out, you start shoveling." He handed me the manure fork, more like shoved it at me, and I took it.

"You're a jerk, Chris."

"Good, glad you're listening."

I stayed far away from the stall until Chris got the large black animal out. The horse handlers watched with amusement.

I knew what Chris was doing. He'd been embarrassed by me on Monday in front of the barn crew and volunteers, so he was here to redeem himself. It riled me up so much that I had half a mind to throw more shit at him.

Dale saw my expression as he leaned in the stall door and looked at Chris who had tied the horse to the outside of the barn and came back in to watch me.

"You better get back, she looks like she may throw that manure fork at you next," Dale said with a chuckle.

Chris didn't look amused as I piled the poop into the wheelbarrow. It was a hell of a lot more than dog poop, but at least it smelled better.

I glared at Chris every time I put a giant fork load into the wheelbarrow as he watched, leaning against the opposite wall with his arms across his chest.

He'd won and he knew it.

My back never hurt as much as it did when I finished with the horse stall. Luckily, Chris only wanted me to clean the one. I spread straw down in the stall and refilled the water bucket, which was huge compared to Rex's, and filled the feed dish.

I went out of the barn to find Chris, who was alone and brushing the horse that was tied to a post.

"I'm finished," I muttered tiredly.

"Good, come here."

I couldn't help it; I rolled my eyes. "Listen, I'm not doing all the stalls today. You guys do this daily; this is my first time."

He laughed and for a second it stopped me. The sound was so familiar but so different from the one I'd remembered when we were in high school. It also made the crow's feet show around his eyes, and for some reason, I thought that was adorable.

"You don't have to clean anymore stalls today, don't worry. Come here and take this," Chris said, stopping to hand me the brush.

I stared at the big black horse, and he seemed to eye me up too. As if we weren't sure of each other.

"No thanks."

"Monica."

Hearing him say my name jarred my attention. His eyes were serious, but his lips were in a small smile. "I promise he won't hurt you."

I felt beckoned, as if my body was moving of its own accord towards Chris. He took my hand, and I wrapped my fingers around the brush. A tingle went down my spine at the contact with his palm. His chest brushed against me as we made a sweeping motion together down the horse's side.

It felt…intimate, as he stood behind me, close enough that I could feel his breath on the shell of my ear.

"Brush down," he instructed softly, and I did. "They can easily spook, so you have to talk to them. If you must go around behind, always touch them so they don't kick."

"Kick?" I asked with a loud squeak.

He chuckled again and seemed reluctant but removed his hand from mine. "Yes, but we'll be fine. He's not a rescue."

I paused, looking at the black beast of an animal. The horse shook his head and looked back at us. "Whose is he?"

"He's mine. My parents got him for me as a graduation gift," Chris said.

I kept brushing, going closer to his beautiful mane. Horses were soft, I realized, and they seemed gentle.

"He's beautiful in a scary, giant dog way. What's his name?"

"He's a good horse. He's never kicked anyone. At least not yet." I snorted at him as he continued. "His name is Jasper."

I glanced at Chris, who was looking at Jasper with kind eyes. He seemed like such a different person from earlier in the day. Relaxed, less angry. There was also no one else around at the moment.

"How many horses are here?"

"Including the one we picked up this week…thirty-six. It's why we have eight men working at the rescue. We have a lot to take care of as you can see."

They definitely did. Jasper was calm and at home here, but the other ones I'd encountered seemed skittish, like the one I'd seen Chris and the vet working with. I'm sure it took lots of work to get them settled in and back to good health.

"My grandma always loved horses," I said quietly as I continued to brush Jasper. It felt comfortable now, almost comforting. "She said they're our spirit animals and if you look into their eyes, you might possibly see yourself."

I thought maybe Chris would make fun of me or say something, but he didn't. He just watched me. For some reason that made it even worse. I made eye contact and felt something race to my stomach where it exploded like fireworks. Whatever look that was, it felt…intense, as if he was searching for something in my expression.

He could see it made me uncomfortable and looked away. "Have you ever ridden?"

"No, absolutely not. And I'm not going to ride, Chris. That isn't part of–"

He laughed. "I'm not going to make you ride, Monica. I was just asking." He loosened Jasper's lead rope from the post and gave it to me. "Take him back into his stall."

I did as he said, and Jasper clopped behind me as I guided him into his stall. It was very intimidating, especially when I went to leave, and Jasper reached across me to get a drink. I squealed and ducked quickly under his neck and ran right into Chris on the other side of the stall. He stopped me with a laugh, both hands on my shoulders to steady me.

We looked at each other and I felt warmness pulling inside me the longer I looked into his brown eyes. *God, how could I ever forget them?* They were soft brown with flecks of gold.

Two lines appeared between his brows as he looked over my face. I cleared my throat, and he dropped his hands to his sides. Silence grew until finally Chris said, "See, they aren't as bad as you think."

"Jasper wasn't bad, but I'm exhausted." I wiped my hand across my forehead and heard my phone ring. I answered it, thinking it was a possible job.

"Hi Monica, it's your mom. I thought we'd see you more now that you moved home. Have you gotten settled?" Her tone sounded very much like my mother: annoyance mixed with worry. My dad was probably pushing her to call me.

I glanced at Chris, who was watching me. "I'm going to step out," I said quietly to him and walked out of the barn.

"Who are you talking to?" Mom asked.

"I'm..." *Shit. What should I say?* I was always good at lying. Don't stop now. "I'm at Long Rhodes Ahead Animal Rescue. I'm talking to them about hiring me for marketing. You know, help them get some more donations."

Yeah Monica...yeah! That was good. Look at you go! Spin that bullshit.

"Interesting. I didn't know they could afford to pay since they are a non-profit," she questioned.

"They are, but they have a few horse handlers they pay," I insisted.

"Well, that's good then." She was quiet for a moment and sighed. "I'm worried about you, Mon. I just want you to get things together so you're a bit more stable. Sam and Emma—"

I reeled back. "I lived in San Diego by myself for several years, Mom. I was stable."

"I mean *settled.* They have Savannah now and we'd like more grandchildren you know."

I couldn't believe this was happening...again. I'd been living back in Cold Spring for barely a month, and she was already down my throat about having babies? I wasn't even dating anyone! When I lived in San Diego, I talked to my parents maybe once a month and I liked it that way. They didn't know I stayed out most Fridays and Saturdays until four in the morning or that I drank a lot. They were distant watchers and only saw what I showed them. Being back here...it's just like it was when I lived at home before I turned eighteen.

"I have to go, Mom. I'll talk to you later."

"We aren't–"

"Love you, bye." I hung up and shoved the phone deep into my pocket.

I was surprised my dad didn't show up to my apartment every week to make sure it was clean and that I was searching for a job and trying to work. Now add to the list, finding a new man and producing a grandchild for them.

I loved my brother and Emma but…but I hated being compared to them. It was something that had been happening my entire life.

Sam went to college. You should go.

Sam went to the police academy. You need to do something good for this country too.

Sam found the perfect woman. Now you need to the find the perfect man.

Sam conceived the best baby. You should too.

I was *sick* of it.

Living in San Diego their words hadn't hit me as hard as they did now.

"You look like you could use a drink," Chris said as I glanced over my shoulder at him.

The summer sun was making his tan skin glow, and it made my heart race. He was truly handsome. Nothing like the men in San Diego who sported fake tans from tanning beds or sprays. Those men were pampered. Chris…he was not. He was hard, rough, and masculine.

"I could drink a beer."

Chris chuckled and continued past me. “Follow me.”

I walked beside Chris as we headed to his house. The front porch had a shoe rack, and a mat filled with boots in all stages of dirt.

He pointed to the porch swing. "Go ahead and sit. I'll be back." I did as he said and sat down, surprised at how good it felt to get off my feet and relax. I looked out across the lawn and saw the sun was getting lower, but it wasn’t late. I'd been at the rescue for over seven hours now and I was exhausted and ready for bed soon. Every day I'd spent here I'd been asleep by ten. Younger Monica would have laughed at older Monica.

It was a beautiful scene, with the horses and cows grazing out in the field. I vaguely heard the dogs barking in their kennels.

I kicked off my boots and pulled my legs up to sit my chin on my knees.

It was peaceful. Comforting even. It was vastly different from living in San Diego or even in the town Cold Spring. You couldn't hear traffic or people yelling, just the sounds of nature.

The front door opened, and Chris came out carrying two brown bottles.

He walked over to the swing and handed over the drink. I realized it wasn’t real beer; it was root beer.

“Really?” I said with a laugh.

He grinned. "You're on probation, remember?"

I scoffed as he sat down next to me, and I realized how close we were. Our shoulders touched and I could smell his masculine scent. *What was that?* It was hay...but it had a spice to it. It most definitely couldn't have been cologne since this man didn't wear it because of his job. Either way, I enjoyed it a lot and caught myself leaning a little bit closer to him.

I took a sip of the root beer and sighed. "I can't even imagine it being beer."

He chuckled and leaned back, rocking the swing a bit. We both stared out across at the rescue.

"It's beautiful," I whispered softly.

The swing creaked as he gently moved his feet. "What brought you back to Cold Spring?" His tone was odd, stiff as if he didn't want to ask but felt forced to.

I snorted and looked over at him. "Want to hear the full truth so you feel better about yourself?" He frowned at me and before he could say anything I started into it. "I got fired from my job. A company came in and bought us out and my position was the first on the chopping block. Without that job, there's no way I could have afforded to stay in my apartment." I took another sip of the root beer and looked out again. "I had spent so much of my time playing someone else.

Playing the girl who dated the hot models and who wore the expensive clothing. I thought that was me, but it wasn't." My voice grew quiet as I really thought of my words and what I'd just said out loud.

It was true though. I wasn't that girl anymore. I didn't think I ever was. I had run away from the hurt and high expectations of my family and tried to fit into life in San Diego, and when I didn't fit in, I'd changed who I was to be like them.

"You're right, I do feel better about myself now," Chris said and as I snapped my gaze to him, I saw he was teasing me. I rolled my eyes.

"Yeah okay. So, you're exactly where you wanted to be after high school?"

He shrugged, his shoulder brushing mine again. "Not exactly, but it isn't as bad as I thought it would be."

I looked at his house, his truck, and the land that he would eventually inherit.

Shit. He was being serious. He was happy with where he was in life.

"You never went to college?" I asked, hoping it didn't sound rude.

"I took a few business classes, but it wasn't for me. What I wanted to learn wasn't something they can teach you in a classroom," he explained.

"So, you want to continue the rescue? Keep doing what your parents have done?"

"That's the plan," he said, taking another sip of his root beer. "It's what I love doing."

He didn't look at me, but I watched his expression, and I knew he wasn't lying. He did love what he was doing. I wanted that. I wanted to do something that made me feel complete. Working in marketing in San Diego had been good, but it never felt like *me*.

"Hey boss," someone yelled.

We both looked up and saw Dale walking over to the porch. He grinned when he saw me sitting next to Chris. "Got another one of those?"

"It's not real beer," I warned, and Dale chuckled.

"This one here doesn't drink so I knew it wasn't going to be anything good," Dale said as Chris stood up.

"Dale," he snapped tightly and disappeared inside. Dale came up onto the porch and leaned against the railing, grinning.

"He doesn't drink?" I whispered.

Dale shook his head no. "Hasn't since he was young."

"Why?"

"Something to do with–"

"Here, take this and shut up," Chris muttered as he walked back out with another root beer.

Dale just kept his grin and opened the soda.

"Did you guys check on the new horse this evening?" Chris asked.

"Sure did. Will checked his foot and it's better, the infection is leaving. Doc said it would eventually, but it just needed some time," Dale assured.

Chris nodded and rubbed a hand across his beard. "We should get Doc out here tomorrow to do another check, just to be sure."

Dale looked between us, and I felt my cheeks flush. "He invited me over for a soda after cleaning out Jasper's stall." I didn't know why I said it, but I did. I guess I was worried about how it looked, though I didn't know why.

Chris glanced over at me, his eyebrows furrowed as if he was confused as to why I'd said it too.

"Whatever the boss does in his spare time is his business. He could use a good time every once in a while. He doesn't get off the rescue often." Dale leaned in closer to me with a playful expression. "This kid here, I've known him since he was only ten years old. He's always been so serious and wanted to be just like his dad, whom he's the spitting image of, inside and out. Anyhow, he has barely gotten to live his life, especially when a young man should." Chris was just shaking his head. "When Chris was eighteen, he got into a rough spot—"

"Dale! Don't you have work to do? Or a wife to go home to?" Chris snapped.

He just grinned again, not affected in the least by Chris's sharp tone.

"That's true. Got myself a home-cooked meal waiting for me. See you both tomorrow." Dale winked at me and left the porch.

A rough spot? Right after high school? Where did that come from?

"Chris, what was he talk–"

"You should probably head home. I'm sure you're tired," Chris said, cutting me off. I looked over but he didn't meet my gaze.

"Sure," I mumbled, standing up with the half-empty bottle of root beer.

I realized I didn't want to go home. There wasn't a home-cooked meal waiting for me or…or anyone for that matter, but that wasn't his problem. It was mine.

"Thanks for the drink. I'll see you tomorrow," I said softly. I handed him the bottle, and he didn't look up at me as I walked off the porch.

"Monica," he called, and I stopped to turn around and face him. He stood up, both root beers in his hands, his expression unreadable. "Take tomorrow off. We don't have a lot going on so there won't be much to do."

I wasn't sure how to take that, but I took it as a good thing. "Okay…boss."

His lip quirked up at the comment and I smiled as I walked back to my car.

Chapter Seven

Birds of a Feather

A day off. What was that? Previously I would have gone and gotten a pedicure and manicure and maybe a facial, but I found myself sleeping half the day and hating myself for it. Finally, around noon, I went to Spring Awake dressed in my normal animal rescue attire. Erin was behind the counter and did a double take when she saw me.

"Almost didn't recognize you, Monica. You okay?"

Did I look that bad?

"Yeah, I'm fine. I was hoping we could chat if you get a minute?" I practically begged. It had been a month since I moved home, and I hadn't made one penny. With my severance pay and my savings, I had enough to pay my bills for a while. And I was making some money from selling my clothes online, but still, I needed to get something under my belt and a steady income.

"Sure, I'll meet you in five."

I smiled and went to the table to sit and wait. I pulled up the presentation on my laptop right as my phone dinged with a text from Phoebe. There was a picture of a very festive piña colada along with a description.

Phoebe: *Yes, I know it's morning and no, I don't care. Miss you!*

Me: *Save one for me. After the week I had, I need one.*

Phoebe: *Ooh, now you must tell me that hot juicy gossip. Too much drama with the New York boys?*

"I've got about fifteen minutes," Erin said, sitting down across from me. She untied her apron and hung it on the chair.

I shut my phone off quickly and smiled at Erin. "Great! That's all I need."

I went over the details of my marketing plan with her, and she was a tough cookie to read. I couldn't tell if I sold her on it or if she was just being nice with her questions.

"If this is something you're interested in, I can do an early post on my social media pages and tag the coffee shop and see if that generates some activity. If it does, you can hire me," I ended, sitting back in my chair.

She chewed on her lip as she thought. "You think one of your posts will get me customers?"

I almost winced. "It sounds narcissistic but yes. I know most of the hashtags that are used and generate more views, and doing short videos are also a big thing right now."

She eyed me a little longer. "Okay. Do the post and let's see what happens. If I get more than five customers from your post, I'll hire you part-time for marketing."

"Really?" I asked, sounding way too hopeful.

"Yes."

"Great! Well, I'll need one of the best coffees and meals on your menu. I'll snap a few good pictures and post them today," I said with a grin.

"I'll be right back." She stood and went back behind the counter.

I couldn't stop my stupid smile. I was going to prove to her that I could do this.

A few minutes later she brought over a beautiful panini and a decorative coffee in a white mug.

"Looks perfect!" I stood up and took a few pictures of it, being sure to have the *Spring Awake* sign above the front door at the top of the photo.

"Got it! You can take it away. I'll get the post ready and tag the store and your personal page. I may even go to a few other platforms to see what we can get from those," I suggested.

She had her hands on her hips as she stood above me. "It's on me. Enjoy. I'll be waiting for those customers," she said before walking away.

I looked back down at the food that smelled amazing and before I could stop myself, I took a large bite of the sandwich.

"Oh, Monica, isn't it?"

Mouth full of food, I looked up to see Skyler, the veterinarian, standing above me. She wore casual clothing but still had her hair up in a clip and away from her face.

"Oh! Skyler!" I almost choked on my panini, not realizing how much of it I had in my mouth and tried to chew it quickly.

"I'm sorry," she said with a small laugh. "I didn't mean to intrude."

I finally finished my bite and put the sandwich down. "You didn't intrude. And yes, I'm Monica."

"How's the German Shepherd doing? I'm going to be headed over to the rescue here in a little bit, but I probably won't have time to check on him," she admitted guiltily.

"Rex is doing a lot better. He's back to himself for the most part."

"Good, I'm glad. I wish it were like that with all the animals I help, but unfortunately that's not the case." Her voice was soft and sad. It made me feel bad for her profession. I didn't like animals that much, but still, to be around the heartbreak of telling someone they had to put their animal down would probably get to me.

"Are you working right now?" I asked, trying to lighten the subject.

"I'm on a quick coffee break between appointments. I'm currently addicted to Erin's coconut chocolate chip frappe. I've dreamed about it at least once this week!"

We both laughed and there was silence. "Well, I better go. It was good to see you. I'm sure I'll see again at the rescue," Skyler said.

Yep, for another hundred and something hours, I wanted to tell her, but instead just said, "See you around."

Had Chris told her the reason I was doing community service? I bet he did. He probably stood in the horse stall and told her all about my incident and how happy he was that he'd gotten to see me shoveling shit.

But things had changed between us since yesterday. Since we brushed out Jasper's coat together then shared a root beer on his porch. I felt a flutter in my stomach at the memory of his nearness.

I shut my laptop, ate the rest of my panini and coffee, and left.

I didn't see Chris the following morning so after I was done cleaning out the kennels, I sat with Rex for a little while. He was back to himself, minus the aggressiveness. He was a little protective of me but even that was getting better.

I went to Jasper's stall and the other horse handlers were standing around in the barn, along with Dale.

I felt disappointed when I didn't see Chris with them. It made me wonder if he got called out for another rescue.

"Whatcha doing in here, little darling?" Dale asked, coming over to lean against the stall.

"I thought I'd brush him a little. I didn't know if Chris was going to make me again, so I thought I'd just do it before he demanded it of me."

He nodded slowly. "You know he's off today, right?"

I snapped my head up. "No? Was it sudden?"

"Keith got back from his trip to Wyoming. He took the day off to visit with him. The boy hasn't seen him in almost two months," Dale said.

"Oh. Why was Keith out in Wyoming?"

"He helps other rescues since we have a big horse trailer. There were about a dozen or so horses and donkeys that were found and he was helping round them up and take them to a farm in Montana. It took a lot longer than they expected."

I nodded. That was a long time to be away from his family and the rescue.

"I'm sure if you leave, none of us will rat you out," Dale said quietly as a young man walked over next to him.

"Can we go home too?" the man asked. He had light brown hair, blue eyes, and a boyish face.

Dale laughed. "No way in hell. Go get Tommy and clean out the other stalls," Dale instructed.

The man rolled his eyes but did as Dale directed.

I smiled softly as I brushed Jasper's coat, and he slowly ate the hay I'd put in his feeder.

"I wondered if we were ever going to meet you," Dale said quietly.

I stopped brushing, not sure if I heard him correctly. I looked at him over Jasper's back and frowned. "What?"

"You were the Monica from high school, right?"

"Yes?"

"The one who stood him up?"

I flinched. "Not on purpose. It was…it was a bad time for me." That was an understatement.

Dale just looked at me and I couldn't read his expression or maybe I didn't want to. "Anyhow, it's been a long time since then. I don't mean to bring up the past."

"Has…has Chris talked about it?"

He crossed his arms over the stall door, looking a little guilty. "Not so much in words."

I stopped brushing to look at him and Jasper nudged his head into me, which freaked me out for a second. "What do you mean?"

"He only talked about it once or twice. It was the day after it happened. The kid was the first one up that morning and had the kennels and barn cleaned by the time we all got in. When I went to talk to him about it, he just said it was a girl he liked who took off and he was sure he'd never see her again. I later overheard Gemma talking to him about a Monica and I put two and two together."

He never thought he'd see me again? Like my parents didn't live here and I wouldn't come back? But I hadn't come looking for him when I did come home. Not that I came home often in the last eight years. Everyone from Cold Spring knew I hated it here and that once I left, I most likely wasn't coming back.

"You took me away from my friends!" I remember yelling at my parents. *"You destroyed my future because you made me move to this dumb town! Once I leave, I am never coming back here!"*

That was of course before getting closer to my grandma. I thought it was the end of my life when my parents uprooted me from California. I had been five years old when we moved to San Diego because of my dad's job. I was so angry at my parents when we came back but then I spent time with my grandma and learned so much from her. She became the only person who knew me and supported me. My parents and Sam, who were pushy and had high expectations, would have overpowered my life without my grandma being present. She was the tether holding me here so when her health went downhill and she passed, I had no reason to stay.

"Unfortunately, I'm the only Monica around," I mumbled.

"I'm sorry, kid. I didn't mean to stir up any problems."

"It's okay, it's nothing."

He didn't look convinced, but he walked away to join the other workers.

I left the barn a little while later and headed towards my car. I was unlocking it when the front door of the main house opened and out walked Keith Rhodes.

He really was a spitting image of an older Chris and wore a Long Rhodes Ahead hat. His brown eyes flashed with recognition as he looked at me.

"Hi Mr. Rhodes," I said, wishing I didn't have to see him. I would have to beg him not to tell my parents the real reason I was at his rescue.

"Monica Locklear, wow. You look a lot like your father," Keith said with a big grin.

"Hopefully minus the broad shoulders and crankiness," I mumbled.

He chuckled. "Your dad didn't say you were home, did you come to visit?"

I frowned. Gemma and Chris hadn't told him? That was shocking. "Um, no. I moved back but I'm here doing community service. Which, by the way, my father does not know about so if you could keep that bit a secret, that would be great."

He looked surprised. "Community service?"

"Long story. Go sit in Sullivan's this week and I'm sure you'll hear all about it." There was silence between us for a moment. "Anyhow, I should go. It was good to see you, Mr. Rhodes."

"Monica, just call me Keith, you're how old now?" he said with a laugh.

I smiled. "Bye, Keith."

A week passed and I didn't see Chris at all, but I kept up with the dog kennels and spent the extra time with Jasper who I ended up really liking. Horses weren't as scary as I originally thought, or at least Jasper wasn't.

After work one day I went in to speak with Gemma and she signed off on my hours for the day since Chris hadn't been around.

"Well, you're getting the hours down. Looks like only a hundred more. That's half!" Gemma said, looking up at me.

"Yeah, time is going by quickly," I mumbled. I didn't want to go home, and I knew Gemma had trails all over the back yard close to the fence line. "Do you think I could walk Rex a little this evening? Off the clock of course."

Gemma's grin was wide. "Of course. Just make sure to put the harness on him and keep your phone on you."

I put the harness on Rex who seemed excited about the entire thing, and we walked out behind the farm and onto the narrow trail. Rex sniffed everything as we walked, peeing at every tree. He would have peed on the electric fence had I not been able to drag him away just in time. He didn't pull on the leash like I thought he would and was an easy companion. It was a hot July day, but I'd opted to wear jeans since I found out the hard way about the bugs. And I didn't own any bug spray because I'd never really spend any time outside.

Once we were past the tree line it opened into a field. I could see the steer behind the fence but could no longer see the farm. It was a beautiful evening as the sun ghosted over the land and the cicadas started their nightly song.

Rex sat on his haunches at my feet and wagged his tail as he looked up at me with adoration. No one had ever looked at me like that before. The love in his eyes could never be replaced. I sat down in the field and Rex laid across my lap as we enjoyed the sun and warm breeze.

The steers were making noises as they came closer to see what we were doing. A bird flew overhead and landed on the fence post not far from Rex and me. I stared at it as it stretched out its wing, until Rex stood up and scared it away. This was why I'd avoided nature so much the last eight years. When my grandma was alive, we used to spend a lot of time outside together.

"Grandma, why did we drive the whole way up here?" I asked, as we passed the sign for the

entrance of the Papscanee Island Nature Preserve and I turned onto the road to the parking area.

When I went to her house after school, she met me at my car, got in, and gave me directions on where to go. I questioned her about where we were going, but she never answered me. I spent almost all my evenings at her house since my parents had become unbearable to be around. They hounded me on where I was going to college, what I was going for, and to not get wrapped up in a guy. The only person to stick up for me was my grandma. She was the only voice of reason with my father. She was the only good thing about moving back to Cold Spring.

I parked by the water of the Hudson where there was a small beach and a wooden bench. Grandma didn't answer me and got out of the car. I quickly followed her and helped her sit on the bench. Her long hair was pulled back into a tight bun and her dark eyes were solemn as she settled into the seat and looked out across the water.

"I used to come here a lot as a young girl," she said softly.

I sat down and didn't take my gaze from her. When I was with her, I felt like my true self. I didn't have to dress or talk a certain way; I could just be me.

"Really?" I asked, finally looking out at the view. The sun shone down onto the river making the water look like diamonds sparkling on top of the surface.

"I've always loved being by the water. It's why I stayed close to the Hudson all these years. Where there is water, there is life, and that's where I want to be." She touched the turquoise necklace that hung around her fragile neck.

"What do you mean?"

She glanced over at me, and her brown eyes were soft and filled with so much love. She clutched my hand in hers. "Water is the source of life. Of you and me. If we are by the water, we will see that it is in our souls to be drawn to it." She gestured around us at the quietness of the world. I took notice of it all with her. It was peaceful. No cars, no people and their voices. As we sat there a bird flew onto a tree close to us and we both looked at it.

Grandma gasped and put her hand on my arm. "There, Monica, the bird, look."

It was beautiful as it tilted its head at us. "It's a sparrow," I said, recognizing it.

She smiled at me, and I saw tears shining in her eyes. "Yes, it's a sparrow. Remember what I told you about them?"

"They are sometimes sent by our passed relatives to show us they are still with us," I said, remembering the conversation.

She squeezed my arm. "Yes, Monica, that's right." Her voice wavered and I could hear the tears in it.

"I love you, Grandma."

She looked at me and a tear slipped down her cheek. "I love you too. Remember that animals are the path to our family who have gone before us. Sometimes, they are our only source of love when people cannot love us. They will be your guide through life so make sure you look for them." She paused and I held her hand tighter as her gaze grew serious. "Look for me when I'm gone."

Rex nudged me as my own tear fell from my cheek, and I quickly wiped it away. I hadn't been around many animals since her death, but those stupid sparrows had been showing up since I'd moved back here. Was it done on purpose? If I knew Grandma, I'd say yes. I'd been in San Diego eight years and never saw one damn sparrow. I move back here, and I start seeing them everywhere. She was haunting me.

A laugh left my lips which seemed to surprise Rex. He rolled on his back and looked at me upside down in that goofy manner that made me smile.

"She'd love you. She would have tamed you within seconds of meeting you," I told him,

Rex flipped around when we heard a horse neigh and glanced up to see someone riding through the field toward us.

The black horse was regal and the man on it looked powerful. It was like a scene from an old western movie, not something you'd see just sixty miles north of New York City. The rider wore a baseball cap and simple t-shirt and I realized quickly who it was.

Chris.

Chapter Eight

The Almost Kiss

As Chris rode toward us on the large horse I noticed he was wearing sunglasses. Rex stood up and barked and I held onto him when they drew near.

Chris reigned in Jasper, and I couldn't read his expression, but he looked surprised.

"What are you doing out here? I thought you left for the day," he finally asked.

I settled Rex and made him sit, which he did. Note taken that it didn't take much to train him. Maybe he wasn't that untrainable.

"Decided to take Rex on a walk. We both needed some fresh air," I answered, not moving from my spot in the field.

He sat there in silence, Jasper reaching down to grab a mouthful of grass, as Chris pulled up on his reins to stop him.

"What are you doing out here?" I asked to help fill the silence.

He looked away towards the horizon at the cows in the field. "Decided to take Jasper on a walk," he said, mimicking my words.

"You can join me if you'd like, or am I going to hog all your fresh air?"

He cracked a smile and dismounted flawlessly. *God, he made that look so easy.*

He tied the reins around a fence post and then slowly sat down next to me. Rex walked over and sniffed Chris then finally settled protectively over my legs with a sigh, not taking his eyes off him.

He snorted. "Didn't think he'd ever be domesticated that quickly," he muttered. I rubbed Rex's head, and his tail swished happily.

"He has been easy to tame and eager to listen. He's much easier than some people I know." I glanced at him, still not able to read his expression behind his sunglasses.

His lip twitched into a smirk. "I didn't think you were a nature kind of girl. I seem to remember you bailing on going to any of the cliff parties," he said, glancing over.

He was sitting rather close to me, and I could smell his familiar scent. Hay and spice. I wanted to inch a bit closer, maybe touch him, but this was Chris. I'd already hurt him once. He wanted nothing to do with me now.

Disappointment filled me at the thought of not getting a second chance with him.

"You and I both know those parties were lame. And how many girls got pushed off the cliff at night? I wasn't about to be a part of that."

He rolled his eyes. "I tried to make sure those idiot Brown brothers didn't do that shit. Your brother has been trying to put a stop the parties for a while now."

At the mention of my brother, I snorted automatically.

"What? You don't like your brother anymore?"

I looked out to the field and saw birds flying across the sky and into the trees. "No, I love my big brother," I murmured. "I just hate constantly being compared to him. He's the golden child who does no wrong and makes all the right choices. Then there's me who fails at her job, her relationships, and just life overall." He watched me and I felt even more pathetic. "Sorry, I realize how that sounds."

He kept looking at me and I wanted to rip off those sunglasses so I could read his expression.

"I don't think I've seen that Monica in a while," he responded, taking off his glasses to stare at me.

"The one who's pathetic?"

"The one who's vulnerable."

When I met his gaze, I felt that sudden shock run through. I didn't have to read his expression. He was seeing through me. He'd done that before. It was such a familiar moment and it caused the same sputtering in my heart that it'd done that first time. That night he'd almost kissed me.

I cleared my throat and looked away from him. "What's your real reason for coming out here? I saw your dad was home." I was good at changing the subject. Chris understood what I was doing and relieved me by looking away.

"Yeah, I thought I'd give my them some time together."

He'd always been close with both of his parents, but his dad was who he always wanted to be like. His dad was his hero.

"Your dad is a good guy, and of course your mom's great."

"He's not bad," Chris said with a laugh and a glance over at me. "Jasper needed to run too, and it finally cooled off a bit outside."

We both looked up at Jasper who was having his fill of the long grass that he could reach from the fence post.

"You said you've never ridden, right?"

I scoffed. "Unless you're counting the ones that are metal and go in a circle, no, and I don't plan to either."

His smile was sweet and made those stupid butterflies swarm in my stomach. "It's not that bad."

"Right. I'm finally able to go into the stall with Jasper without freaking out."

He looked at me and I felt his gaze again, making a tingle down my neck and spine.

I swallowed. That *déjà vu* feeling went through me.

"I'm going to ride out past the pasture to check on the cattle. Be careful out here," he said standing up quickly and grabbing Jasper's reins.

"Okay," I said dumbly as he hopped onto the back of the black horse. He gave a nod as he went back to the trail and followed it along the outside of the cattle fence.

As I watched him, I petted Rex's head and frowned.

"It's too loud in here!" I yelled out to Sophie, who was on her fourth shot in the two hours we'd been at the Brown's party.

She was already drunk from the looks of it and making out with the youngest Brown boy.

"It's not loud! I don't know what you're talking about!" she slurred.

I looked for Natalie and found her sitting on Ricky's lap on the couch, about to start making out. I ignored them both and went out the back door to the pool.

I was not in the mood to be here tonight. My parents and I had gotten into a fight this morning before school. Of course, it was about college and what my major should be. They didn't like that I wanted to study marketing, but it was something that interested me. I could not do blood so being in the medical field was a big no. Being a lawyer was even worse. I couldn't be professional for that long, even if the pant suits looked adorable. I was a great liar though so that would do me well. But I hated the idea of spending the next 10 years in school, so it was another no. I tried to talk to Sophie and Natalie about it earlier, but they kept saying it would be alright, and I realized they didn't want my negative vibes. They were too excited about tonight, so I'd kept my feelings to myself.

There were very few people sitting outside since it was a little chilly. Mr. and Mrs. Brown had just opened the pool and then left for the weekend, giving their boys the opportunity to throw a big party.

The bass of the music thumped loudly even outdoors, so I went to the other side of the pool to get away from the noise. It smelled like chlorine as I sat down and took off my flip flops. I hadn't gone home after school, not wanting to talk to my parents, so instead I went to Natalie's. She let me borrow a pair of white shorts and a pink top that was more of a crop top over my long torso. It was a little too cold to be wearing shorts, but Natalie insisted that we all wear them to the party.

I dipped my toes into the water and was surprised to find it warm. The pool lights shone up from under the water and danced across the surface.

"Isn't it a little cold for that?" The voice startled me and I turned around to see Chris Rhodes standing behind me.

I felt a thrill at seeing him again. "It's not bad, but don't tell the Brown boys that, or they'll probably start throwing people in."

Chris chuckled as he sat down next to me but kept his feet up. He was wearing his Cold Spring

High School football sweatshirt, jeans, and his signature cowboy boots. His thick dark blonde hair was styled and didn't look as if he'd been wearing a baseball cap all day. It looked soft and part of me wanted to run my fingers through it.

"What'd you come out here for?" he asked, looking over at me with those sweet brown eyes.

I bit my lip. "It was getting a bit crowded in there." I shivered.

"You're cold?" Before I could say anything, he pulled off his sweatshirt in one swoop and handed it to me. His undershirt slipped up and I saw the tan skin of his stomach for only a moment.

"Are you sure?"

"It's too cold out here for what you're wearing," he scolded.

I pulled it on over my head and untucked my black hair. Chris kept his eyes on me. I was engulfed by the scent of his cologne, which I recognized as a popular body spray for men. It made me want to take a deep breath.

"Thanks," I said shyly, realizing he could probably see what I was doing.

He cleared his throat and looked down at my feet swishing in the water.

"Do you have your major picked out for school?" he asked after a few moments.

I almost flinched at the topic. It's as if he knew what had pissed off my parents that morning.

"Marketing, I think," I answered.

He looked surprised, "That's a good major. You'd have plenty of opportunities with that."

The praise surprised me, and it did something inside my chest. "Yeah, I think so too."

"And you're going to college in San Diego?" His question was quiet and eager.

"I'm not sure yet."

Hope sparked in his eyes. "What do you mean?"

I sighed and pushed my hair behind my ear. "My grandma is really sick right now and I'm thinking of staying an extra year to be with her. I just don't want to leave her alone." I paused, giving myself a second. "I've hated it here my whole life, so it surprises even me that I'm considering staying longer."

"It's not that bad here," Chris said.

I shrugged. "I guess it isn't. But if I do stay, I can't live with my parents anymore so I'd ask my grandma if I can move in with her."

"Your parents are that bad?"

I scoffed. "They have all these expectations of me to be exactly like Sam…" I looked out at the water again and focused on a leaf floating on the top. "We just got into a fight today about them wanting me to go to school to be a doctor or a lawyer and I just don't want to do either of those jobs."

"I wouldn't trust you to stitch me up or represent me in court, so I think marketing is a good choice," Chris said to lighten the mood.

I laughed and elbowed him in the ribs playfully. He caught my arm, and I felt his warm hands through the layered fabric of his sweatshirt before he let go.

"They don't even know I'm considering taking a year off." Panic filled me as I looked at him. "Please don't share that with anyone. No one knows I'm thinking of staying and I don't want it to get back to my parents."

"I won't." And I knew he was telling the truth. The understanding in his eyes and his empathy took my breath away. I was sharing all of this with him for no reason…I didn't do this. Even Natalie and Sophie had never heard me express this much of my life to them.

"Enough about my woe-is-me *life. What about you? What are your plans?"*

He sighed and leaned back on his arms, and I turned to look at him. God, he was such a hot guy. His forearms stretched, making the green shirt tighten and cling to his chest. He had played football of course and was decent at it. He tended to be either the safety or a linebacker, though Gemma was scared he'd get hurt. She was always there at every game, and I'd seen her several times as I cheered.

"I'm going to head to community college to take some business courses then see what I want to do from there. My parents don't really care what I do, as long as I enjoy it."

Yes, Gemma and Keith Rhodes were every kid's fantasy parents. "Do you think you'll go back to the rescue and take over?"

"Maybe. I guess we'll see." He smiled at me, and it was that contagious smile that made me grin back.

"You should come out sometime and let me show you around. My dad just rescued a litter of puppies, so we have to bottle feed them for a few weeks," he said with joy.

"Puppies?" I asked in surprise.

He finally sat back up. "Yeah, some asshole dropped them off on the side of the road. If Dad can figure out who did it, he's going to let the Cold Spring Police know."

I scoffed. "It would just be perfect if my brother finds the culprit who dropped off puppies and sends him to jail. They'll erect statues in his name and people will name their children after him."

Yikes, that sounded so bitter.

He snorted and it broke out into a laugh and then we were both laughing. That was always the case when I was around Chris Rhodes. He made me happy. He'd always been there, but we hadn't spent much time together, especially by ourselves. And this...this was nice.

"I'm sorry, I do love my big brother," I explained after the laughter died down.

"It's okay, I get it."

Did he? It felt like he did.

We were smiling at each other, and I watched as he got closer to me. Tingles spread down my neck and into my spine as I held my breath. This was different. I'd kissed and been with a few guys, but none had made me feel like this.

His expression grew serious as he got closer and lifted his hand to tuck the hair behind my ear that had fallen beside my face. His hand was gentle and soft as it brushed my cheek. Warmth seeped into my limbs and heat started in my chest. We maintained eye contact and I felt his breath across my lips that caused a zing of pleasure in my stomach.

"Monica," he whispered, and I felt my heart wanting to leap out of my chest.

"Chris?" I responded, breathlessly.

"Can I–"

"Monica! Get in here! Soph is throwing up in Mrs. Brown's vase!" Natalie yelled out towards the pool, startling us both. We broke apart and I saw pink stinging his cheeks.

"I'll be in," I called to her, and she went back inside. Chris had pulled back and I saw with disappointment that the moment was over. "I guess I need to go get her."

"Yeah, go ahead, I'll catch up with you later," he said as I stood up and went in to find Sophie. I bit my lip with a smile until I saw Sophie clutching

a very expensive vase to her chest. Her face was pale and there was a green stain on her pink shirt.

"Don't look at me, I look horrible!" she wailed.

I rolled my eyes skyward. "Let's get you home."

"That was a long time ago," I whispered as I traced the black dot on Rex's head. I looked up and could barely see Chris on the horizon. He and Jasper were just a small spot on the green landscape.

Where had that contagious smile gone? Or did he have it and not want to share it with me anymore? Rex licked my face, and I laughed and pushed at him.

"I guess that's probably the only kiss I'm going to get."

Chapter Nine

Road Trip to my Feelings

Another week passed but I couldn't spend much time at the rescue. I was getting so many hits on my post from Spring Awake that people were flocking to Erin's coffee shop.

"I can't believe it!" Erin exclaimed as we stood beside the counter at her cafe. She'd had at least twenty people come in and specifically order the items that I posted.

"You're amazing!" Erin said.

"I just shared it. It's your food and coffee that bring them back," I replied.

"Well, you're hired. I'd love you to work at least fifteen hours a week. We can set up a spot in the back or if you'd prefer, you can be out here in the cafe."

My mouth dropped. "Are you serious?"

A job! A real job!

"Absolutely. You've surprised me, Monica," Erin said with a genuine smile. "You've changed a lot since high school."

I wanted to scoff and say that the move home was what really brought me off my pedestal but didn't.

"I'm taking that as a compliment. As for where to work, I'd say keep me out in the cafe. I don't do well being put in an office anymore."

She raised an eyebrow at that. "Working at the rescue making you outdoorsy?"

I thought back to the walks in the open air that I took Rex on every day. I looked forward to that time in nature; it made me think a lot of my past and my grandma. It centered me in a way.

"Yeah, something like that."

Even though I didn't go into the rescue that morning since I was meeting with Erin, I still decided to do my walk with Rex. Gemma and Keith were outside when I arrived, and Gemma looked happy to see me.

"Coming to walk Rex?" she asked as I got out of the car.

"Yep, I think he'd get upset with me if I didn't."

Keith chuckled and it reminded me so much of Chris.

"Well, be careful out there. The ticks are starting to get bad," Keith advised as I smiled and walked back to the kennels. I'd finally bought bug spray, and I'd doused my bare legs and arms in it before leaving the house. It was too hot to wear pants and when I did finally put shorts on to walk Rex a few days ago, I'd regretted it immediately. Who knew the bugs loved my blood type? It looked like I had chicken pox by the end of the walk. The next time, I didn't make that mistake.

Rex was overly excited, and it took me an extra minute to put on his harness. Once we were headed out into the field, I let him sniff and take his time on our walk.

"Soak it in buddy. Now that I've got a job, I may not be able to do this every night," I said to him, but he just wagged his tail and peed on a tree stump.

We got to the end of the trail where the cattle grazed and were just about to sit down when we saw someone walking behind us.

It was Chris.

"Hey," I said, surprised. I had come out here a lot, but Chris had never joined me since the last time he was out riding Jasper.

He got closer and I saw he had something in his hands. It was a bottle of bug spray. He wore long pants with his boots and a short-sleeved t-shirt. It was too hot for pants and boots, but I never saw him wear anything else. Probably because of how bad these bugs were. I subconsciously looked down at the red bites speckling my legs.

"Here, I thought you'd need this. It's tick season and I saw you were wearing shorts again," Chris said, handing it to me.

"I got some after getting eaten alive the other night. I drenched myself it in before I left the house, but thanks." He wasn't wearing his sunglasses, so it was easy to read his expression.

His hat still shielded his eyes though. “Where have you been? I haven’t seen you much.”

“I had a lot of paperwork to do for Mom. She took some time off to be with my dad, so I was dealing with adoption applications,” he explained.

My heart almost plummeted. “Any for Rex?”

He looked at Rex, who was sitting by my side wagging his tail happily. “No, none for Rex. He’ll be hard to adopt. He’s not a puppy and he’s a bigger dog.”

“Oh,” I said, feeling bad. “He’s a good dog now. He just needed a little help. People just need to see that. You should take some videos of the dogs to kind of showcase their personalities and post them online. It might be helpful in getting more applications.”

His eyebrows raised at that. “That’s actually a good idea. I’ll pitch it to my mom.”

“Who does your marketing anyhow?” I asked, intrigued, shifting on my feet. Rex pulled at me to go sniff a leaf that had fallen, and I followed with Chris at my side looking amused.

“My mom. She only does some though since it’s not her main job,” he said as he put his hands in his pockets. We walked towards the farm, Rex leading the way.

“There’s so much more she could be doing to get more donations and adoption applications,” I said.

“How?”

I didn't get to answer him because his phone started ringing. He pulled it out and answered it right away. "Chris Rhodes," he responded. Then he frowned.

"Where? How many? Okay…I can be up there in about two hours. Tell the shelter they need to get warm milk and bottles immediately; we don't know how long it's been since they had food. Yes. I'll see you soon." He hung up and sighed.

"What was that about?"

"Puppies were found in Albany, and they're at a kill shelter. I have to run up and get them. We haven't had puppies in a while." He scratched his neck, looking distracted. Then he dropped his hand and glanced towards me. His eyes were alight with something that warmed my stomach. "Come with me. I'll add it to your community service hours."

I raised a surprised brow. "Really?"

"It's not far and I'll need help."

He wanted to be alone, in a car, with me, for four hours? I'd be stupid not to take him up on it though. Especially since it would cut down my hours.

"Deal. Let me take Rex back to his kennel."

Chris let his mom know what was going on so she could call Skyler to come check the puppies in the morning. After collecting supplies and a cage, we were on the road in the red truck headed toward Albany at seven in the evening. It was slightly awkward as we sat in silence. I turned on the radio and of course, it was on a country music station.

"You haven't changed much," I said with a laugh. "Still into country."

"Who wouldn't love country?" he said in mock offense. "It talks about dogs, heartbreak, love, and beer."

I laughed harder and I felt the tension break between us. I glanced over and watched the sun dance across his face as we traveled north. "Do you normally go on these trips alone?"

"It depends," he said, looking over his shoulder to pass a vehicle. "If it's two or three dogs, normally I can handle it. I put crates in the back and load them up. If it's any other animal, normally Dale or Mom come with me."

I remembered him going as a kid along with his parents sometimes to pick up animals. He'd been pissed one day at school that they'd gone without him.

"I'm sure it's lonely if you have to travel by yourself."

I watched him stiffen from my words and I realized he'd heard that before. "I've been alone for years, it doesn't bother me anymore," he muttered.

"Me too," I said, and he scoffed. "No, I'm serious. Yes, I had boyfriends in San Diego, but they didn't know me." As I said the words, the truth of it settled within me. "All my friends out there just wanted to be friends with me because I had a good job and knew the best places to go clubbing. None of them knew me, which meant…. I felt alone.”

Oof, this trip was not going how I thought it would. There was something about Chris that made me spill all my secrets. If Grandma was still around, she’d say he was a gatekeeper to my soul and whenever he was near, he would unlock it and let it spill out to relieve me. “I've been single since Emma and Sam's wedding.” I didn't know why I told him that but as soon as the words came out, I felt my face flush. And what made it worse was he didn't say anything

The sun set and the music played softly in the background. The longer we didn't say anything the more comfortable I got. Perhaps it was because I hoped he'd forgotten what I’d told him.

“Do you remember when we were at the Brown’s party?” I asked suddenly.

He shifted in his seat, not glancing over at me. “It’s been years since that party.”

He didn’t answer the question, so I continued. “You had just rescued a bunch of puppies and told me to come see them. What breed of dog were they?”

He seemed to relax. “They were a rottweiler mix. We didn’t know the exact breeds, but they all got homes within a few months.”

Didn't remember my ass.... he literally just spouted off what breed of puppy they were from over eight years ago. He remembered everything from that night. Just like I did.

"I wish I would've come to see them. Maybe I would have realized I liked dogs," I said softly.

And you. Maybe I would have started to like you quicker. Maybe you would have been my other reason not to jump ship when my grandma died.

What good would that have done? I would have fought with my parents even more about staying for a boy. They didn't even want me to stay for Grandma, let alone a farm boy. There was no way I would have stayed.

"Are you admitting you like dogs now?" Chris asked, glancing over at me.

"I wouldn't say I'm a dog lover but I'm a dog liker."

The laugh that rang out from Chris was sweet and contagious and it reminded me so much of high school.

My phone rang and I pulled it out to check and answered it when I saw a picture of Emma. "Hey! What's up, Emma?"

"Are you home? Brynn and I were going to stop by to talk about the next few posts for the store. We had a lot of feedback from your last one! We want to get you more involved with Feather Blue."

I grinned widely. "I'm not home and–" I looked over at Chris and he shook his head. "I probably won't be back until late tonight. I could meet tomorrow though."

"Sure, but where are you? Are you in the car?" Emma asked, intrigued.

"Um, yeah. I'm riding along with Chris to Albany to pick up puppies that were abandoned. We won't be home until late tonight."

"That sounds like fun! Make sure you use protection and have fun with him." Emma's words were suggestive of course and I prayed he hadn't heard it.

"Thanks, Emma," I said shortly, heat burning my cheeks. "Bye."

"Love you, Monica! Bye!"

I hung up and tucked my phone back into my pocket and faced the now pink and purple sky.

"Who was that?" Chris asked, trying not to sound interested.

"Emma, Sam's wife."

"You mean your sister-in-law?" he corrected with a small laugh.

"Yeah," I said stupidly. "Sister-in law. It's weird to think he's married."

"Don't you like her?"

"Oh yeah, I like her more than my brother," I countered. "Brynn planned a great bachelorette party for her in Albany, and we had a lot of fun. I got to know both of them more during that trip."

And realized tequila makes me think I can change tires even though I've never changed one in my life.

"They seem good together."

I kicked off my boots and put my feet on the dash. "Yeah, they are."

She was perfect. Beautiful personality inside and out. She was a great wife, daughter-in-law, and an amazing mom. So many things I'd probably never be.

I brushed my hair behind my ear as I looked out at the river that we followed.

It was silent for a second or two and he kept glancing over. "I think this is the quietest I've ever heard you be."

My jaw dropped and I couldn't stop my laughter. "Shut up! Not everyone can be quiet and moody like Chris Rhodes. I still remember in speech class you would brood in the corner because you didn't want to get up in front of everyone."

"No shit, Mrs. Hinley was Satan. She hated me."

"She hated you because you argued with her about your speech!"

"She secretly hated me because she had my dad in her class in high school and he did something to piss her off." He waved a hand. "Thank god she retired."

I just laughed, throwing my head back on the seat. "High school feels so far away but then it feels like yesterday."

He rubbed his hand over his jaw and scratched his chin. "Yeah, those were the days."

I turned towards him. "Whatever happened with football? Didn't they have a team at community college?"

I saw him stiffen. "I played a few games then stopped."

"Why? You were pretty good. Was it your parents?"

"No."

I waited. The music played in the background, and it was harder to see Chris with the sun's fading light.

"Chris?" I asked, softly.

"I couldn't play football anymore."

"Couldn't play?"

"I got hurt, couldn't run," he replied shortly.

Hurt? He got hurt? When? How? I looked over at him as if I could see his injuries.

"We're almost there," he said, distracting me before I could ask more questions.

We pulled into the parking lot of a small white building that had 'Albany Shelter' displayed across the front. We got out and Chris grabbed the cage from the back of the truck, and we walked into the shelter. It was loud and noisy from all the barking dogs and the attendant at the front desk was a man looking to be in his 70s.

"I didn't think we'd be hearing from you this soon, Randal," Chris said as he put the cage down.

Randal grunted and I saw his balding head had a few wisps of gray hair. “I’m glad you came. There’s five of them and they are a little spooked. Better to be careful and not keep them with the others for a bit. We think they are around six weeks so they won’t need bottle fed but they will need to be introduced to food mixed with water. I’m thinking they haven’t had much so far,” Randal explained as he guided us back into a small room. It smelled like antiseptic and cleaners.

In a cardboard box in the corner by a heater were five puppies about the size of my hand. Three were gray and white and the other two were white with a few black spots. They whined and yipped when we came in and one puppy stood up against the box to see us.

I went over and crouched down to touch him. He didn’t pull away but sniffed my hand then nibbled at me playfully.

Wow, they were adorable. I couldn’t remember if I’d ever really touched a puppy before.

“Better be careful or else the wife will decide to keep all them little guys,” Randal said with a laugh.

I quickly spun around and at the same time Chris and I both said,

“She’s not my wife.”

“I’m not his wife.”

Randal was surprised by our outburst and stared at us.

I swallowed when Chris looked at me, his light eyebrows creased.

Randal cleared his throat. “Anyways, they’re all yours. I’m sure you’ll need to get them dewormed and put on a healthy diet,” he added.

“Thanks for letting us know. I’m sure we'll find homes quickly,” Chris said, as he leaned down to pick up the box with of puppies. He slid them into the cage, and they started yipping more.

My heart broke. I didn’t want to see them scared.

I cooed and put my fingers through the cage so the one watching me could bite at my finger again.

“Good, I appreciate it. You can let yourselves out. I have to close up.” Randal waved as we headed out and I opened the side door of the truck so Chris could put them comfortably on the back seat. We got in the truck and started home.

We rode in silence, not wanting to wake the puppies. I looked at the road signs and suddenly recognized where we were. My chest grew tight.

“Chris, wait,” I said, stretching out a hand to put on his arm.

“What?” he asked, alarmed.

“Slow down…turn right, please.”

He glanced over, concerned, but my eyes were only on our surroundings. He did as I asked, and we drove a short distance then pulled into a small parking lot beside the Hudson river. The headlights of the car illuminated a bench and before I could stop myself, I got out of the truck.

The night air was warm and humid as I moved towards that bench. I looked at it, my hand running along the smooth, worn wood.

Bugs made noises and a breeze blew in from the river. I sat down when my legs felt too heavy and stared out toward the water. As my eyes adjusted to the darkness, I felt the tightening in my chest grow worse. I closed my eyes and took a breath, then another, then another. This was the last place my grandma and I visited together. When I first saw that little sparrow and she'd explained its meaning. The sparrow that kept showing up everywhere, reminding me that Grandma was still here.

Then…only then did the tears come. I wasn't weak, I rarely cried. I could count on one hand how many times I'd cried. The first was over a history test I'd failed and my parents got upset about. Another was when my parents told me we were moving to Cold Spring, and then…. when my grandma died.

It was almost as if the sobs had been stored up all those years and finally the plug had been pulled out.

"Monica?" I didn't look up when I heard his voice; I didn't want him to see me this way.

When Chris pulled me to my feet and brought me into his warm embrace, my tears flowed heavier. He held me tightly and it made me feel for once that I was safe, that I was going to be okay.

"The-the stupid bird, the stupid river," I blubbered against his shirt, resting my face against his chest.

"The bird?" he asked quietly.

"L-long story."

His entire body was pressed against me, and it took everything not to hold him tighter.

Way to try to take advantage of him being nice, Monica.

Once my sobs slowed and embarrassment creeped in, I stepped back. I immediately wished I hadn't because he dropped his arms from around me. He was frowning but I saw sympathy in his gaze. "I'm sorry…I never cry."

I wiped the remaining tears and sniffed several times as he continued to look at me. He didn't say anything and that almost felt worse than him questioning what the hell was wrong with me.

I crossed my arms and looked out at the Hudson. "This…this was the last place my grandma and I visited together before she passed."

The words hung heavily in the air and the heat in my chest almost felt like it would choke me. I hadn't felt this bad when he was holding me.

"It was special, and I wish I would have taken advantage of that time and...I miss her so much sometimes that it hurts." I finally broke and the tears came again. "She was one of the only people who I felt understood me and the only one who kept my parents from completely overtaking my life. And she's gone. She's gone and I'm back here without her and I need her. I need her now more than ever but.... she's not going to come back." She may be here in sparrow form, but that bird could never hold me and tell me not to give up.

He again pulled me into his arms, and it fully hit me how much I'd missed him too. It reminded me that he was definitely my gatekeeper. I'd never been this open with anyone or cried with anyone like this. Even when I'd broken up with Jay and he said some hurtful things to me, I'd just laughed.

After reigning in my emotions, I quieted, as Chris's hand rubbed circles on my back in a comforting way. I leaned back and he let me go completely, stepping away.

"You okay?"

I nodded, but didn't say anything as we got into the truck and headed home.

When we got back to Chris's house, it was around midnight. We hadn't talked at all for the rest of the ride home, but I felt the change between us again. It was.... I couldn't describe it.

Comfortable, forgiving, sympathetic. When we got out of the truck, I opened the back door for him, and he slowly slid out the cage.

"Door is unlocked," he said as I walked ahead to open it. He'd left a light on, and I was surprised to find an open-concept house with logs on the walls, old-style appliances, and hardwood floors. It looked like a cozy cabin. In the living room was a giant TV and several couches big enough to hold thirty people to watch a game. Also in the living room were several baby gates put together to make a puppy pen, along with blankets and bowls, set up and ready to go.

There were photos on the walls of the rescue, his parents and him, friends, even horses.

He carried the cage over to the pen and glanced at me when he set it down.

"Can you help me get them in here? I want to get some water and food before they sleep," he said.

I pulled off my boots, walked over beside him, and stepped inside the pen. He handed me the puppies one by one, and I nestled them into the comfy blankets. They whined and seemed tired.

When we had them all in, Chris took the blanket out of their cage and put it in the pen with them.

"Shouldn't that be washed?"

"No, sometimes they need something that smells familiar, like each other. I'll take it out in a few days but for now, it'll stay."

Chris went to the kitchen to get food and water while I sat on the floor and petted one of the puppies who wanted to play when the others were sleeping.

It struck me then that there were no other dogs in the house.

"Chris, do you have a dog?" I asked, looking over my shoulder at him. He was filling up bowls with food and his concentration was adorable as he measured it out.

"No."

I laughed. "Seriously? You work at an animal rescue."

"Exactly," he said, laughing with me. "If I want a dog, I'll go get one out of the kennels." He came over with three bowls of food and water and placed them inside the pen as I stepped out. We sat down on the floor and watched them wake up, their small tails wagging as they started eating. They made pig-like noises, and I chuckled.

"It's actually easier if I don't have a dog in the house. For moments like this when we bring in puppies. It could spook them, or they may not get along. So, I choose not to have one."

It made sense, but then again, what did I know about dogs?

I rubbed my eyes and yawned. He was sitting close to me again as I leaned back against the couch. "I'm sorry for keeping you out late."

I shrugged. "It's okay. I haven't stayed up this late since I moved back. I've turned into a nine-to-fiver."

He scoffed. "Try being a 5am to 9pm person."

"No thanks. That's a hard pass."

As the puppies finished eating, they found their way to the blankets and started to fall asleep.

"Would you…." I stopped and looked at Chris who was waiting for me to finish my sentence.

"Would I what?"

I pressed my lips together looking into his soft brown eyes, a flush creeping up my neck. "Would you care if I stayed over to make sure the puppies are okay?"

He was hard to read again with that blank, almost surprised expression. "Um, yeah, sure."

"I don't have to, I'm just worried—"

"No, it's fine. You can stay if you want. I have a spare bedroom," he offered, as his cheeks tinted pink.

"Um, no, it's okay, I can just sleep on the couch. I can honestly sleep anywhere anytime. Ask my college roommate. I once fell asleep during a rave and she was stunned, especially when the cops came, and I still didn't stir. Now I did have a lot of tequila in my system, but still, I can sleep anywhere." I didn't shut up and I realized why I was going on and on. Even I was embarrassed by asking to stay.

"Okay, um, I'll get you a blanket and pillow," Chris said before standing up and going to the hallway that I assumed led to the bedrooms. He came back out with a big fluffy blanket and a comfortable looking pillow. He put them on the couch behind me.

"There's water in the fridge and the bathroom is down the hall. There's an extra toothbrush in the closet," he pointed.

He looked at my clothes, my shorts, tank top, and long sleeve flannel shirt. "Do you want something else to sleep in?"

His clothes? He was offering me his clothes to sleep in? I almost started to blush until I realized I'd slept in many men's clothes! This was nothing new! But it was...this was Chris Rhodes. I still had the sweatshirt he'd let me borrow years ago. This should be no different.

"Um, a t-shirt, maybe? I'll give it back in the morning. I'll get up early and head out. You probably won't even see me," I explained.

Something flew across his expression, but it wasn't there long enough to read.

God he was frustrating.

"You can take tomorrow off, no need to do kennels," he said as he shifted on his feet.

"Are you sure?"

"I think you got plenty of hours in today. Thank you," his voice was soft and surprising.

"N-No problem."

He awkwardly stood there for a moment then went to the hallway and into a room. Moments later he returned with a Long Rhodes Ahead Animal Rescue t-shirt in a light gray. I smiled and took it from him with a muttered thanks.

"You know, I still have your Cold Spring High sweatshirt," I said softly.

His eyebrows rose. "Huh."

"I won't keep this one. I'll make sure to give it back," I said quickly.

He gave a nod. "Night, Monica." He didn't say anything more as he headed back to the hall and shut the door behind him. I took a deep breath and stared at the puppies all piled into a circle, sleeping dreamily.

I was in Chris's house. Sleeping over. But not in his bedroom. Was he taking off his shirt and pants right now?

I felt my body warm at the thought and threw my head back against the couch.

"Shut up, Monica," I whispered angrily to myself. *You're staying because it's late and you want to make sure the puppies are okay.*

I stood up and walked down the hallway and found the bathroom. Across from it I saw light under the door, and I knew he was in there.

What if I just knocked? Would he be shirtless lying on his bed with his strong arms tucked under his head?

That zing was turning into a zap through my entire body as I thought of Chris. *No…you're here to watch over the puppies, nothing more.*

I shut the bathroom door.

Chapter Ten

I've Already Seen Your Boobs

The puppies kept me up a lot during the night as I tried to soothe them when they whined. I figured it was because they were someplace new and were scared. Chris had turned up the heat in the living room to keep them warm, so I ended up taking off everything except the big t-shirt Chris gave me. I was exhausted so when six o'clock came I felt groggy and not quite sure where I was.

When someone knocked at the door, I groaned, keeping my eyes closed. Then they knocked again, and I angrily stood up from the couch and walked over to the front door.

It better not be my parents or I will be pissed. They were probably wondering where the hell I was all night and if I was waiting to tell them something.

When I swung open the door, I blinked several times trying to understand what was going on.

Skyler, Dale, and Will were standing on the front porch and all their jaws dropped when they saw me.

It hit me like a gallon of cold water splashing in the face.

I wasn't at my house. And I wasn't fully clothed.

I shut the door without a word and turned around in shock.

Oh no! No! No! No!

At that moment Chris came out of the hall, his chest visible for just a moment as he pulled on a shirt. He blinked at me a few times then quickly looked away.

"You've got to be kidding me!" I yelled as I went to the couch to grab my discarded clothes and dress quickly.

"Did you strip last night?" Chris asked, his voice tight as he tried not to watch me slip on my clothes.

"It's hot in this damn house Chris! Oh, and by the way, everyone on your porch just saw my half naked body! Looks like I'm going to get two hundred more hours of community service!" I snapped. "That Will kid better be over eighteen!"

His eyes bulged. "You answered the door like that?" he demanded.

Finally clothed, I turned to him with fire in my eyes. "I was half out of my mind because the puppies kept me up last night! Excuse me for answering *your* door for you! And, by the way, where the hell were you?"

When he stepped closer to me, I noticed his messy hair and it made me want to run my fingers through it. "Unlike you, I was getting dressed before answering the door."

There was a twinkle in his brown eyes, and I recognized the look enough to know it was definitely desire. I swallowed.

A softer knock sounded, and we both remembered there were people still standing on his porch.

He walked over and opened it up. "Come in, the puppies are in the living room," Chris said as Skyler came in first, her face a little red. Then Dale and Will stepped in, and both just grinned at Chris and patted him on the shoulder as they passed.

"No wonder you didn't meet me in the barn this morning. Had your hands full last night I guess," Dale said to Chris.

"It's not what you think," he muttered but Will just gave me a wink.

"Good god," I prayed as I sat down on the couch with my head in my hands.

Skyler cleared her throat and came over to sit down on the floor by the puppies. She opened her vet bag and started examining them.

"Listen, what you guys saw was not what you think. I slept on the couch with the puppies all night. That's it, end of story," I said to everyone.

Would this get back to Gemma and Keith? My parents? God, another incident that made me want to start wearing footie pajamas to bed every night so I wouldn't be indecent if I opened any door.

Will and Dale were grinning, especially when they noticed the t-shirt I was wearing.

Shit.

"She's right, nothing happened. So, get those damn smirks off your faces," he snapped at the two. "Also, why the hell are you even here? Shouldn't you be working in the stables?" he demanded of Will.

Will just shrugged.

"Randal at the shelter said they were about six weeks old. Is that what you think?" I asked Skyler, trying not to look at Chris. He'd practically seen me naked but so had some fourteen-year-olds and a lucky Cold Spring tow truck driver, so it really wasn't a big deal at this point.

"I think so, maybe almost seven weeks. They seem in good health," she explained as she picked one up and checked it. They yelped and murmured as she gently looked at each one. "Pitties mixed with something. It's always the pit bulls that are left." She shook her head in sadness. After inspecting them she turned towards Chris. "They all look good. They don't have fleas, but we should start them on heartworm medicine as soon as possible. I'll send in a prescription and let Gemma know when she picks up her regular stuff."

Chris leaned against his kitchen counter with his arms crossed and nodded. "Thanks, Doc. I appreciate it."

"No problem. I'm going to go check on the new horse's foot. I'll see you guys later," Skyler said as she left the house.

Will and Dale stood there, not moving, Dale with a smirk on his face. “So, we want to–"

Both Chris and I said "no" at the same time and Dale just kept up his smirk.

"Both of you can go. I'll be out to do the kennels after a while," Chris announced.

"Let's go son, I see we aren't welcome," Dale teased, putting a hand on Will’s shoulder to push him out the door. After they left, I got down on my knees to pet one of the puppies.

"I'm sorry, that was not how I wanted my morning to go either," I said before he could say anything. I stood up and reached for my boots.

"Stay for breakfast," Chris said quickly.

I stopped halfway through putting on my boots and looked up at him. He was still standing in that same position, back against the counter, arms crossed, but his expression was puzzling. It seemed soft and almost sweet. I realized he’d even put on his boots this morning before coming out to answer the door.

I narrowed my gaze. "Is this some sort of pity breakfast because you just saw the outline of my boobs?"

His eyes widened and he choked on his words for a second. “N-no.” Then his shock turned into a smirk. “I've seen them before anyhow."

“No, you haven’t!” I retorted standing up.

There was that twinkle again in his eyes. “It was the Johnson’s house party in August junior year. Some asshole boy threw you into the pool, you came out soaked."

My jaw had lowered as I vaguely remembered that situation. I'd been pissed and slugged the kid who'd thrown me in. Of course, I'd been stupid enough to wear a white t-shirt and no bra because back then I rarely wore a bra.

"Shit," I muttered, and his face lit up even more. His gaze traveled down my body then back up to my face.

"Breakfast now?"

Breakfast was at the main house, and I was thankful it was just Keith and Gemma who were there. In the kitchen Gemma was laughing at something Keith said as she set the table with cups and coffee. She looked up when we walked in.

"Look who I found," Chris said as I came in behind him. "Thought I'd have her join us this morning."

Gemma grinned. "Of course! Do you drink coffee or tea?"

"Better be coffee, no one can come into a Rhodes house and drink anything but," Keith jested.

"Coffee, with two creams and two sugars," I answered with a smile.

Keith gave a nod of approval, and I realized he wasn't wearing a hat. He still had a full head of light brown hair, though it was getting gray.

Standing by his dad, Chris was almost an exact replica, even down to the jeans and t-shirt. He filled two cups with coffee and came back to hand me one.

I sat down and inhaled the drink, as the rest of them layered bacon and eggs onto their plates. It seemed so normal, so *family,* to be eating a meal together, and it shocked me. My family rarely did this. Someone was always too busy doing some activity, but when we did sit down together, the kitchen table became a place where I would get grilled about my life and what I was doing. As I got older, I avoided home all together.

But this…here right now, with the Rhodes family, felt good.

"How are the pups doing?" Keith asked both of us.

I couldn't answer since I had a piece of bacon in my mouth. I didn't realize how hungry I was until I started eating Gemma's breakfast. It was delicious. How long had it been since I'd been awake for breakfast and actually wanted to eat?

"They are good. Doc said all are healthy and should be fine. She wants to start them on heartworm medicine just in case," Chris explained. His arm bumped into mine, but I didn't care. The touch was nice, even if it was just an accident.

"What time did you get back?" Gemma asked.

"Around midnight," Chris answered before taking a sip of his coffee.

Gemma looked at me and her smile was almost a smirk, and it reminded me of Chris. "So, I guess you spent the night and that's why all my workers are whispering about you two this morning?"

Chris spit out his coffee and choked as his dad handed him a napkin. My face grew red with embarrassment. "It's not what it looked like, I promise you," I answered quickly.

She chuckled and Keith had to look away so he wouldn't laugh. "I know it wasn't."

"It's the first time Chris has had any woman stay over in his house, so that's why Dale is getting entertainment over it," Keith finally said.

Chris had cleared his throat and got himself together. "I'm going to kill Dale."

"I'm the first woman?" I frowned, glancing over at Chris who wouldn't look at me.

"Really, Chris, it was obvious she stayed. Her car was still sitting outside the house and she's wearing the same clothes she wore yesterday. Least you could have done was share some clean ones with her," Gemma scolded.

I'd taken off his shirt and given it back before leaving the house, so Gemma obviously didn't hear about my "shirt-only fashion show" earlier.

"We didn't sleep together!" we both said at the same time.

I took another breath, my face and neck as red as the barn outside. "I slept on the couch to watch the puppies. It was too late for me to drive home anyhow."

"We don't care what you guys do. We're just happy you're finally getting along again," Keith said.

"Yes, and not throwing shit at each other," Gemma said with a wink behind her coffee mug.

Keith looked confused as Chris nudged his leg into me again. This time I knew it wasn't an accident as I looked at him from the corner of my eye. His lips were twitched up into a smile.

It felt like we were both teenagers again and had secretly tried to stay the night at each other's houses but got caught.

Okay, I changed my mind, I don't want family breakfasts anymore.

But something still floated back to my thoughts...*he'd never had a woman stay over before? I was the first?* At least the first they'd seen, right? There had to have been other women. Chris was a good-looking guy, and when he wasn't being an ass, he really was sweet.

"Anyhow, today is going to be a busy day. We have the horse feed shipment coming in," Gemma said, redirecting the conversation. Chris seemed relieved at the change of subject.

"I'll have Will and Steve work on that. I have to keep an eye out on the puppies, so I'll need to go back and forth," Chris said.

I finished the meal and sat back and listened to them. It felt…nice. Even after the embarrassment of them finding out I'd stayed the night at Chris's house.

"How many puppies are there?" Keith asked.

"Five," I interjected.

Gemma looked concerned. "And they are pit bulls mixed with something?"

"I'm thinking maybe a lab," Chris stated.

"They may be hard to home. We should start sharing the news," Gemma said.

"I have an idea." I figured now was a good time to pitch my idea. Chris glanced over at me, an eyebrow raised. "Let me get Brynn Price to take a few photos of them, then start posting on social media. We can give them temporary names, show some cute personality traits, and see what kind of response they get. Are you friends with any other rescues?" I asked the three.

"Well, yeah, we have connections with different rescues in almost all states," Keith said.

"Get them to repost and we should have qualified applications rolling in," I ended.

They all looked at me, surprised and impressed and…some expression from Chris I couldn't figure out.

"I think it sounds like a good idea," Keith commented. "You don't have enough time to do all of it, Gem. Let Monica work on it."

"Really?" I asked, surprised.

"I say why not," Gemma agreed. "I'll let you lead this up, Monica. Get Brynn to take some pictures then I'll give you access to our social media accounts. You can come in here and work on it," she said pointing to the main room where her office was. "I'll add that to your hours."

When Chris's knee knocked into my leg again, it stayed against me.

When breakfast was over, Chris walked me out to my car.

"Do you mind if I stop by this evening to check on them? I think I need to spend some time getting to know them so I can figure out what to post."

"That's fine, just park beside my truck over at the house, don't park here."

I snorted. "We really got those rumors flying. I thought the culprits were the Browns, but I guess it might just be the rescue's workers doing all the gossiping in Cold Spring."

"Yeah, they have nothing better to do," Chris mumbled, looking over my shoulder at the group of them. I glanced to the men who were winking and hooting at us as Chris flipped them the middle finger.

"Can I have your number?" I asked suddenly.

Chris looked at me in surprise. "My number?"

Do not blush, do not blush! You are twenty-six years old, and this is for professional use. Asking a man for their number isn't a big deal.

"Yes, so I can let you know when I'm coming over. I don't want to just stop in," I said, trying not to blush anymore.

"It's the same one," he said softly, his brown eyes light.

"Same one? As in the same phone number you've had since high school?" I clarified.

"Yes."

For some reason, I was surprised it hadn't changed. I looked at the contacts in my phone and found Chris's number.

I still had it? I guess that's all thanks to modern technology that transferred all my contacts every time I got a new phone.

In my phone, his name was under *Chris Rhodes (Hottie from Spring.)*

Yikes, I didn't clean out my contacts ever.

"I have it," I said, quickly putting my phone away. "I'll text you."

He nodded and stepped back as I got into my car. I watched him walk over to the barn workers who were making obscene gestures at him, and he just shook his head.

Chapter Elven

What We Don't Know Will Hurt Us

After I took a five-hour nap at home, I went into Spring Awake to get more coffee and to chat with Erin about the business.

She looked excited as she came to "my" table and set a piña colada looking frappe in front of me that had a piece of pineapple on the edge of the cup.

"I introduce you to the new and improved virgin piña colada! It's actually a white mocha with coconut and chunks of pineapple," she explained proudly and sat down to join me.

"It's beautiful!" I said, inspecting it. "I think your followers are going to love it. Let me get some pictures."

I took a few then handed it back but she shook her head.

"It's yours, try it."

I eagerly took a sip of the drink and moaned in delight at the amazing taste. "Erin…this is the best. Everyone will be headed here to get this. You should add it full time to your menu," I suggested, taking another sip.

It was the perfect time to bring in a last-of-summer drink as we headed into August. She smiled at me. "Maybe. I would consider that if it takes off in the next few weeks." She paused a few moments. "You aren't as bad as I thought you were," she said.

I stopped and frowned. "What?"

She shifted in her seat. "In high school you were a lot different. You were always popular and so…perfect. I don't mean that rudely but you're more…down to earth now."

I sighed and shut my laptop. "I was far from perfect. I just made it look that way on the outside. I'm a little too comfortable with failure at this point in my life." I paused. "I have a lot of regrets from high school." Making fun of her and others, bailing on Chris…and the list could go on. "I know I didn't treat people the best but I'm trying to make up for it."

"The past can stay in the past. Only the future matters now and how you treat others," Erin said with a genuine smile. She would have been a much better friend than Natalie or Sophie. Why hadn't I hung out with her? Then it hit me: Sophie had made fun of her, and it spiraled from there. Erin could see I was different, now if I could just prove it to Chris. There had been so much that I didn't tell him that would have made him hate me less. I also knew there was a lot I didn't know about him.

"Erin, can I ask you something?"

"Sure."

"Has Chris Rhodes dated since I left?"

She thought for a moment, her fingers dancing over the table. "Maybe a few dates but I can't say I remember seeing him with a 'girlfriend' you know?"

My frown increased. "No girlfriend at all?"

She shrugged. "I go to Sullivan's a decent amount and Scarlett tells me everything. I don't think we ever discussed him and a girl before. He was pretty hung up on you, especially after you left. Also, Chris had a lot happen after high school so he may not have had time."

"Like at the rescue?"

She looked at me and her smile turned down and her eyes became sad. "No, not the rescue. You didn't hear?"

My heart thumped a little more. "Hear what?"

She pressed her lips together and was quiet for a moment. "Chris was in a bad car accident the fall after we graduated. He injured his left leg pretty badly. It's what pulled him out of college and why he didn't go back."

A car accident? What? How had I not heard of this before? He'd said yesterday he'd gotten hurt and couldn't play football, is that what he meant?

"I-I didn't know."

"It really shook up the town since Chris was well known. I thought maybe your brother would've told you even if you were living in San Diego. Chris hasn't been the same since the accident."

"I didn't have much communication with my family after I moved," I whispered, still reeling at the information. I hadn't talked to my parents until the week of Thanksgiving that year. Instead of rehashing everything about our fight, we all pretended nothing had happened.

Chris had been in an accident, and no one told me, not my parents, not Sam, not even Chris himself.

Was that the other reason he was mad at me when I came back? I hadn't even called him after I left. I had wanted to and maybe that was why I never deleted his number out of my phone.

Erin said her goodbyes and walked back behind the counter to serve more customers.

I took my time gathering my things and going back to my apartment. I changed into jean shorts, a t-shirt, and a flannel shirt before slipping on my boots and heading back out the door. I sat in my car with my finger hovering over his name and the text icon.

I hadn't deleted him from my phone. Why? Could I chalk it up to never deleting people? When was the last time I'd had my finger hovering over his name?

It was the day I left. The day after the big fight with my parents.

I didn't want to tell them. I'd waited all week, more like avoided the conversation. I knew it would probably go badly but I was doing this for

Grandma. Not them. Not even for me, but for her. I'd seen Grandma the previous day and she wasn't looking like herself. She was thin and weak, and she needed me, or maybe I needed her.

I had decided a while ago that I was going to postpone college till the following spring. If she was still okay by then, I'd delay another semester and start in the fall. All I knew was that I wanted to be here with her. I planned to move out of my parents' house and into her place then get a job somewhere in town. Maybe Chris had some ideas.

I smiled to myself thinking of how nervous he was to ask me out, but he didn't need to be. I'd wanted to go out with him for a long while and tomorrow was finally the day. I wondered where we were going. Part of me was glad I was holding off going to college. Chris and I could explore whatever was going on between us.

I heard the front door open and my parents talking. My blood ran cold, and my hands felt clammy as they came into the kitchen where I stood.

They both were smiling, a rareness for my father, but he was looking at my mother.

"Monica! What are you up to?" my mother said, dropping her purse on the counter. "We missed you at the tribal meeting. You know you only have a few more of them left before you leave. You really should come to another."

Here goes nothing.

"That's what I wanted to talk to you and Dad about," I started. My father frowned and crossed his arms.

Don't let him intimidate you. "Oh?" he said.

I took a breath. "I decided I'm going to wait to start college until at least the spring semester."

There, I spit it out.

There was silence. My mother's mouth hung open; my father didn't move.

I shifted nervously on my feet.

"Why?" my father asked, his voice hard.

"Because I want to help Grandma. She's still really sick and I don't want to leave her until she's back on her feet again."

My mother looked concerned, and she glanced up at my father who still stared at me.

"No." It took me a moment to realize what he said.

"What?"

His head shook back and forth. "You're going to college, Monica, at the end of the summer."

Shocked by his demand, I stuttered, "Y-You don't get a say in this, Dad."

His look could have burned me. "Yes, I do, Monica Locklear. Use that tone one more time..."

My blood boiled. "I'm not going. I already told my college that I won't be starting until next year. It's done."

My mom put a hand on my dad's arm as if to keep him from leaping across the room at me.

"Is this about a boy, Mon? We just don't want you to throw your life away so young," my mom said softly.

I gritted my teeth together. "No, I mean, I have a date tomorrow but I'm not staying because of him. This is about Grandma. I want to be with her, Mom. She means the world to me." I felt my eyes sting with my confession.

"Honey, I just don't think–"

"You're going to college, Monica. This isn't even a discussion. Locklears do not fail, they achieve."

God, I could have quoted my father saying that.

"I'm not failing, Dad. I'm just trying to take care of Grandma! You should be happy I want to be with her. I'm going to go to college, I'm just delaying it a year at most," I defended.

He shook his head even as my mom tried to tell him to stop.

"You won't go if you don't go now. I've seen this before and you won't be one of those people."

"Those people?"

"People who aren't successful with their life. You have too much potential. You've already wasted enough time partying and cheering while not focusing on your education," he snapped. "You will not be in my household if you don't go to college." His dark eyes threatened, and I felt about to burst. I was done listening to him. I was done with them.

"I wasn't staying here anyhow," I said coldly.

"And where will you go, Monica? You're eighteen! You don't have a job or hardly any savings! Would you please just listen to us? We are trying to help," my mom pleaded. I could see she was trying but my dad was not.

"No," I ground out. "I will not leave Grandma. You may not give a shit about her, but I do! I might be the only one–"

"Don't you dare finish that sentence, Monica," my dad's words were ice cold, and I shivered.

My hands were curled into fists by my sides, and I felt a sudden brazenness. It was almost as if Grandma was pushing me from far away to stand up for myself. "I'm going to pack up my things and go to Grandma's tonight."

My father's phone rang loudly in the silence that followed my statement, and he didn't even look at it until it was on the last ring. His expression changed when he saw the caller and answered quickly.

Did I have time to run upstairs and pack a quick bag? Grandma would leave the porch light on for me and she'd probably make me a cup of hot chocolate. She was always good at that kind of comfort. Unlike my stone-faced father.

I'd have to text Chris tonight and tell him to pick me up at her house tomorrow instead of here because I'd be gone after tonight.

"What time?" my father's voice cut into my thoughts, and I blinked, looking between my mom and him. "O-okay. Who found her?"

My mother's hand went across her mouth as tears shined in her eyes. It struck me my dad's voice had cracked which wasn't like him. A deep dread filled my stomach, making it feel as if there were boulders inside weighing me down.

"Okay. We'll be over shortly." He hung up his phone and stared at it for several seconds before looking at my mother. They somehow communicated and when my mom looked at me, I knew what that phone call was.

She took a step forward, her hand outstretching. "Monica–"

"Who was that, Dad?" I demanded but I knew. I knew what it was about, but I needed to hear it. Maybe I wanted to hear him say it was about someone else and not her. Not when I'd finally gotten the nerve to speak up. I wanted to tell her that.

"Dad? Who was that?" I asked again but this time I sounded broken.

"It's Grandma."

I felt my knees weaken and Mom caught me as I started to cry. She held me, patting my back.

She tried to calm me down, but I was angry, sad, and hurt. I hadn't been with Grandma like I promised her I would. We had plans to do movie nights and for her to teach me how to sew and make turquoise jewelry and hear more stories from her childhood. This wasn't supposed to happen!

My mom rubbed my back as I felt my dad's eyes on me. When I finally looked at him, he was emotionless again. "You're going to go to college, Monica. Not in the spring but at the end of the summer." I felt those harsh words clear down to my bones and it made me angry. I pulled away from my mom, standing up straighter, staring him down. I could see in his expression a crack forming at the news, but his thoughts were still on my choices and his reputation.

"I'm going upstairs."

I left them then and went up to my room where I quickly packed all my bags. Then I got on my computer and booked my flight to San Diego. When I clicked the purchase button, I got my phone out and messaged a friend from my childhood that I'd kept in touch with through the years. I asked if she could pick me up in the morning in San Diego when my flight got in. I could barely see her reply with an excited "absolutely!" because the tears were back again.

I didn't want to spend one more day here with my parents knowing she was gone. My buffer, my comforter, my friend. The one person who knew me better than I even knew myself.

The next morning Sophie picked me up early and I left a note for my parents saying that I couldn't stay and went to California. I added that I was contacting the school about starting in the fall instead of next year. When I was in my seat staring out the window at the airfield, I thought of Chris. I closed my eyes tight as I remembered his contagious, sweet smile that made butterflies flutter in my stomach.

Our date!

I picked up my phone and pulled his name up into a text and had my fingers hovering over the keypad.

What would I say? I can't go on our date? I left for California early? Sorry, Chris, I got into a massive fight with my parents because I wanted to date you and take care of my Grandma? I was already a failure to my parents. The last person I wanted to be a failure to was him.

I had to say something. I couldn't just let it go.

My fingers wouldn't type anything. I reread our last few texts. He had been asking me about going to a party and if I'd be there. I'd responded of course, I wouldn't miss it.

I wanted to go on that date. I wanted to get to know him more because of how he made me feel, but it was too late.

I felt the stinging again behind my eyes and took a few deep breaths then turned off my phone. He would hate me for not saying goodbye, but I wasn't good at goodbyes.

As I came out of my thoughts, my fingers were still poised above the keypad. I stared at an empty conversation with Chris. Our old text messages had probably been archived or deleted, and I felt a little guilty. I couldn't change what happened even if I wanted to, but I knew now things were different. *I* was different.

I typed out a text to him: *Is it okay to stop over and check on the puppies?*

It didn't take him long, maybe seconds, to respond.

Chris: *Sure.*

Chapter Twelve

You're Infuriating

I parked next to Chris's truck beside his house as he'd asked me. I wasn't sure why, but my nerves were on edge as I stood on the porch.

The questions still rolled around in me about his accident. *Why hadn't he said anything? How badly was he hurt? How had it affected him?*

I knocked and inside I heard him call out 'doors unlocked' which I took as a come in. I did and the house was still warm, and Chris was standing in the open kitchen mixing something in a pot. He wore a t-shirt and jeans. It struck me then that I'd never seen him in shorts, even on the hottest days he was working on the rescue.

His hair was mussed as if he'd just taken a shower, and he'd quickly run his hands through it. The puppies were in the living room, barking and yipping and playing, and it made me smile.

I slipped off my boots and padded into the kitchen to see what he was making. It felt so…domestic. As if I lived here too and was coming home to him.

A warm feeling went through my stomach and a longing in my heart. It stopped me in my tracks long enough for me to shake it off quickly as I peered into the pot he was stirring. It looked like some sort of stew.

"Is this for the puppies?"

He glanced over at me, his lip twitching into a smile. "No, it's beef stew, for humans to eat."

I felt my jaw drop a little, realizing I had just insulted him. "Oh, I-I'm sorry, it looked—just ignore me, I obviously haven't been around enough people lately to realize how to converse properly."

He chuckled, his deep laugh making his shoulders move. "Now that you insulted my dinner, you have to eat some."

"Oh, I don't want to intrude. I didn't realize you hadn't eaten dinner yet," I said in surprise.

He gave me a look, and those brown eyes narrowed playfully. "No excuses, Locklear. Get two bowls from the cupboard." He pointed behind him and I didn't object considering I was hungry.

I grabbed two white bowls from the shelf and brought them over to sit on the counter beside him. He ladled in the stew, and it smelled like basil and beef. My stomach growled automatically.

"There's soda in the fridge," he instructed.

I grabbed two from the fridge and saw it was well stocked with soda and healthy foods, and of course no alcohol.

I turned to the lonely table that sat behind the couch. It had two chairs but on one side there was a pile of paperwork, as if no one ever sat there.

I went over and flipped on the light above the table and moved the paperwork aside. I glanced at the papers and saw vet bills and…physical therapy bills for him.

I cleared my throat and set the two drinks down then went over and collected a few napkins. I glanced at Chris's leg, but of course it was covered with his long jeans and his boots. When my eyes rolled back up to his face, he was watching me.

"Everything okay?"

"Yes, everything is fine," I mumbled, embarrassed I'd been caught.

He brought over the bowls, and I dug in quickly. "This is really good. Definitely a strange time for soup in the middle of summer, but still good," I said around a mouthful.

He smiled. "When you're single and don't want to make food every night, this normally does the trick."

I wiped my mouth and took a sip of my soda. "When I was in San Diego, I rarely ever made my own food. I ate out a lot."

All those late-night Chinese food or pizza runs. So unhealthy but convenient. Sometimes I'd ask a guy out and have him take me to an expensive restaurant just so I could eat a good dinner. Then I'd dump him.

Yikes, that just sounded horrible. Old Monica was a bad person.

I finished up my stew and leaned back in my chair. "I'm sorry, I didn't mean to stop in and eat your food and crash your night. My plan was just to check on the puppies and leave."

He was still eating and his eyebrow raised. "You haven't even looked at them since you saw the stew."

I pressed my lips together. "Okay, so maybe I'm a sucker for a good meal. Or a guy cooking a meal."

The last part was a bit much to say to Chris but luckily, he took it well and laughed again. His muscles strained on his arms as he crossed them.

"You can't tell me there weren't a few of them in San Diego."

"Cooking men? Good god no. None of them could cook, not even a microwave pizza."

He shook his head at me and took my empty bowl to deposit into the sink. I finally moved to visit the puppies. They saw me and started barking and jumping and I laughed and petted them as they tried to bite my fingers.

"They seem good," I mentioned as Chris came around the other side of the couch and sat down, propping his feet up onto the coffee table. I glanced over hoping to see something on his leg from the accident, but I didn't. His boots were a nice pair, not scuffed or dirty like his work ones. He hadn't shown any signs of an injury, but I also hadn't been looking.

I was upset at Chris for not telling me about it, even a text or quick phone call. But what could I have done from San Diego? Would I have come back? If I could have stayed with Gemma and Keith…maybe. But I couldn't be that mad…I hadn't reached out either, why would he contact me?

One of the puppies kept going after the others, wanting to play. He wasn't wearing out very quickly as he bit the ear of another one. He had little white paws but the rest of him was gray.

"This one is a troublemaker," I pointed out.

Chris agreed. "Little bastard grabbed my pant leg when I was switching out their water."

I laughed. "He'll be a hard one to adopt. But the one in the corner seems calm."

"I think that's a female. They are always easier to find homes for," Chris said.

I glanced over at him. "What happened with Rex?"

Chris was watching the puppies as they played but he seemed the most relaxed I'd ever seen him. "He came in a litter of puppies but he was the only one not to get adopted out. Once he got a little older and showed aggression issues, we weren't able to find him a home. We have some dogs that will never get adopted, which is fine. My mom and dad make sure they have a good life while they're here at the rescue."

I had no doubt about that. His parents truly were amazing people. Even with the rescue they always made sure to put Chris first. You could see the great relationship they all had.

"I've always been jealous of you," I said softly.

Chris turned toward me and frowned. "Why?"

"Your parents."

He realized what I meant, and his expression softened. "Ah, I see."

I looked down at my dirty fingernails, avoiding his eyes. "The day before...the day before our date...I got into a horrible fight with my parents." *Was I about to do this? Was I about to tell Chris why I'd stood him up?* "Remember how I told you I was thinking of staying another year to take care of my grandma?" He nodded in answer. "I told my parents that night. They didn't agree with that...they thought there was a boy keeping me here, not just my grandma." I looked at Chris to see his expression and he was frowning but intently listening. "In the middle of our fight my dad got a call...my grandma had passed away." I felt that call down to the marrow of my bones since the memory had been so close to the surface lately. It was almost as if she was still trying to be the buffer between us, even after death. "My dad told me I was going no matter what. His focus had still on me even after receiving that news...so I went to my room and booked a one-way ticket to San Diego. I had Sophie drop me off early Friday morning at the airport and I didn't come back for my grandma's funeral."

During the conversation, Chris's eyes moved to the puppies. When I looked over, I saw his jaw clench with the memories of that Friday.

"They'd told me I'd wasted so much time and hadn't spent enough time on my education," I started slowly, my heart breaking a little. "They said.... if I didn't go to college, I'd be a failure and Locklears don't fail." I swallowed, biting back tears that threatened to overtake me. "I was hurt, and I couldn't stand to be in the same state as them anymore. I was selfish and I should have called you. God, I thought about it so much on the plane, but I couldn't bring myself to call and let you down too."

I waited for him to look at me, but he didn't. I did something that I knew could be bad, but Monica Locklear didn't back down. I reached across and took his hand. He let me and I felt an overpowering sense of relief that he didn't pull away.

"I was ashamed and hurting and I didn't know how to explain what happened."

"It's fine, Monica. It's been years." His stiff voice didn't replicate his expression. His hand held mine even though the rest of him was facing away from me.

"Chris," I said softly. He looked at me finally and I saw him try to cover everything up. "What happened after I left?"

"I moved on."

I didn't know why but it hurt me, his words hitting me a little too close to home. He hadn't moved on. Gemma said he hadn't dated, and he'd been in a car accident.

"No, you didn't."

His eyes narrowed. "I did. As soon as I realized you'd left town, I moved on. In case you aren't aware, the world doesn't revolve around you, Monica."

"I'm well aware of that," I said angrily. "Pretty sure moving on means finding a new girl and as far as I can see, you haven't found one."

He sneered. "Just because it doesn't look like it doesn't mean there weren't many."

"You're disgusting." I pulled my hand back from him, realizing we were still touching, and right now, I didn't want to be near him.

"Don't act innocent now, I know you had lots of men in San Diego," he retorted.

"So what? I'm not flaunting it!"

"God, you're infuriating!" He stood up and went to the kitchen.

"What are you going to do? Chug a sprite? Get some alcohol like a real adult!" I yelled, standing up. He turned around and his eyes were heated.

"You...." His jaw was clenched so hard I thought it was going to crack.

I went over to my boots and shoved them on. "It's always a mistake to ever spend a minute alone with you. I thought we could be two freaking adults, but I forgot that one of us is a child!"

Before I grabbed the doorknob to leave, Chris clutched my shoulder and whipped me around to face him. His eyes were still angry, but a beautiful infuriating brown and his lips were in a tight line.

His hand was gentle as it let go of my shoulder and encircled my waist, bringing me up against him. I let out an unsteady breath as my body leaned close to him. That zing became a painful pleasure coursing through my body as his gaze softened.

"It is a mistake being alone with you," he whispered against my lips, and I felt myself losing all sense of my surroundings. My thoughts were focused on every part of him that was touching me, which at this point was almost everything. Our bodies lined up almost perfectly and I felt the muscles in his legs, stomach, and arms as we stood completely still.

We stared at each other and my heart beat loudly against my chest as the feelings zapped every nerve ending in my body. We hadn't even kissed, but I felt like I would die from the anticipation before we even got there.

When had I ever felt like that around a guy? Sure, that first little bit of coiling in my stomach when I'd kissed someone for the first time, but this…this was intense…and different.

I waited, our breaths mingling, our bodies unmoving as we stared at each other.

His eyes traveled to my lips and just as quickly as we got there, he moved away, my body growing cold from the separation.

I watched him swallow and run a hand across his beard. "Do, um, do you need me to walk you to your car?"

It was almost comical the way he asked and the timing, considering where we were just moments ago.

"Uh, no," I finally answered. Feeling confused, surprised, and…I wasn't sure. Something had shifted between us, and I wasn't sure what it was yet.

I left the house and when I stepped onto the porch a cool breeze touched my cheeks. I realized how flushed I'd been. Whether from the fighting or the almost-ravishing, I wasn't certain.

Six in the morning came quickly as the alarm buzzed in my ear. I hadn't slept well and kept waking up, thinking of being at Chris's house and our heated conversation. I showered and dressed quickly.

When I pulled into the rescue, Chris and Dale were unloading a horse from a trailer. Chris glanced over and a look of surprise went across his face.

Great, it was going to be awkward now. Would my red face give away my thoughts of him pressing his body against mine as he caged me against the door last night?

I prided myself on making things more comfortable, so I walked over to the two of them as Will struggled to get the lead rope on the brown horse who didn't seem to like him.

"What's going on?" I asked. Chris kept looking at me, but I stayed focused on the horse who looked slightly insane.

"Keith had a friend that was getting rid of this one. Can't tame him it seems, so before they turned him into glue, we got him," Dale said with a grin.

"He looks dangerous," I commented as he reared back, and Will did a "whoa boy" to halt him.

"Yep, and that'll be the fun part," Will called out with a grin. "He's too young to not try to train. He has potential, he just doesn't know it yet."

"How's that going to happen?" I asked.

This time, Chris finally spoke up after staring at me. "We'll put him in the round pen and do some groundwork to get used to people. Then we'll try a saddle. We won't break him in like ranchers do, we'll work with him slowly."

I turned to look at Chris and when our eyes met, I saw how much our relationship had changed. Even if we'd fought and bickered and I'd almost stormed away, the way he'd held me close to his body had changed something inside him. I know it definitely changed me.

Maybe I needed to treat Chris like a wild horse and go slow. I couldn't break him overnight; it had to come with time.

My expression must have changed because he cleared his throat and looked back at the horse and Will.

"We'll go in and get his stall ready. Take him into the pen to get him used to it for a bit," Chris instructed.

I went to leave for the dog kennels, but Chris stopped me. "We need help with the horses today. Kennels can be done by another volunteer."

I know he saw the surprise in my gaze, but I nodded.

I followed him to one of the new stalls and we cleaned it out together in silence. Occasionally, he would brush past me, his body lighting mine up like wildfire. I caught a smirk on his face when he came behind me to reach for something and his breath tickled my ear. I had gasped quietly as he said "sorry" but not really sounding very sorry.

I filled up the water bucket with cold fresh water and Chris brought in hay. No sooner did we finish up than Will came into the barn, cursing while holding onto the lead rope of the horse.

"Get out of the way, he's not liking it in here," Will yelled as he brought a very upset horse in behind him.

Chris grabbed my arm and pulled me into the tack room as Will tried to guide the pissed horse into the stall. He barely got out of the way as the horse gave a small buck when he got into the stall. It wasn't until he saw the grain that he dove headfirst into the bucket to noisily eat it.

Panting, Will pulled off his baseball cap and ran his hand through his hair. "Shit, he's going to be fun."

It was then I realized that Chris still had a hold of my arm. He realized it too and let go, clearing his throat as he stepped back into the aisle. "Be careful with him, Will."

He nodded, hands going to his hips. "Boss lady wanted me to see if you'd ride out to check on the cattle. She said one of the mommas looked ready to pop and she wants to make sure the calf is okay," Will said.

He nodded. "I was planning to do that today. We'll go this morning."

"We will?" Will asked.

"I'll take Monica."

Will just grinned. "Never do anything without a buddy, right Chris?"

He must have given him a glare because Will put his hands up in mock surrender and backed up. "I'm going, I'm going."

We watched Will leave the barn and I finally looked at Chris. "Why am I going out to the fields with you?"

He shrugged and didn't look at me as he went to the tack room to collect something. When he emerged, he was holding something that did not look like a saddle. It was more like a foam, thin pad.

It made me a little nervous seeing Jasper after witnessing the new horse. I did feel more comfortable with Jasper at least. I could walk beside him and be fine.

"I thought you'd want to do something other than clean out dog kennels," he offered.

But I knew that wasn't the case. He wanted to spend time with me, and I wasn't about to say no because truth be told, I wanted to spend time with him too.

Chapter Thirteen

A Rescheduled Date

Chris explained that the pad he had was actually a bareback saddle and it was much bigger than a regular saddle. He showed me how to place it onto Jasper and the importance of tightening the girth strap. Then he guided Jasper out of the stall and into the pen. He turned and looked at me. His eyes were.... present, calm, as if he'd come to some resolve over the night about me. I felt a warmness sweep across my body. He had something in his hands, but I didn't get to ask what it was.

"You ready to get on?" he asked.

All warmness left me as I stared at him. "What?" It was more a strained screech than anything.

His lip quirked up into a smile. "You're going to ride today. It's the easiest way to get to the cattle."

"Oh no, not going to happen." I backed up with my hands raised. "I'll walk."

He just smiled more. "You won't ride alone; I'll be behind you."

"On that? That isn't even a real saddle! It's a maxi-pad on a large creature!" I squeaked.

Squished on that foam pad in front of Chris? Well, that didn't sound too bad, but I also wasn't looking to die today. Bareback? Technically that's exactly what this was.

Chris tried to cover his laugh and failed. "I promise, it's safe."

"I don't know about this," I said quietly.

Chris walked over to stand close to me, so close I felt heat radiating off him.

"Try it, I won't let anything bad happen."

I believed him, and that was scary in itself.

"Okay, but if I end up in the hospital, that counts toward my community service hours!"

A chuckle of laughter bubbled out of him before he could stop it. "Put your foot into my hand, I'm going to give you a leg up." He cupped his palms and bent his knees a bit. "Grab the loop and swing your leg over the other side," he instructed.

With shaky hands I grabbed onto the loop, put my foot in his awaiting hands and swung myself up. My butt landed onto the back of Jasper harder than I anticipated. I squealed and leaned forward as I felt him shift.

Chris laughed. "Put your feet in the stirrups. Good. Now hang tight a second."

"Wait! Why?" I demand as he went beside the barn to grab what looked like little stairs.

He climbed up the block and settled in behind me. There was not much separating us as we pressed very closely together. I froze in surprise as I felt his breath on my ear and the back of my neck.

"Oh," I said unsteadily. "This is…close."

I felt tense, but like last time, that zap of pleasure roared down my spine and throughout my limbs wherever our bodies touched.

"Is that okay?" His voice sounded hoarse and gruff in my ear, and it made me shiver even though the weather was warm. I looked at him over my shoulder and I saw how close we were. His brown eyes shown with those speckles of gold, and I felt my breath catch.

God he was beautiful, in his masculine, wannabe cowboy way.

"Yeah," I croaked.

"You can grab onto his mane, it won't hurt him."

I touched the horse's mane and was astonished at how thick it was.

"We use these pads for training riders. We used to do more horseback riding lessons, but we lost a lot of our good horses," Chris mentioned as his arms went on either side of me to grab the reins. I held my breath as he lightly nudged Jasper with his heel, and he started to walk slowly; the motion of the horse jarred me for a moment.

"Horse riding?" I squeaked, trying not to focus on the fact that I was sitting atop a gigantic animal that could easily kill me. I held onto Jasper's mane so tightly, my knuckles were white.

"We used to offer lessons to kids. It was a way to earn more money for the rescue.

Unfortunately, there's only about three horses we trust, and we use them too often to also teach with them. We stopped giving lessons years ago."

Chris's body moved into mine every time Jasper stepped, and I slowly felt the tension ease out of me. It wasn't comfortable but it wasn't as scary as I thought.

We trotted towards the path to the cattle. It was the same path I took Rex on in the evenings. The sun's rays warmed us, and the breeze blew my hair back. I sighed in the silence.

"It's beautiful," I said once we got into the field, and I saw the fence line.

The clip-clop of Jasper's hooves was relaxing, and I realized maybe this was a part of my heritage that I didn't know and was finally coming out. Grandma always said that horses were a window to our soul. They were a part of us. I hadn't been around them to understand it, but maybe she was right. I felt free and part of me wished to start galloping so I could know how it felt to ride through the field as fast as I could.

I shifted to find a comfortable position. Chris's hand immediately went to my hip and stopped me from moving.

I jumped from his hot hand. "Is something wrong?"

"Don't shift," he said, sounding strained.

My heart picked up. "Will it spook him?"

Good god, the last thing I wanted was to get bucked off the horse. There were way too many famous people who fell off horses and died or broke something. I didn't want to be one of them.

"No," he said tightly. I looked over my shoulder to see his expression and saw his jaw clenched. "Just.... stop shifting."

I raised a brow and saw his cheeks tint pink. I turned back around, realizing what he meant.

Ooh…that's why. I couldn't help it, I smirked. "Been that long, Rhodes?"

"Shut it."

Maybe he did like me. Maybe he was just hiding it. Well, when you're riding this closely on the back of a horse, it's hard to hide.

"You guys should make more trails," I said, to relieve him of embarrassment. "It would be nice to have some places around the property away from the kennels where volunteers can walk the dogs."

He cleared his throat twice. "That's not a bad idea. We'd have to keep up the trails though because the vegetation will try to take over."

We got to the edge of the fence line and stopped. Chris got off first. He turned and looked at me as I sat up there alone, surprised how cold my back felt without him there.

"You're going to get off similar to how you got on. Feet out of the stirrups, swing your right leg around and climb down," he instructed, making it sound easy-peasy.

I felt my stomach quake a little and I was nervous. “I got you, Monica,” he said from below me and I trusted him.

I did as he said but as my left foot came out of the flimsy stirrup, I lost my balance and slid off very ungracefully. Chris caught me, his hands going way up under my shirt as I slid down the side of Jasper. He pulled me back up and quickly took his hands away as I started laughing.

“If you wanted to feel me up, you could have just asked,” I joked, my breathing fast.

He looked mortified. “That’s not–”

“Chris, I’m kidding. Getting off a horse is a lot harder than getting on,” I said looking at Jasper who was already grazing in the field.

“It gets easier, I promise.”

I turned back to him and saw that he’d taken at least a step away from me after having his hands under my shirt.

It was comical to see how embarrassed he was at touching me. Little did he know, I enjoyed it. When was the last time I’d had a guy’s hands on me? A year? How long had it been since Emma and Sam’s wedding?

“She’s right up here,” he said hoarsely as he started walking up to the fence. A big brown cow was on the other side and then I saw the calf. Small and still a little unsteady on its legs.

"Do you ever have to get Skyler out here to help with the birthing or do they do it alone?”

Chris leaned his arm on a fence post as he looked at them. “It depends. Normally they do just fine by themselves, but with some of the cattle we’ve rescued, they’ve needed more help because of health problems.”

I reached a hand through the fence and just grazed the top of the cow. She mooed and moved away, the calf following after her.

"You just touched a cow," Chris said in surprise. I looked at him, now fearing what I'd done.

"Do they bite?"

His eyes were wide and had a look of astonishment. "Some do but I'm surprised you touched her without asking first."

"Can you ride cows?"

He started laughing and drew in closer to me, his shoulder brushing against mine. "No, not unless you want to get kicked off. Believe me, many have tried."

I smiled and watched the cows and the sun shining over the fields. No noise except for the sounds of nature and the cows. The hot breeze blew my hair away from my face.

During certain times, I remembered my grandma going out to the mountains, staying overnight, and calling to the ancestors. It was her place of peace. I'd never understood it considering I liked indoor plumbing, a comfortable bed, and no bugs. But now, looking out across the open terrain and feeling…complete, I understood. I'd been addicted to city life, partying with strangers, drinking, and staying up until the sun rose, but I hadn't experienced the opposite side. I hadn't taken the time to enjoy Cold Spring when I was young because I'd hated that we moved here. I would have been a much different person had I just tried to live happily here. Would that have happened if I'd stayed another year with Grandma? Would I have ended up with Chris? Living in his house on the property? Helping with the rescue? A deep need filtered through me, and I looked over at Chris who was staring out at the calf. He was relaxed, his muscled arms hanging over the fence, his eyes shaded by his hat.

"Do you ever wonder what would have happened if we'd gone on that date?" I spoke it out loud before I could stop myself.

He was quiet for a moment, still not looking at me. "Yes and no."

"Explain."

He sighed. "Yes, because I think about it more often than I should, and no because I know you would have been resentful towards me if I'd been the reason you stayed." The answer sounded as if he really had thought about it for a long time. It shocked me.

He had liked me for a while in high school, but I'd kept myself distant. Was that because I knew if I fell for him, it would have been over for me? That I would have stayed here and maybe regretted it later? Though, San Diego did nothing for me except empty me of life. Grandma knew that would happen too and she tried to warn me, but I didn't listen.

I wanted my chance again, I wanted a "redo."

I turned to him and saw him watching me. "Why don't we try that date again?"

He raised a brow. "Are you asking me on a date?"

I shrugged. "I mean, not exactly, I'm just rescheduling the old one."

"Rescheduling?" he repeated in shock.

I bumped into his shoulder and gave him a warm smile. "Yes. Rescheduling."

He softened, looking at my lips for a moment before going back up to my eyes. My heart beat a little harder at his expression as he stayed quiet for several seconds. Part of me felt a little fear because for a moment, I was afraid he was going to say no.

"Alright."

"Really?"

"Sure, why not?"

Sure? Cause that's exactly what I wanted every man to say when I asked them on a date. He ignored my look and continued, "Meet me here at seven tomorrow evening."

"Meet you here? As in the rescue?"

He nodded.

"This isn't some sick joke where you make me clean kennels instead?"

He laughed and amusement shined in his eyes. "No, I'm not that cruel."

I smiled and looked out across the field, for once feeling happy about where I was in life.

I didn't know what to wear on my date with Chris. He didn't tell me what we were doing, so I wasn't sure how I should dress. I decided to go to Feather Blue and pick out an outfit and talk to Emma and Brynn. They were both there helping a customer when I walked in. Emma grinned and waved as she opened a fitting room for the lady.

I went to Brynn for some help. Her brown hair was curled, and she wore a pair of feather earrings that matched her dress. She and Luke had been married almost a year now and I wondered if they'd started thinking about having a baby. Seeing her best friend Emma with Savannah might be that incentive. But I wasn't about to ask her about kids. No one wants to hear that question as much as everyone asks it.

"Hey, we weren't expecting you," Brynn said.

"I know, I wanted to look at some of your new items, and I had a question for you," I started. "The Rhodes just rescued some puppies in Albany this past week. I thought maybe you could get some photos of them so we could post them on social media. It might help them get adopted quicker. Could you give me a price estimate to do that?"

Brynn looked surprised. "Puppies? I've never photographed dogs before. Unless you count a few of Molly." She paused a beat. "Let me stop over with my camera and take a few, free of charge. If this is for the Rhodes, I don't mind doing it as a donation."

"Are you sure?" I asked with surprise.

She nodded eagerly. "They helped me when I found Molly. I don't mind giving back."

"Thank you! Just text me and let me know what days work for you and I'll talk to Chris. They are at his house right now; I can send you the address."

Brynn smiled knowingly. "The community service at the rescue is working out great for you, isn't it?"

"Yeah…it is." And I realized I wasn't lying.

"Monica! It's good to see you. Are you coming to dinner at our place on Sunday? We invited your parents too," Emma said as she came to hug me.

"Oh, this Sunday?" I asked when she pulled back. I did not want to get grilled by them and I knew they still hadn't found out about my incident with the law yet. I wasn't sure if I wanted to deal with it. "I don't think I can make it. I have a lot of stuff to do for Erin."

"How's it going with you marketing for the shop? I know the few posts you did for us were great!" Emma said, glowing at me.

"It's working out well for her. We're doing some themed coffees for holidays."

"I hope it's like that chocolate coconut one," Brynn said wistfully.

Emma and I both laughed.

I looked at the rack of tops and found a pretty teal one that I knew was a good color for me. It was a bodysuit with short sleeves and a lace front that would show just a little cleavage. It would be cool with the warm weather and look good for a somewhat casual date. It would also match Grandma's necklace that I still wore, mostly hidden under my shirts. It had become part of me, something I never took off.

"This is adorable. I'll take this."

That evening, I slipped on the top and black shorts then added my black sandals. I opted to let my hair down and stared at myself in the mirror. I almost looked like California Monica. The teal blue of my blouse heightened my golden skin. I pulled Grandma's necklace out from under my shirt and it matched beautifully.

On my way to Chris's, I thought of what we could be doing tonight. Would it be a homemade meal? Or maybe he was taking me into New York City?

When I pulled into the driveway, Dale and Chris were standing close to the barn. I thought for a moment that he'd forgotten about the date and was still working with Dale until I realized he was cleaned up. He didn't have a hat on, and his hair looked combed. I parked in front of Chris's house then walked over to them.

Dale grinned at me. "Well, hi beautiful. I hope you weren't planning to go out with this sorry sucker. Why don't you go for someone older that will appreciate you more," he smooshed.

I laughed. "Sorry Dale, I think you're out of my league."

I looked at Chris and I saw him staring at me, starting at my toes and ending at my face. I felt a rush and trained my knowing smile on him.

He looked good tonight. He'd trimmed his beard, gotten a haircut, put on his nicest jeans, and added a nice maroon short sleeve t-shirt. He even had on clean cowboy boots, not his scuffed-up ones.

"Are you ready?" I asked, hoping the sexy tone of my voice made him squirm a little.

"S-sure," Chris stuttered, clearing his throat as Dale patted him on the back.

Monica still got it!

"Have fun tonight," Dale said with a wink as we headed to Chris's house.

"So, are you making dinner?" I asked, glancing over at him.

He hooked his fingers into his pockets. “No, we’re going out.”

He opened the door of his truck, and I got in, surprised that we weren’t even going inside. When he got in and started up the truck, I looked over. “Why did you make me drive over here if we’re going out?”

Chris smirked. “Had to make sure you were going to show up.”

I rolled my eyes, but I couldn’t fault him. What was that saying? Fool me once shame on you, fool me twice, shame on me?

“How are the puppies doing?”

Chris backed out of the driveway, and we headed towards Cold Spring.

“Good. Skyler is coming out next week to give them shots. We can start adopting them out after that.”

Once we were on the road, he didn’t try to touch me, even though I sat very close. Close enough to encourage him to. But instead, he kept both hands on the wheel.

“I talked to Brynn today. She said she’d take a few pictures of them. She might be able to come out next week.”

“I think we could do that. You really think it’ll work?” He finally glanced over at me but didn’t linger.

“I hope so.”

He turned back to the road, and we drove past my apartment into the parking lot of the Cold Spring Diner.

"This is where we're going for dinner?" I asked, surprised.

He got out and came around to open my door. When I slipped out and looked up at the neon lights of the old diner, it took me back to high school.

The music blared from the old radio sitting on top of the coffee maker. Sophie had convinced the cook to turn it to her favorite station and turn up the volume.

Natalie and I sat in a booth as Sophie raced back to us with a proud grin on her face. She slid into the seat next to Natalie and pulled a bottle of vodka from her purse.

Natalie giggled and I pushed my glass over so she could add it into my soda.

"Quick! Before anyone sees!" Natalie whispered.

Soda sloshed over the table as she poured the alcohol into my glass. As soon as she moved on to Natalie's drink, I mixed mine with my straw and took a large sip.

"Perfect," I said with a laugh.

Natalie and Sophie looked behind me as a group of five guys, all from the football team, shoved their way into the diner. Since we were cheerleaders, we felt it was our duty to get to know them.

Especially the cute ones. I couldn't actually date, but I could make out, hang out, and flirt with any of them just as long as Sam or my parents never found out.

"Ooh! Yes!" Sophie squealed. "I thought they would be here tonight!"

"You brought us here specifically for them?" Natalie asked, pulling her shirt down to show more of her cleavage.

She winked at me. "Maybe." She leaned out of the booth and whistled at them. "Over here!"

The boys pointed towards us and came over to stand next to our booth.

"Well hello ladies," a smooth-talking Brown boy said, looking towards Natalie's cleavage.

"Hi Kyle, what are you doing here?" Sophie asked, twirling a blonde lock of her hair in her fingers.

The other boys standing around Kyle weren't nearly as good looking. They were nice but were jocks and I wasn't exactly fond of jocks.

The bell dinged again on the diner door, and I looked over my shoulder. Walking in was a tall, dark blonde-haired boy. He had on his letterman jacket and as he turned to glance towards us, his soft brown eyes connected with mine.

My mouth opened in surprise, and I saw a light in his eyes as he smiled. Something shifted inside me, something odd and different. I felt heat rise to my cheeks as his eyes didn't waver from mine. He was tall and thin and when he walked, I heard the clacking of his cowboy boots against the floor. I'd seen him before in classes but didn't know his name.

"Rhodes! About time you got here!" Kyle Brown said as the boy walked up next to him.

"Sorry, had to help my parents."

Kyle rolled his eyes and started conversing with Sophie and Natalie while leaning in very closely. He was probably trying to get a better view of Nat's boobs. The Rhodes boy slid in next to me at the booth and I looked at him with a smirk.

"And who said you can sit down next to me?" I asked, with a flirty tone.

His smile was contagious and heart clenching as he looked over at me. "I said I could sit here, and it didn't look like anyone else was going to."

He reached for my cup and took a sip, and I stared in shock. He almost coughed but kept it together as he set it back down on the table.

"Well, that should teach you to steal someone's drink," I jested and took a swig of it.

He cleared his throat. "Looks like you take your soda strong."

I giggled. "Just a bit."

He put his arm over the back of the booth, and I almost swooned at his manly scent. It was intoxicating.

He stared at me, still smiling, recovered now from the drink. "My name is Chris."

I bit my lip. "Monica."

I blinked several times, looking at Chris sitting across from me in the familiar diner. It had changed a lot since I'd last been there, but it still had that familiar smell of brewed coffee and stale cigarettes. The seats were still bright red but with a few tears in the leather. The man in front of me was different from the one back then. He was cute when he was young, boyish even, but now…he was manly and devastatingly handsome. He'd grown and his jaw had filled out, no longer round and youthful. The lines between his eyebrows were new along with wrinkles around the corners of his lips. *Ugh, those lips.* Full and thick and very kissable.

"You okay?" Chris asked, grabbing two menus.

I cleared my throat, averting my gaze. "Yes, I'm fine. It's been a while since I've been here."

He stared at me, those eyes not nearly as shiny and happy as they had been the night I'd first met him. We both had changed so much since then.

"So, what's my budget?" I asked.

He chuckled, looking at the menu. "Unlimited budget."

"Ooh," I cooed and looked at mine. Nothing was over fifteen dollars at Cold Spring Diner, and I realized that even the prices hadn't changed much since I left. “I guess that means I’ll have to get the most expensive item on here.” He glanced up and raised a brow. “The pancakes with bacon.”

He shook his head, a smile on his lips. “Forgot to tell you that you’re paying tonight.”

I laughed and so did he. It was almost a glimpse of him from all those years ago.

“Christopher! How are you doing?” Our waitress, an older lady with a badly stained apron, came to our table and pulled a notepad from her pocket. Her gray hair was pulled into a bun at the nape of her neck. She had a kind smile.

“I’m doing well. How’s Mr. Smith?” Chris asked, sounding concerned.

She sniffed a little. “He has good days and bad. Thanks for asking. What can I get you both?” She finally looked at me and recognition flared in her gaze, but she didn’t say anything. We gave her our order, and she left.

“Christopher?” I questioned with a smirk.

He rolled his eyes and leaned on the table. “She’s known me since I was born, it’s the only name she calls me.”

I nodded. “Is something wrong with her husband?”

He grew serious. “Yeah, he was diagnosed with cancer last year. He’s been fighting it, but it hasn’t been going well.”

I felt empathy for her, and I glanced over my shoulder to see her humming as she cleaned some cups and stacked them. The diner wasn't that busy since the crowd that ate here was mainly over the age of sixty and were probably in bed and almost asleep by now.

Our food came and we ate and talked, and it felt as if no time had passed between us. That it hadn't been eight years, I hadn't bailed on our date, and he hadn't gotten into a car accident. It was the two of us getting to know each other again.

"That was a horrible night! How could you even think it was one of best parties you've been to?" I exclaimed, laughing as I drew my knee up next to me on the seat.

Chris laughed, that smile melting me even more. "Listen, as a farm boy, running from the cops and diving into Mike's pool, it was the best!"

We laughed so much that my stomach hurt. How long had it been since I felt this happy? I couldn't even remember.

"Lucky you got away with it; I wouldn't have. I swear Sam has always had 'Monica Radar.' It tells him where I'll be and what I'm doing."

He winced, stacking my plate and his, and pushing them towards the edge of the table. "Didn't he come pick you up at the Walter's party that one time?"

I scoffed. "Yep, and told my parents. He was such a snitch," I muttered, shaking my head.

Mrs. Smith came by and asked if we wanted dessert, but he told her no and got the check. Just to pick on him, I said, "What if I wanted dessert?"

He gave her his card, and she walked away. Then he looked at me. "You'll get dessert."

It almost sounded sexual, and I couldn't help the twinge that rolled through my stomach. He realized his tone and how he'd said it and his cheeks turned slightly pink. It was adorable to see him blush considering what a manly man he was. Even his beard couldn't hide it.

"N-not like that." He cleared his throat and was interrupted by Mrs. Smith giving us the receipt. She looked over at me with a sweet smile. "You take care of this one. He's a good man, and tell your brother I said hi."

"I'll tell Sam," I mumbled. She knew who I was, but she probably didn't know my name.

As if he could see my irritation, he caught my eye as we were walking out of the diner. "She upset you." It wasn't a question; it was a fact.

I looked straight ahead towards the truck. "No, she didn't upset me."

I went to reach for the handle, but he nudged my shoulder with his own. "Let's go on a walk."

I frowned and followed him, his hands shoved into his pockets. I left my hands free, hoping maybe he would try to hold one. There hadn't been many dates in my life where the guy hadn't already tried to cop a feel at this point.

We went out to the water and walked on the sidewalk. It was a warm evening but with the sun setting, the balminess was bearable.

"I could tell whatever she said bothered you," Chris continued.

"It's not what you think."

He glanced over. "How so?"

I took a deep breath. "It's just that my brother is well known here in Cold Spring to the point that I'm only known as Sam's sister or Officer Locklear's sister. She didn't even know my name."

It was quiet between us for a few minutes. "I'm not trying to be an ass, but you realize you didn't live here very long. No one had time to get to know you other than as Sam's sister," Chris explained. I glanced over as we got closer to a small ice cream shop by the river.

"I was still here from 8th grade until–"

"A week after graduation," he finished for me, a hurt expression on his face. He looked away quickly.

"Yeah," I finished lamely. "That was five long years of my life."

We paused outside of the bustling ice cream shop and glanced in the windows to see people lined up waiting to be served. Several kids came out of the store, ice cream cones in hand, laughing and giggling, as the doorbell tinkled in the summer breeze.

He was standing so close to me now that I felt the warmth of his body.

"Monica, you kept everyone at a distance. I didn't even know who you were until sophomore year," Chris said softly. "You were in my algebra class and sat in the back alone and didn't talk to anyone."

I frowned. "You were in that class?" He nodded slowly. "I don't remember seeing you."

"I don't think you saw anyone in that class. Your head was down a lot, and you did the work and left."

I pressed my lips together. I remembered the class. It was a challenging one but I'd taken it because algebra wasn't my strong suit, and I knew I had to get a better grade in it. Sophie and Natalie didn't take it, so I didn't have any of my friends in there with me. I knew without him saying it, I was a different person when I was around them. If I didn't take notice of him in my class, I was there just to get a good grade, focus, and leave.

"I wasn't *that* distant," I fought back.

He let the conversation go and gave a nod towards the shop. We ordered ice cream from the menu then went back outside to walk along the river. We didn't talk and it was mostly because I was thinking over everything he'd just said.

I ate my ice cream slowly, savoring the sweetness. It reminded me of when I was a teenager and Sophie, Natalie, and I would come here after being at the diner. It was the best local ice cream shop and was the most favored in town.

Had I really kept everyone at a distance? I still partied with Sophie and Natalie, and I let them in, right? I'd gone on a few dates to the movies with Zane and made out in the back of his car. I made out with Evan at Sophie's seventeenth birthday. But…none of them really knew me. Sophie and Natalie knew about my grandma, but they didn't know how close she and I were. They knew I hated my parents most days, but they didn't realize I was thinking of staying another year to be with my grandma. It wasn't until…until I started to talk to Chris that I felt someone knew me. It was as if he actually saw me.

He finished his ice cream, and we stood in silence, looking out over the Hudson. There was only a sliver of a moon, but stars dotted the sky.

"I guess you're right," I mumbled, throwing my ice cream cup into the trash can.

He leaned over the railing and glanced over at me. "What am I right about?" His gaze was directly on me, and I felt it clear to my bones.

"I did keep everyone at a distance." I took a breath. "I wasn't planning to stay, and I didn't want to get attached to anyone. Of course that didn't work. I was going to stay for my grandma…and for you."

He gave a nod, his eyes dark.

"Care to tell me anything else about myself I didn't know?" I questioned, crossing my arms.

He smirked and straightened to move closer to me. I knew it was going to happen; Chris was finally going to kiss me. His eyes softened and I leaned in, watching his expression.

"You are one of the most beautiful women I've ever met," he said quietly.

The air rushed out of me as I felt the weight of his gaze. "I knew that," I mumbled.

His lip moved up in amusement and he stepped away. "Let's get you back to your car."

I may have stood there stupidly, realizing he hadn't kissed me, even as I heard his boots clomping on the cement walkway.

He had just gotten that close to me but didn't kiss me? Hell, he even complimented me! I finally made my legs move and caught up to him. I was so confused I didn't utter another word as we got into the truck and drove down the road.

"Thank you for a fun night," I said finally as we got close to the rescue.

He looked over and flashed me an old Chris smile. "You're welcome."

"I may not come in tomorrow morning," I mumbled with a yawn.

"It's Saturday. Take the day off," he encouraged.

When we got back to the house, I felt awkward getting out of his truck and going towards my car but we both paused at the walkway to his house. He still hadn't kissed me, and I hoped he still would before I left.

Chris was quiet as he pushed his hands deep into his pocket again.

"Thanks again for the evening, I had a nice time. It brought me back to when I was a teenager," I said.

"It was our original date. I thought since you made me wait eight years, you had to suffer through the first date I planned."

I laughed loudly. "You're serious? That's what you had planned?"

"Are you saying eighteen-year-old Chris doesn't know how to woo a lady?"

"Diner, ice cream, and a walk by the Hudson?" I looked up at the sky like I was thinking. "It may have worked on eighteen-year-old Monica, but… it works for this Monica too."

He shook his head with amusement. "Get home safely." His voice had dropped an octave, and I pressed my lips together.

"I will."

He turned toward the house, and I fished my car keys out of my purse then paused to look at his retreating back. Was he really not going to try to kiss me? Or touch me? The most he'd touched me was a hand to my lower back. But not even a hug goodbye? This wasn't like anything I'd experienced before. A man not trying to grab me at any point?

Not a boob grab, butt, leg? He'd practically hid his hands from me the entire night.

I put my purse on the roof of my car and called out. "Chris!"

He stopped on his porch and turned around to face me. I couldn't see his expression with his back to the porch light, only his silhouette. But his broadness, his long legs, and powerful arms were easy to notice. I walked closer, frowning as I stared at him.

"This was a date, right?" I clarified.

"Normally when the man pays and he takes you to the restaurant, that means it's a date."

I opened my mouth, still confused and slightly annoyed. "So why the hell didn't you kiss me? You had your hands shoved so far into your pockets the whole night!" He stepped down from the porch as I continued. "You buy me ice cream, say I'm beautiful and then wave goodbye from the porch? How do you think that makes a girl feel?"

"Like I'm a gentleman?"

I scoffed. "No! It makes me think you're not interested! And maybe you aren't, and that's fine but tell a girl." I was exasperated by him.

His lips formed an amused smile as he watched me. "This is what I would have done eight years ago, Monica. I would have let you decide where it goes from here."

I just stared, still not understanding, and turned my back towards him. He didn't say he wasn't interested but he didn't say he was…what did his riddle mean?

I would have let you decide where it goes from here.

Was this him putting the ball in my court? Was he saying if I wanted him, I had to chase him now? Son of a bitch! And I thought women were complicated!

I turned back towards him, and he was still watching me.

Fine, ball's in my court buddy? You're about to get your socks blown off.

I stalked towards him, and he reached for me as I put my hands on either side of his face and kissed him.

Chapter Fourteen

A Kiss Worth Waiting Eight Years For

Sparks flew and that fire erupted in my stomach. His hands tightened around my waist, drawing me in closer to him and our lips moved as one. He tasted of mint, and it had my head spinning not knowing which way was up or down. It was only him and the press of his lips to mine.

I opened my mouth, and his hands tightened on me, urging me to keep going, so I did. Tongues meeting, retreating, connecting until I heard a growl from Chris that made my toes curl.

We slowly broke apart and when I opened my eyes, I saw surprise.

"That was eight years past due," I whispered, breathlessly.

It was more than I could have ever imagined it would be. Had I let him kiss me at the pool that night, I would have been lost to him forever. He would have ruined any other man I tried to be with had I kissed him then. And now, I was still forever ruined.

I wanted to push him into the house and let the last eight years be gone and pick up where we'd left off, but I stopped myself.

He dipped his head and kissed me softly, not urgent like the first kiss, but as a promise.

"I should go," I whispered, between his lips.

"You should." His deep voice made my insides curl with delight. He nipped at my bottom lip, his hands ghosting down my back. "This is why I kept my hands to myself tonight," he said quietly as his fingers moved down on my back. "Because I knew I wouldn't be able to keep them off you."

I closed my eyes, a shiver of pleasure running over me at his words, his touch. "That explains a lot."

He chuckled and to my disappointment, he stepped back, but he didn't look away from me. "Text me when you get home."

Still stunned and overwhelmed, all I did was nod and walk to my car. I got in and drove down the road toward my apartment. My smile was wide, and it hurt my cheeks as I remembered every moment. His warm hands, his lips, his big body...his smile. That twinkle in his eyes that said "finally." He didn't have to voice it because I felt it. Whatever havoc was running through me, was running through him too.

How would tomorrow be? How would it be when I got back to cleaning those kennels? Would he pretend tonight never happened? Panic rose in me and part of me thought perhaps I'd imagined what had happened.

No, I hadn't because my lips were still tingling from that kiss and the press of his hands on my back…that was real.

Don't overthink it, just let it happen.

When I got home, I threw my purse on the counter and pulled out my cell phone. I texted Chris, my fingers flying over the keys.

Me: *I'm home. Thanks for a nice evening. (smiley face)*

That felt silly, so I erased the smiley face before sending the text. I then wished I'd sent it, so I texted again with the smiley face. *God I was pathetic!* How many men had I been with? Why was this one turning me into a virgin teenager again? I walked into my bedroom to change clothes and the minute I heard the buzz on the counter, I flew back out to the kitchen and grabbed my phone to see who'd texted.

> Phoebe: *Girlllll, we need an intervention! What's going on with you? You're working at an animal rescue?? Isn't that where like…animals are??*
> Me: *Long story, but yes. And if it makes you feel better, there's a hot guy who works there that I'm seeing.*
> Phoebe: *Oh, thank god! I thought we were going to have to send you to an insane*

asylum. Roger that, Officer Monica, we have finally landed in normal territory.

I laughed and went back into the bedroom to put on an oversized t-shirt and shorts. When my phone buzzed again, I didn't race for it, but when I saw Chris's name pop up instead of Phoebe's, my heart leaped.

Chris: *Good. I think we should do this again.*

I grabbed a water bottle from the fridge and laid down on the sofa on my stomach to look at his text.

Me: *You mean the kiss or the date?*
Chris: *Both.*

My insides definitely did a few flips and turns. I wanted to see him again, and soon. I wanted to make sure what we'd felt was real and it hadn't been a hallucination.

Me: *Lucky for you, I work part-time and only have a few hours left for my community service.*
Chris: *Sunday?*

The texts were almost sent at the same time, and I relished how excited he seemed to be together again.

Me: *I think that works with my schedule*

I smiled as I saw his chat bubbles come up, then disappear, then reappear.

Chris: *I'll pick you up at 5.*
Me: *5? Isn't that a little early for a date?*
Chris: *Not for someone who runs a rescue.*
Me: *Got it. Is this a casual date?*
Chris: *I think you know me enough to know there's no such thing as formal dates.*

I laughed out loud, knowing he was right. I texted a quick *I should've known* with a smiley face.

I waited for another response but when I didn't get one, I went back to my bedroom and slid between the sheets. It was difficult to shut off my brain but when I did, I only fell into dreams of Chris.

My grandma would've said that there is a reason for every dream we have. There's an ancestor behind it trying to guide us to the right path. It reminded me of when I'd told my grandma the dream I'd had about Chris when I was only seventeen.

"I just had a weird night," I explained to Grandma as I got her some tea and sat in the chair across from her. They were mostly uncomfortable and needed to be reupholstered, but Grandma refused to pay for that.

She eyed me over her glass, her brown eyes twinkling. "What type of weird night?"

"Vivid dreams."

She placed the teacup and saucer on the end table and clasped her hands into her lap. "There are never weird dreams, Monica. They all have meaning. Explain it to me."

I leaned back into the chair, my legs stretched out in front, clad in only a shirt and the tiny shorts my mother hated.

"It was about this guy," I mumbled. Grandma raised a thick eyebrow at that. "It's not like that…well, I don't know. He showed up at the diner when I was with Soph and Natalie last night. I'd seen him before, but I'd never spoken to him or knew his name. He was handsome and we had a great conversation and flirted. Next thing you know, I'm dreaming *about him."*

"Oh?" Grandma cooed with an amused smile. "And how did this dream go?"

"Really?" I complained.

She gave me a hard look. "Have I taught you nothing, Monica Locklear? Sit back, close your eyes and replay this dream, now."

I decided to humor her and leaned my head back onto the uncomfortable chair and closed my eyes. I thought of the dream I'd had and tried to replay it out loud.

"We were at a bonfire outside," I said softly. I could see Chris sitting beside me, his smile and eyes making me feel so different than anyone else I'd encountered. "Chr–uh, the guy is sitting beside me and he's staring at me, as if there's no one else around us."

"When you look into his eyes, what do you see?" Grandma's voice cut into my mind and echoed around my thoughts.

I leaned in closer to him to see into his brown eyes and there...a flicker of something.

"An eagle," I whispered.

Then I felt the tiniest spit of water splash on my face. I turned to look up into the night sky and watched lightning streak across as the rain hit heavier.

"It's raining but I can still see the moon," I said.

I looked back to Chris who had his hand outstretched to me. "Take my hand, trust me."

"He's...." I trailed off, looking at him longer but not reaching for him. "He asked me to trust him."

The rain hit harder, dousing the flames even more and my fear of the night awakened.

"Take my hand," he encouraged again but I kept looking to the flames. It was about to go dark. I couldn't, I had to get away, I couldn't wait to see what would happen when the fire went out.

"Monica?"

I couldn't tell who'd said it, Chris or Grandma, but I stood up and opened my eyes without taking his hand. Grandma was sitting straight, watching me. My hands shook as I stared out the window in her living room.

I calmed myself and sat back down in the chair, avoiding her gaze.

"Well, do you want to know what it means?" Grandma finally said.

"I don't think I want to."

"Too bad." She slapped her hands down onto her lap, startling me. "He is one with nature and animals. He is courageous and will bring harmony to your life."

I rolled my eyes. "Yeah, okay, Grandma."

She leaned forward, her eyes wrinkling at the corners. "The rain is for the love that will develop between you and that moon represents protection over you both if you are together. If one leaves, it could bring harm to the other. That is why you must stay."

My phone buzzed and I was thankful for the distraction. I looked at the screen and saw it was Sophie calling me.

"Sorry Grandma, I have to take this, it's Soph." I didn't wait for her response. I ducked into the other room and answered her call. "Hey, Soph, what's up?"

"Moni! You're not going to believe what happened. Kyle Brown just kissed me!"

I was the good friend and asked her questions about it, trying to sound eager to hear more but really, my thoughts were on what my grandma had said. She'd never steered me wrong, but she believed things, ancient things, that I wasn't sure I did. All I knew was that Chris was hot, and I liked him more than any other guy I'd hung out with. There was nothing more to it.

The weekend came and Sunday quickly approached. I looked through my closet, trying to find something cute that wasn't jeans. I found a short black dress that was more a summer dress than one for the club and grabbed a sweater in case it got chilly.

My phone rang and I answered it quickly. "I'm here. Are you ready?" Chris asked and my stomach did a somersault.

"Almost, come on up," I responded happily.

I ran out of the bedroom and removed the coffee cup from the table and grabbed my shoes to slip on just as I heard the knock on the door.

I grinned as I swung it open to see Chris standing in the hallway. I hopped on one foot, trying to get my sandals on.

Shit…he looked good. Those boots, jeans, and a nice black t-shirt. It wasn't a polo shirt and for as long as I knew Chris, he never wore polos. He was not dressy or preppy. He was…a farm boy. He didn't wear a hat, and his hair looked light and fluffy and still a little damp on the ends. I didn't know why that was so hot but knowing he was just in the shower…

"Sorry, I'm almost ready. Come in," I gestured, and he stepped in, clearing his throat as he eyed me up.

"You look beautiful," he muttered as I shut the door behind him.

"Thank you. Give me one minute, I just need to grab my earrings." I went back into my bedroom and collected a pair of hoops then came back out to see Chris standing with his hands in his pockets glancing around the room.

"It's a nice place. It's small but I don't need much," I said to him.

He went over to my window that overlooked the road below. You could see a little of the river from here but not much.

"It's loud," he commented.

I scoffed and came up next to him. His shoulder brushed mine and I liked that connection. Cars traveled by the house as the sun shined and we looked out the window together. “Compared to the rescue, yes. Sometimes I forget how quiet it is there until I come home and try to sleep.”

I felt Chris move to clasp my hand. The contact made me lean against him until I wrapped my arm around his forearm. He turned his head towards me, and I leaned in. His lips pressed into mine, not urgent, but savoring. His hand moved to cup my cheek and guide me closer until his hand was tangled in my hair and I was stretching on my toes, hungry for more.

Finally, we broke apart and I leaned back, trying to catch my breath.

Chris looked just as winded as he untangled his hand from my hair and brushed it behind my ear.

“Hungry?” he asked, staring at my lips.

“Starving.”

He smirked and unfortunately, we left my apartment, still holding hands. He opened the truck door for me, then ran to his side to get in. We immediately reached for each other again.

“Where to?” I asked.

His hand tightened in mine comfortingly. “There’s a brewery that just opened. I thought we could get some food there. It’s by the river.”

“A brewery? You don’t drink though?”

“No, but the view is nice, and I heard the food is good.”

We were seated at a table close to the river on the brewery's porch. We ordered our food, and I sipped my water as he took a drink of his soda.

"Why is it you don't drink? I'm sure I remember seeing you at some of the parties with a beer," I asked, curious.

He shrugged and looked out over the water, his arm up on the back of his chair. It was such a relaxed, manly pose. "I don't like the taste anymore."

"College would have changed that," I muttered before I could stop myself.

He scratched his bearded chin. "College wasn't for me."

He'd mentioned before that he didn't finish because he'd gotten hurt. By hurt, I assumed he meant in the accident. He still hadn't told me about it. Well, if Monica Locklear was anything, she wasn't shy about asking questions.

"I heard a rumor that you were in a car accident after we graduated." There, I got it out.

Of course, the waitress appeared at that moment with our food and placed it in front of us, but Chris didn't reach for his fork. He stayed relaxed, leaning against the chair and looked at me. I couldn't read his expression other than seeing that he was frustrated.

"When did you hear this?" His voice was tight.

"A few weeks ago."

We just stared at each other, and I knew he could see the empathy in my gaze. “I didn’t know it happened until I came back. Not even my brother told me.” I didn’t know why I needed to tell him that, but I did.

“Did you hear anything else about it?” His voice was strained as I watched him.

“No.” It was true. Erin didn’t really say much more other than he was in an accident and that he was badly hurt.

I saw his shoulders relax a little and he started eating without saying another word. Was that all he would say about it? I had more questions, more concerns, and I wanted them answered.

We finished dinner almost in silence. When we got back into his truck and began driving down the road, I finally spoke up again.

“Are we just not going to talk after I brought up the accident?” I questioned, annoyed.

“There’s not much to say about it,” he said tightly.

“You mean you don’t want to elaborate on how it happened and if you were hurt?”

“You didn’t care back then, why would you care now?” he snapped.

I flinched. “Chris, I didn’t know about it. No one told me.”

"I find that hard to believe." His jaw was stiff, and I could see his hands gripping the wheel a little harder than before.

"Chris," I whispered again softly, putting my hand on his arm. I scooted closer on the bench seat. "I didn't know. I would have texted or called you or sent a carrier pigeon, *something*. But no one told me."

He was quiet and I felt him relaxing under my touch. "Sam was the one who found me."

My heart shattered for a moment at what he was saying. "What?"

Stiffly, he nodded in the darkness of the truck. Realization hit me. *Sam hadn't told me.* He knew I liked Chris. He'd heard the conversation and argument I'd had with my parents about dating him. I pushed off the rise of anger and focused on the present.

"What happened?"

I didn't think he was going to tell me at first until he took a small breath. "I was coming back from a party…drunk. It had just rained so the roads were slick. I don't remember much after I hit the tree other than knowing something bad had happened and I wasn't sure if I was going to make it." I heard the strain in his voice, and it broke my heart.

"How did Sam know?"

"A neighbor down the road heard the squealing of tires and the crash when I hit the tree.

They called 911 and Sam was the first one on the scene. He...he talked to me while we waited for the ambulance. Even some of that has left my memory," he trailed off.

I swallowed hard past the lump in my throat. "Were you injured?"

He shrugged. "I'm fine now."

It wasn't an answer, but I knew he had been. I didn't know what else to say as I looked at his profile in the car and could feel his pain. I leaned against his shoulder and wrapped my arm around his forearm and didn't say anything else.

When we got back to my house, he walked me up to my door. He held my hand as he looked at me and I realized I didn't want this night to end.

"Do you want to come in? It's still early," I said looking at my phone.

"As much as I want to, I can't. I have to be up early tomorrow morning." I knew he was telling the truth, but I still saw a sadness that lingered over him from our conversation. I hadn't meant to cause that. "Will you be in tomorrow?"

"Yes, I still have about fifty something hours left."

His lip finally curved up into a smile. "I'll see you then."

He leaned in and brushed his lips gently against mine and it ignited every nerve ending in me. Chris's hand trailed down to wrap around my waist and pull me towards him until our bodies were flush against one another. I urged him on by speeding up the kiss and pooling my arms around his neck.

"Come in," I encouraged between kisses.

He chuckled and it vibrated my lips. "Not tonight."

He pulled back reluctantly and cupped my chin. His eyes looked over every part of my face until I felt like I was going to melt under his gaze. "I've waited a long time to kiss you, now I want to take my time."

That made my toes curl, and I hummed a reluctant acceptance. He gave another kiss and stepped away. "Have a good night."

I leaned against the doorway and watched him go back down the stairs. I stood there until I knew he was gone, then went right down myself and got into my car.

The effects of the kiss had drifted away as rage filled me.

Sam.

My own brother had known about Chris and kept the information from me.

Chapter Fifteen

You Should Have Told Me

I closed the door quietly behind me and tip-toed in, heels dangling from my hand. Graduation night had been a bit crazy, and I was still buzzed after several drinks.

"It's after 2am," a voice called out.

I squealed and jumped, turning to the voice. Sam stood in the hallway, arms crossed, looking very much like our dad.

"When is your house settlement?" I hissed. "With you living back here, it feels like you're my unwanted second father."

"You've got to get serious, Monica. You've graduated now."

I rolled my eyes. "Don't worry, I'll still be the family disappointment and you'll still be the favorite, Sammy."

Yikes, tequila and I were not on the same team.

He shook his head at me. "Stop it. You're being childish. If you get your act together and stop partying and going out with guys, you could be better than this."

His words hit me hard, and I ground my teeth.

"Let me help. We can hang out on Friday next week. I'll help you prep for college. We can create a plan and see about a second major."

I barely heard him, I was so angry. He was my big brother. I knew he was trying to help but it was degrading.

"I can't, I have a date "

He frowned. "With whom?"

"Chris Rhodes. I like him, he's a good guy. I'm not canceling on him to work on shit that is pointless." Shit. I couldn't say anything else. Sam and my parents didn't yet know I was planning on putting off college for a year.

Sam just tilted his head in disappointment. "Dating? Really? You know that's not a priority right now."

"Neither is more college prep! I already picked my major and I'm not going to go for anything else. I don't need your help with a plan." I walked to my door and was about to go in when Sam's words made me pause.

"If you're leaving, why date someone who lives here? You'll just hurt him."

Because he didn't yet know that I wasn't leaving for at least another year.

When I pulled into Sam and Emma's driveway, I was shaking. I went to the front door and knocked heavily, and Emma opened it in surprise.

"Monica! It's good to see you–"

"Is Sam here?" I cut her off.

She could see me fuming and she stepped back and motioned me in. "We just got finished with dinner."

Sam came out of the kitchen wiping his hands on a dish towel.

"Monica, we weren't expect–"

"Why the hell didn't you tell me Chris was in a car accident?" I yelled. I hadn't meant for it to come out that strongly, but I was over family, over Sam, and over anything that tried to get in the way of my happiness.

I saw several different emotions play across my brother's face. Worry, sadness, guilt.

"It was confidential—"

"Don't play that cop bullshit with me! The whole town knew Chris had been in that accident, but you purposely decided not to tell me. Why?"

Emma was behind me, and I could feel her curiosity but also weariness. I didn't even realize that Savannah was probably asleep upstairs, but I really didn't care.

Sam's expression softened. "Because I didn't want it to interfere with college and distract you."

"That wasn't your decision to make!" I yelled, feeling like I was going to combust with anger. "You knew I cared about him, and you withheld that information from me!"

"What could you have even done, Monica?" he said, his voice getting harder.

"I would have come back." And I knew I would have too. I would have stopped whatever I was doing and flown back.

He shook his head. "You hated it here, Monica. You said every day for years that you couldn't wait to leave."

"That was before!" I snapped.

"Before what?" he demanded.

"Before Grandma and Chris."

His eyes grew dark. "If you cared about Grandma, you would have stayed for her damn funeral and helped!" His voice boomed, shaking the room. "Instead, you left and Mom, Dad, and I had to pick up the pieces."

"I left *because* of you three!"

The words hung heavy in the air as Sam and I stared at each other. Then a piercing cry echoed down the stairs as Savannah woke up. Sam blinked as if he had just realized what I'd said, and that Savannah was screaming. I heard footsteps padding quickly towards the stairs and suddenly felt guilty for being so loud and waking the baby.

I felt ashamed at first for what I'd said to Sam, but it was the truth. If it hadn't been for that big fight with my parents, I would have stayed. If Sam had told me about Chris's accident, I would have come home.

"You should have told me," I said quietly and before he could respond, I left, slamming the door behind me.

That night I lay awake in my bed for hours thinking about everything. About Chris's accident, Sam, my parents…my grandma. By the morning, I was tired but the prospect of seeing Chris again gave me energy. I got up early and added a little makeup just because I wanted to look cute in case Chris would find me at the rescue. It was silly really, especially considering he'd seen me absolutely drenched in sweat and smelling of dog poop.

I drove over and went straight back to the kennels and cleaned all of them. When I was on the last one, Chris and Keith stepped into the building. I felt those feelings riling up in my stomach at seeing him again. When we made eye contact, he smiled knowingly.

Part of me was relieved because I'd been worried his feelings would change if we spent time apart, but it looked like they hadn't.

"Hey," I said, brushing a hand across my face to get the hair out of my eyes.

Keith smiled warmly. "Nice to see you here. I thought you were finished with your hours already."

"Not yet, I'm getting close," I said. I looked back to Chris's face, and he was watching me with those eyes that made me want to drop everything and run into his arms.

"We stopped by to see if we had any kennels open. The pups will soon be ready to move from the house," Chris explained.

"Have we found homes for them?" I asked.

"Not yet. Gemma wants to know if you have some info to post about them online. She'd like to talk to you after you're done," Keith said.

"I'm almost done."

"Great, see you in the house." Keith waved, and Chris gave me a nod before he strode off after his dad.

After I finished, I sat with Rex for a little while, then went into the Rhodes' house. Gemma was on the phone and Keith and Chris were sitting at another desk looking over documents. Chris stood as I walked in, and Keith looked surprised by the gentlemanly gesture.

"Do you need something to drink?" he asked me.

I smiled. "Water?"

"Come with me."

Keith paid no attention to us and neither did Gemma as she raged on the phone to someone about an electric bill for the stables.

I followed Chris into the kitchen, and he got a bottle of water from the fridge and turned to hand it to me.

"Thanks, I drank all of mine," I said, opening it to take a drink.

The tension between us grew and he moved forward to take the bottle from my hands and placed it on the counter. He stepped closer and kissed me. It was soft and sweet, but my head spun like I was on a rollercoaster. He leaned back just a little, our lips apart but almost touching.

"All I think about is you, I can't get you out of my head," he whispered.

I looked up into his handsome face. "Do you *want* to get me out of your head?"

His hands flexed at his sides as if he wanted to put them on me but fought the urge. Just that gesture made my skin heat and my heart thud in my chest. I wanted him so badly, I could feel my own body trying to lean closer to him.

"No." It was a hoarse *no*. His lips descended on mine again and I pressed my palms against his chest urging him to move quicker. I wanted him to touch me and not stop.

"Hey Chris?"

We broke apart quickly as we heard Gemma walking towards us. He cleared his throat, and I grabbed my water to keep my hands on something other than him.

Gemma came into the kitchen not even looking at us but at her phone. "Can you get Monica and come in here?"

"Sure," I answered her, and she finally looked up blinking, as if just realizing I was here.

"Oh! There you are, I didn't know you came in."

Gemma looked between a blushing Chris and me and frowned but didn't say anything as she turned and walked back into the office.

I started to follow but Chris quickly stopped me with an arm around my waist. "When can I see you next?"

I bit my lip. "I'm free whenever."

He kissed me quickly then we went into the living room where Keith and Gemma were sitting at the desk.

"We got a call from the Nebraska rescue. They just got in two horses that are in rough shape. They have no room there and they need training," Gemma explained, running a hand over her forehead.

"Chris and I will leave first thing tomorrow," Keith announced.

My heart sank. So much for seeing each other. Chris stood beside me frowning but his shoulder brushed mine and I knew it was him making that connection between us that we both craved.

"I'll get Will to help with the trailer today," Chris said, then put his hand on his head. "Shit, the puppies. They aren't quite ready to be moved out to the kennels yet and they can't stay alone in the house while I'm gone."

"We can put them in here," Gemma suggested as the five dogs around us wagged their tails.

"That'll be too much for the pups. We don't want them to become dog fearful," Chris mumbled.

"I could take care of them," I offered.

Chris turned to me with a surprised look. "Can you have them in your apartment?"

My landlord was a sweet man, but I don't think he'd allow one dog, let alone five. "Oh, no."

"You can stay at my place then. If you're willing to watch over them for about a week," Chris said.

"Stay at your place?" I asked, my voice a little high.

Gemma and Keith didn't seem upset or surprised by him saying this. "Yes. My house is already set up for them and there's food for you and the dogs. We can count this toward your community service hours."

That would surely tick off most, if not all of them.

"Do you have an issue with that, Monica? We know you have your own place and all," Gemma said.

I shrugged. "I don't see why not. It'd be easier for me to get to the rescue. I'll even have Brynn come by and take some pictures too. She said she could come this week." Chris smiled at me, and it felt like it was just the two of us in the room together, until Keith cleared his throat, and we snapped out of it.

"If you need anything this week, Gemma will be here, and Doc is only a call away."

I nodded. "I'll let you guys talk it out, I'll head out to Jasper's stall," I mumbled awkwardly.

"Meet me over at the house before you leave and I'll give you a key," Chris said, stopping me with a hand to my wrist.

"A key?" It took me a moment as my stomach unraveled, to realize what he was saying.

"So you can stay there this week?" he said slowly.

My face flamed. "Oh right! Yes. Um, I'll be over afterwards."

He let me go and I went out to Jasper's stall and fanned myself. Being in the kitchen, with his hands on me, and getting a key to his house…this August heat wave wasn't the only thing heating me up.

Chapter Sixteen

Temporary House Guest

It was so hard to concentrate on cleaning the horse stall. I didn't see Chris until I'd finished and went to his house. To my dismay, Dale was there, and I knew we weren't going to have any time alone before he left.

"There's the puppy wrangler," Dale said with a grin.

Chris stood next to him on the porch and watched me with a light in his eyes. "Come in, I'll show you where the dog food is."

We went into the house, Dale following behind us.

On the kitchen counter was a big container of food and a lone metal house key. "Give them a few scoops of food with water every day. You can sleep in my room which is the first door on the right down the hall," he pointed.

"Thought she already knew where that was," Dale said smugly behind me.

Chris glared as I just closed my eyes for a brief second. "Don't you have any place to be right now?" Chris snapped at Dale.

"Not really, I'm actually off for the day," Dale answered.

"Go help Dad get the halters ready."

Dale just grinned. "I'll be on the rescue most of the week, so you let me know if you need anything, Monica."

"I will," I said softly.

Dale left the house and shut the door behind him as Chris stood there watching me.

"I'm totally going to go through your underwear drawer," I said humorously.

He cracked a smile as his hands wound around my waist, pulling me against him. My body grew lax and pliable in his arms.

"Just don't let me see you take any."

I barely heard what he said before he leaned down and kissed me. I held onto his shoulders as the kiss deepened, and I lifted myself onto my toes. He was tall, one of the tallest boys I'd ever kissed and there was something so feminine about reaching to kiss him that had me melting.

His hands went further down my back, and I ran my hands through his hair at the nape of his neck.

The puppies barked loudly, and he slowly retreated, nipping my bottom lip.

God, this man was going to be the death of my feminist spirit. I wanted to beg him not to leave and stay with me, but I knew I couldn't ask that.

"I should be back in a week," he said breathlessly, still holding onto me.

I blinked, looking up at him, trying to focus. "Is there anything else you need me to do while you're away?"

He thought for a moment, looking behind me at the door. "Just the regular stuff and the puppies, I think. Check with my mom. She might need something, or she might get lonely. If you go in and check on the horses, don't get close to the new one. Will said he's being rather aggressive and it's taking longer to get a saddle on him."

I nodded. "I guess a house party is out of the question, huh?"

He chuckled and before I knew it, his hand was slapping my butt, which made me jump. "No parties."

I came back the next morning and was sad to see Keith's truck and the horse trailer gone. It would be weird to not see Chris this week, especially staying in his house without him being there. I went to his place first and dropped my bag on the couch as the puppies got excited to see me. They jumped around and bit at my fingers as I put the bowl of food in the middle of their pen. Chris had cleaned up a bit from the day before and I saw a note on the kitchen counter.

I went to it and read:

There's some food in the fridge and drinks. Help yourself to anything in the house.

P.S. Don't look in my underwear drawer.
Chris

I laughed, grabbed my bag and went back to put it in the bedroom. When I opened the door, I wasn't surprised to see such a plain, manly room. It had gray walls and a plaid comforter. He had old dressers that looked like they'd been with him since he was a kid and several photos on the wall of horses, dogs, and family.

It was very much like Chris. This was how I had envisioned his room even as a teenager. I went to his closet and opened the door and looked in.

I was definitely being nosy, but I couldn't stop myself. I saw a few boxes on the top shelf with labels that read *Sports, Fillauer, Photos, Tax Docs.* Hanging on the clothing rod were shirts, slacks, coats and partly hidden at the end was a jacket. I reached in and pulled it out.

It was his letterman jacket. The one he'd been wearing the first time I'd met him at the diner. The white and blue colors of Cold Spring High School had faded, along with the polar bear patch on the front. I traced the letters of his last name on the back of it.

My thoughts drifted to my grandmother and the dream I'd had of him. The lightning and the moon with the eagle...it was all too much, and I put the jacket back and shut the door.

It had been a different life for both of us. I'd moved and he had…he had been in a car accident, and I just looked like a jerk for not knowing it had happened. For not being there for him when I should have been.

I hadn't heard from Sam after the night I'd gone over to yell at him and even Emma had been quiet. I was angry though and I had a right to be.

I cared about Chris back then and Sam knew it.

I went out to the puppies who were mostly asleep after eating their food. I stared at them with a small smile.

On the third day staying at Chris's place, I checked in on Jasper after cleaning the dog kennels. Will and Dale were chatting outside of the new horse's stall looking concerned.

"Hey, everything okay?" I asked, coming up to them.

Will had his hat off and his sleeves rolled up. "This thing threw me off and I almost lost a hand. He's not trainable."

Dale looked concerned. "We'll have to wait to talk to Chris about him when they get back. He may be one that isn't adoptable and stays here on the rescue."

I turned and looked into the stall where the horse stood in the corner, watching us with dark eyes. I felt bad for him. He was in a new place with people he didn't know. I leaned into the door of the stall and cooed at him.

"You aren't bad, are you?" I asked the big beast. He shifted his weight from one foot to the other staring at me.

"Be careful, Monica. He seems nice but he's a biter," Will said, showing his gauze-wrapped hand.

I winced. "Yikes."

"Let's give him some more time to accumulate to the environment and try again in a few days," Dale suggested to Will.

"There you are," Gemma said, coming into the barn and looking right at me.

"Hi boss lady," Dale said with a sweet smile.

She patted his arm as she walked past him, straight to me. "You've ridden, right?"

My eyes got big. "One time, with Chris."

"Good. We've got to go check on a calf and give it a shot. I need a partner to ride with me, and these boys need to go home," she said, nodding to Dale and Will.

"Oh, okay." I didn't know what to say. I could easily say no to Chris but to Gemma, I couldn't.

"I don't know how to saddle–"

"Don't worry about that. Will, get Jasper ready for her while I get Sundance."

Within twenty minutes, we led the horses out of the barn and Gemma gracefully swung up onto her horse's back.

Shit, how was I supposed to do that? I'd only gotten on a horse one time and Chris had helped. And it took me five minutes to calm down and keep from panicking.

Just do it, Monica. Think about Grandma and what she would do.

Grab horn, put foot into stirrup, swing leg up and over.

I did just that and landed with my butt right in the saddle.

"Look at you," Gemma said with a big smile. "You look as if you were born to ride a horse."

Even I was surprised by how easily I got on Jasper. I guess I'd learned a lot from watching the other workers saddle and ride since I'd been at the rescue.

"Follow me. We're going out to the pasture on the right by the wood line," Gemma instructed, and I followed behind her, holding the reins tightly in my hands. Jasper followed Sundance and I realized it was mostly him doing his own thing and me just along for the ride. When the path widened, she motioned me to ride up beside her. I urged Jasper on with my heel, remembering how Chris had done it, until I was beside her.

"We used to go on lots of rides when Chris was young. It took a while after his accident to get back on Jasper, but with some coaxing, he did it. He and Keith usually come out to check the cows when we get a new one, but I like to come out too.

Helps me get out of the office and away from the paperwork for a little while."

The accident.

"It's beautiful out here. You guys should turn these into walking trails and get the volunteers to walk the dogs out this way."

"Chris told us your idea about that. I like it. I just wish we had more volunteers. Other than our community service candidates, which aren't many, we don't have a lot. We do pay the horse handlers and if they clock out and stay late, we have them for volunteer hours."

I frowned. They had a lot of animals to care for, why weren't there more volunteers?

"You market that you're looking for help, right?"

She chuckled. "As much as I can, but I'll admit, it could be more. I want to see if we can adopt out these pitties first and if you help me with that, I'll use you for more. I heard through the grapevine–"

"The Brown family grapevine," I muttered under my breath. The Brown family were the gossips of Cold Spring.

"–what you're doing for Erin at Spring Awake. I may not be able to pay you right away but once we get more donations coming in, I could," she suggested.

I smiled. "I'm good with that. I have Brynn stopping in tomorrow to take photos of the puppies."

"Good." She smiled again at me and paused as we got to the fence where the cows were. "You know I always liked you, Monica." I glanced at her. "You were a good kid, with a good heart."

Did she really see that or is she just saying it?

"I was a shitty kid," I said with a snort. "I let kids get bullied and may have also bullied a few."

She shook her head. "You may have done that but that didn't define you. Keith and I know how much you took care of your grandma. We also know your parents were hard on you."

I swallowed a lump in my throat. She really did see me. Like Chris had.

"They still are hard on me, but I've dealt with them for this long, why stop now?"

She laughed and got off her horse. "Get your butt down here, Locklear. We've got some shots to give."

Gemma was amazing. We laughed as we tried to wrangle the calf in our arms and my feet got stepped on a lot. Eventually we were able to get its shots done, and it ran along to its mother.

We rode around for a little while on the horses and Gemma encouraged me to pick up my pace on Jasper to a trot. When I did, I felt adrenaline run through my veins and I found myself laughing and feeling pure joy. I wasn't scared anymore, and that was… freeing.

We got back to the barn, and she told me how to unsaddle Jasper. I got the hang of it quickly and took the saddle off and put it in the tack room. The horse handlers were gone for the day and even Dale and Will had left.

Gemma and I walked back towards the main house. "I'll see you tomorrow," I called to her, as I headed for Chris' house.

"Hey, wait, come join me for dinner. This big house gets lonely without Chris or Keith; I could use the company."

"Are you sure?" I asked, feeling like an intruder.

"Yes, come on. I was planning to make cheesesteaks."

We didn't eat at the dining room table like I thought we would. Instead, we ate in front of the TV with the dogs sitting at our feet waiting for any morsel we dropped. The cheesesteaks Gemma prepared were amazing and mouthwatering.

We laughed at the show on TV and when it went to a commercial, she leaned back and sighed. "It's nice having company," she said, smiling over at me.

It was nice being with a parent who wasn't trying to act like my parent. "I'm sure it does get lonely when Keith is away."

She nodded. "I'm hoping he'll slow down a bit and stay home, but I won't hold my breath. Chris is trying to take over more because he knows it makes me happy when his father is home."

"Was this always Chris's plan? To take over the rescue?"

"Oh yes. It's why he was going to college. He was taking business classes to learn more about how to run the rescue and get ready to eventually take it over," she explained.

"He stopped when the accident happened?"

She paused and sighed. "Yes. He…he couldn't walk so there was no way he was able to go back to college."

He couldn't walk? I was living it up, enjoying my life in San Diego and he'd been home, suffering. "Did he go to therapy for his leg?"

She shifted, not looking at me. "Yes, lots of it. Unfortunately, he couldn't go up or down stairs for a while, so we helped him build his house on the property. It's one floor as you know."

I hung my head. "I didn't know any of this happened."

She glanced over at me. "The accident?"

I nodded. "Sam kept it from me, so I didn't know until recently."

She was quiet for a little bit. "The town was very supportive and helped us raise money for his hospital bills. Your parents being one of the donors."

I scoffed without being able to stop myself. "Oh great, so even my parents knew, and no one told me."

Despite me being annoyed, she chuckled and patted my hand. "I always wished I had a daughter."

"Well, I'm sure my parents would gladly give up their failure of a daughter so you can adopt me."

"I think that would be weird considering what's going on between you and Chris."

I glanced up quickly in surprise as she gave me a knowing smile. "I may seem distracted all the time, but I see it." She winked and stood up, grabbing my empty plate. "I think we need some ice cream."

I stayed at Gemma's until we'd eaten a bowl of ice cream and watched another episode of a funny sitcom. I finally went back to Chris's house and took off my shoes and headed straight to the bathroom after feeding the puppies.

I was sore from riding and my bones felt like putty. I filled up the impressive big bathtub, turned on the jets and slowly sank under the hot water.

I sighed with happiness and leaned back against the back of the tub.

I could get used to this. It was a full bathroom with double sinks, the tub, and a separate walk-in shower. It was a girl's dream.

My phone buzzed on the floor by the tub, and I looked down to see Chris's number pop up. I grabbed it and answered.

"Chris's temporary house guest, how can I help you?"

He chuckled. "I called to check in. How are the puppies doing?"

I heard one bark from the open bathroom door. "Fat and happy, I think. I just fed them."

"Good. You doing okay?"

I looked at my toes poking out from the water in the tub and used my free hand to pour in some soap. "Oh, I am doing amazing. Your mom fed me cheesesteaks and ice cream and now I'm soaking in your tub."

He was quiet on the other end of the phone for a moment, and I was worried we'd gotten disconnected.

"Chris?"

I heard a door shut and wind blowing softly against the phone. "Are you telling me you're naked in my tub right now?"

I felt a ripple of pleasure run down my body at his deep words. "No, I decided that would be weird so I'm fully clothed."

His chuckle was gruff sounding. "I need proof of that."

I felt a thrill run through me as I pulled my phone away from my ear, turned on my camera and snapped a picture. I made sure my arm was across my chest, not showing too much and sent off the picture.

"Proof coming in a few seconds," I told him. I waited, my teeth biting my lip.

"Shit, Monica."

I grinned to myself at the feminine pleasure it brought me knowing how much that had teased him. "See, fully clothed."

"I'm never daring you to do anything again."

"Probably shouldn't. I don't say no to dares normally. Ask my college friends," I said with amusement.

"Wait, you were with my mom all evening?"

I blinked. "I'm soaking naked in your tub and you're thinking about your mom?"

"Monica," he growled. "No…I'm trying not to think about you naked in my tub."

I laughed. "Yes, I spent the evening with your mom. We went riding out to the field to give the calf its shots then we had dinner together. It was really nice."

"She didn't break out the baby photos?" he asked reluctantly.

"Oh yes, right after she told me you peed the bed until you were twelve."

"Now I know you're just messing with me."

I laughed again, loving this banter between us. I wished he was here. It was only a week, I could do that, but I didn't want to. His pillow and sheets smelled of him and it felt so…domesticated to be here in his house, waiting for him to come home. It seemed so…real, or how real it could be.

"Now, how's it going out there? When are you coming back? You owe me a date."

Chris and I talked for over an hour and by then I was in his bed falling asleep when we finally said goodnight. That night I dreamed about him being there beside me as I sat in his tub soaking, and his hands moved under the water to touch me.

Chapter Seventeen

Stay Tonight

Brynn came over the next day and took pictures of each of the puppies separately. I tried to convince her she needed to adopt one, but she said she'd had a hard time convincing Luke to agree to their border collie, so another one was out of the question. He apparently was not a dog person but claims he's a "Molly" person now. In other words, the man only likes *his* dog.

Gemma came over to Chris's house and we worked on the social media postings of each puppy. She was on the floor checking out each one and cooing at them.

I used Brynn's photos of the puppies and created details for each one. Within minutes of posting them, we had over ten shares and several comments.

"They are adorable, aren't they?" Gemma said, holding one in her hands and rubbing between its eyes.

"They are adoptable," I sang with a grin.

Gemma just smiled and shook her head. "Keith doesn't care how many dogs I have but the five in the house are plenty."

"I thought it was odd that Chris didn't have a dog."

"When he's away, he doesn't want me to have to come take care of them. I don't leave the rescue often since there's a lot to be done. Keith is the one who picks up and goes when there's a new rescue. And since Chris sometimes goes along, he doesn't think it'd be fair to the dog."

I respected that. How nice would it be to have Rex though? To actually have a dog to come home to? To cuddle with? My drunken nights and awful hangover mornings had been spent alone or sneaking out of a guy's apartment. That reminded me of my walk of shame when Brynn had to come get me the day before Emma and Sam's wedding. I'd gone back to that guy's house and fell asleep on his couch after drinking too much. I was not myself and didn't want to go back to my parents' house or Sam's. He'd been pissed at me for not answering my phone and had given me a lecture almost in front of Brynn. It wasn't a good time.

"Glad to know it isn't about Chris's commitment issues," I finally said.

Gemma snorted. "No, but he definitely has those too." She looked up at me and I saw something in her expression that made me frown. "He seems very happy of late." She sighed and continued. "Sometimes my son reminds me of a wounded animal. When someone gets close, he strikes out at them until they've been bitten or too scared to come back. As his mother, I hope he finds someone who makes him feel safe when he's feeling wounded and is willing to stick around through it."

My mouth opened in surprise from her words. She knew her son so well, better than probably my parents knew me, and part of that made me jealous.

I didn't have time to figure out something to say because my laptop beeped several times and then Gemma's phone rang. She answered quickly.

"Long Rhodes Ahead Animal Rescue, this is Gemma." She paused, her eyes widened, and she grinned at me. "Yes, we have 3 males and 2 females available. You saw the social media posting? That's great! Yes, she sure does have a personality!"

I bit my lip and smiled as I glanced back at the emails that were coming in about the pitties.

By the end of the week, three of the puppies had been adopted and were slowly being picked up by their new families. Each family had to undergo a background check and a home visit before the dog was picked up. The process was thorough to ensure all animals would be safe and with the right people.

I watched a family with two kids love on one of the puppies. The parents surprised them by allowing them to pick one and they cried with happiness. It was sweet to see how excited they were, and the puppy seemed just as happy, licking their faces and wagging its tail.

Chris called every evening to check on things and I gave him updates on the puppies and how things were going around the rescue. When they were finally on their way home, he called to talk while his dad slept beside him in the truck. He said they were taking their time driving.

I had settled into a routine at Chris's house, and I liked being there. I knew where the cups were, I washed laundry, hung out in the living room and watched TV. I felt settled and comfortable for once.

When Friday evening came, I'd decided to take Rex for a walk. I hadn't been able to spend much time with him since I was taking care of the puppies, and I missed our walks.

Rex's tail swished with happiness as he sniffed every blade of grass and fence post he could find. The sun washed over the rescue in orange and red, and I heard the neighs of the horses and the moos of the cows. It was peaceful. I hated the idea of going back to my apartment, but I loved the idea of seeing Chris again.

Rex's head snapped behind us and I glanced back to see someone walking the trail, following us.

It thought it might be Will. He had been having issues training the new horse and just needed a break. But Rex's tail wagged, and he pulled on his leash until I finally turned around.

It wasn't Will, it was Chris!

The moment I saw him, my heart leaped in my chest and ached to be with him.

"Hey stranger!" I called with a big smile. I walked fast towards him, and I saw him grinning underneath his baseball cap. His clothes were dirty as usual, and his flannel shirt sleeves were rolled up.

Chris quickly reached me, pulled off his hat, wrapped his arms around my waist, and kissed me. I stretched my hands around his neck and held onto him as tightly as he was holding onto me. His lips were soft and warm, and it made my entire body melt. He smelled of horses and that familiar scent that was unique to him.

Rex barked and jumped, excited to see him too. We finally broke apart for a second to look at one another. Chris's smile was big and beautiful and breathtaking.

"I think you missed me, Chris," I said breathily.

He chuckled and put his cap on his head. "Maybe." He didn't remove his hands from my waist. "We got back a little bit ago and got the new horses into a stalls that Dale prepped for us. Mom said you were out walking Rex."

I nodded and glanced at Rex who pawed at Chris again. Finally, Chris patted his head and scratched his ears with one hand, the other not leaving me.

"He was getting lonely since I've been spending so much of my time with the puppies. But there's only two left and we have people coming tomorrow for them."

He looked surprised and amazed all at once. "I didn't think it'd happen that quickly."

"I'm just that good." I winked, and he gave me a grin that made my toes curl.

I was falling a little too hard for him.

We went back to the kennels, and I dropped off a very reluctant Rex in his cage and left a few treats for him. We then headed back to his house and as we walked there, I felt tension rising between us. Not the bad kind of tension but the really, really good kind of tension. His hand coasted down my back idly and a shiver ran over me.

I slipped off my work boots before I went into the house. The last two puppies barked happily when they saw us.

"Two females too," I noted to him as I went over to pet them. He took his cap off and put it on the kitchen counter. "I think by tomorrow they'll both be adopted."

"Stay with me tonight," Chris said suddenly.

My head jerked up to him and I saw his expression of desire and…something else. My stomach coiled with anticipation. There was no way I was keeping my hands to myself.

"O-Okay," I stuttered stupidly.

He walked over and I stood up to face him. He cupped my cheek and kissed me lightly then pulled back to look me in the eyes. "All I've thought about this week was you in my house, in my tub, and in my bed."

I swallowed at his low, almost growling words. Whoa…my ovaries were exploding at that very moment.

"Sounds like you were a little jealous."

He chuckled softly and ran his hand down my side to my waist. "I'm going to get a shower, are you hungry?"

He let me go and stepped back.

Oh boy, yes, I was definitely hungry, but it wasn't for food.

"No, I ate before Rex's walk."

"Good." And the look in his eyes made me know exactly what we would be doing as soon as he left that shower.

He disappeared down the hallway and I heard a few doors opening before the bathroom door shut behind him.

I suddenly realized I hadn't moved for several seconds so as soon as I heard the shower turn on, I bolted to his bedroom where I shoved most of my clothes back into my bag and picked out a cute pajama set that was satin and lace. I quickly changed, made the bed, stashed my shoes in the corner, then looked out at the room.

My things were mixed with his. It was such a weird feeling that filled my chest. This was commitment. Or just puppy sitting, I wasn't sure. I didn't think many people were going to sleep with the owner of the dogs though, so this definitely wasn't just that.

The bathroom door opened, and he came into the bedroom. He wore a tight white t-shirt that displayed his nice, sculpted chest, long sweatpants, and socks on his feet. It had been the first time I'd seen him without his boots on.

His longer hair was slightly wet, making it look darker. He saw me and eyed me up in the scant clothing I wore. It didn't leave a whole lot to the imagination, but it was also extremely hot in his house. He threw his towel into a bin and walked over to me. I radiated with anticipation as he reached for me. We kissed hungrily, pressing our bodies against one another in a desperate way.

It'd been too many years. Too many pent-up days of being around each other and feeling something but not acting on it. I liked Chris. When was the last relationship I had that felt like this? Never. I wasn't going to hold back from it. I was going to give my all because he was everything I'd ever wanted.

His hands roamed my body, cupping my butt and squeezing.

Oh yeah, he was a butt man for sure.

I had my hands under his shirt, feeling his solid muscles as he let out a sigh, my fingertips grazing his chest.

He lowered me onto the bed, holding himself up with one arm as the other was too busy touching me all over. I ran my hands through his hair, loving how soft it was to the touch and enjoying the scent of the body wash he used.

He was intoxicating.

I lifted up his shirt and he pulled it off with one quick pull, only breaking our kiss for a second. Next was my shirt where he lavished my chest with kisses that had me gasping. Then he lowered my shorts and sat back to look down at me.

I was in good shape; well my body was. Maybe not my stamina but I had a nice body, and I was proud of it. Even more so now with the look in his eyes as he watched me below him.

He traced a finger over my skin, his eyes following it from my collarbone down my chest to my thigh, all the while I held my breath. When he looked up at me, he leaned down to kiss me. It was desperate.

I ran my hands down his hard chest until I got to the top of his sweatpants. When I started to push them down, he stopped me.

"Don't."

I frowned. "I hate to tell you this but what's underneath them, we kind of need to complete this thing."

His brown eyes looked slightly panicked but he blinked it away quickly. "They don't have to be off the whole way."

His leg injury. Did he not want me to see?

I brushed his hair from his forehead and kissed him softly. "Okay."

He looked relieved as he continued the kiss I'd started. His gentle hands, his sweet lips, his strength made my head spin. It also made me realize that I was falling for Chris, and quickly.

His hands bracketed my thighs as his head lowered to kiss across my stomach, my hips until finally he was there. *Right* there.

I gasped and gripped the sheets.

Holy shit. How long had it been since I'd done this? From the noises that were coming out of my mouth I'd say a while.

Chris's beard scratched across my sensitive flesh until I couldn't keep my hands to myself. I shoved one into his hair and heard his growl of approval.

"Chris," I whispered, my stomach quivering, my peak coming a lot quicker than I wanted it to. It was embarrassing when men came a little early, was it the same for a woman? I honestly didn't care at that point because this sexual tension between us for the last few months had been my foreplay.

One of his hands reached up and before it could even get to my breast, I shattered. I swore I saw stars, heavens, galaxies, or any other magical thing that was in the sky. I slowly peeled open my eyes, my chest heaving with the aftermath. Chris's expression was deliciously smug.

"You're ruining me," I panted out as he crawled up my body to hover over me.

"That's the point."

Thank god we never got this far when we were in high school. I'd never be able to sleep with another man again without thinking of him.

I reached below and he let me but his other hand was poised on the waistband. I paused and made him look at me. His eyes were vulnerable and excited all in one.

"I won't take them off, I promise."

That sentence seemed to give him what he needed. He removed his hand as I leaned up and kissed his lips. My fingers slipped below to grip him, and his mouth opened in a groan.

Wow. He was hiding this all this time?

I watched Chris's eyes as he focused on me as I rubbed up and down. His lids grew heavy until finally he stopped me with a hand over mine.

"Been that long for you too?" I asked with a smirk.

He didn't answer, just leaned down to nip at my collarbone and the base of my neck. "I want to be inside you."

I shuddered at those hoarse, manly words that vibrated across my chest.

If this man asked me in that same voice to ride a horse naked or run through a tick covered field, I would have.

He lined himself up and kissed up the column of my neck before looking me in the eyes. "I'm on birth control," I said quietly as I ran my hand across his cheek and into those locks of dark blonde hair.

I saw him swallow and nod to that. This had been everything I'd dreamed about and wanted. Any and all fears were gone, and it was just the two of us. Our bodies and our heartbeats pounding against our chests.

We kissed, our lips hovering then meeting slightly. He pushed in little by little, and I brought my legs up further on his sides. His breaths matched my own at the invasion of joining our bodies.

Finally…finally he was seated fully into me, he paused and we both let out a relieved, pleasure-filled sigh. Tingles washed over every limb as I looked into his eyes.

His expression was just as desperate as mine. He lowered his head to kiss across my breasts, still unmoving in me.

"Monica," he groaned and that almost made me orgasm a second time.

I moved my hips, and beautiful friction made me gasp. He smiled then let his lips coast to mine where he feathered them lightly across. Then…he pulled back and pushed back in, and I couldn't help the somersault my stomach did at the feeling.

I gasped again and made noises I'd never heard come out of my mouth before. This was…this was so different with him. I leaned my head back and closed my eyes and felt it build again in my lower belly.

Chris's one hand moved to my hip and his steady rhythm picked up. It was slow but fast and made me feel *everything*.

"God, Monica, you're making this hard for me to last," Chris ground out.

I couldn't help my smile and laugh. I looked at him and saw the sweat beading on his forehead. I leaned up and kissed his throat and nipped at his Adams apple.

He groaned and I loved that sound. I wanted to implant it into my memories forever.

"I'm not going without you," he muttered, and his hand moved to the apex of my thighs. The touch sent a shiver down my spine, and I arched my back.

I could no longer focus on him but his fingers…wow, those fingers were doing amazing things to me. Strumming and circles.

I was falling. And not just in the mental sense, but the physical sense too.

"Chris, I'm going to—"

I didn't get to finish before we both hit our finale, and we let out a groan. We clutched each other tightly, the waves slowing, our breaths the only sound in the room. His head dropped to my neck, and I felt his kisses across my damp skin until they met my lips.

Then he pulled back, and I brushed his hair back from his forehead and met his gaze. His eyes were still dilated but there was surprise behind them and an open vulnerability.

"I'm sorry…that wasn't long," he said, his voice deep.

I smiled. "You make up for long things in other areas.

I woke up and rolled over to touch the bare spot on the bed, then sleepily opened my eyes. I was alone but I could hear the puppies howling and barking and a deep voice talking to them.

I smiled as I moved and felt that soreness that only comes after sex.

They always talked about how good it was when you found your person, but I didn't quite believe it. I'd had my fair share of men through the years, and all had been similar. But this time…it felt different. We'd shared a past and maybe knowing that, made the sex even better.

I stood up and slipped on my pajamas and went out to the living room to see Chris making something on the stove. He was shirtless with just his sweatpants on that sat low on his hips. He'd kept them on the entire time, even when we went to sleep. It hurt me a little that he felt he needed to cover up his injury. I didn't want to mess things up by asking him about it, so I didn't say anything. I wanted him to *want* to talk to me about it.

"Good morning," I said with a smile.

He looked up and his hair was messy and a piece hanging in front of his eyes. It was probably from my hands. I came around the corner to look at what he was making, and he put his hand around my waist to draw me close.

"Did you sleep okay?" he asked, his voice husky.

"Once we got to sleep, yes."

Only about an hour after the first round, we'd gone again. This time a different position and up against the bedroom wall. Who would have thought that he could carry around a five-foot-nine woman like a ragdoll?

I felt his chest shake with laughter before he kissed me. It was a good kiss. I wrapped my arms around his neck and tried to deepen that kiss. God, he made me wild; he made me want things I hadn't thought about.

A home and him. A life together. I could almost see it, which should have scared the shit out of me, but it didn't. I'd been living my life so selfishly since I was young. I bought expensive brands, made sure my makeup was perfect, my apartments were stylish, and I went to all the exclusive bars. But not anymore. Coming back to

Cold Spring had changed me, a lot. Working at this rescue and even reliving some of the hard memories from my teenage years had changed me. It made me want something I hadn't thought of.

We pulled back so Chris could take the bacon out of the skillet, but he kept his arm around me. I looked over at the puppies who were happily playing together.

"Oh shoot!" I said with a gasp. "The family will be here soon to see them!"

Chris looked alarmed. "Here?"

"Yes! I figured I'd let your mom sleep in today and I'd deal with the family."

I ran to the bedroom to change quickly, and Chris was behind me, but he didn't dress in the room. He grabbed his things, and I frowned as I watched him limping away from me to shut the bathroom door. I had to give him time.

After brushing my hair and putting on a new shirt, I heard a knock at the front door.

"I'll get it!" I called to Chris who was just finishing up.

I went to the door and opened it to find Gemma and two families eagerly waiting on the porch.

She looked as surprised to see me as I was to see her. "Good morning! This is Monica. She's our marketer for Long Rhodes Ahead."

I was surprised that she'd called me their marketer. One of the families had two kids and they kept looking around me for the puppies.

"Come in! The puppies were just fed so they are pretty lively." I stepped aside and let them in. The kids ran to the puppy pen and the parents laughed behind them as everyone came into the living room.

"I thought you were going to sleep in today," I said quietly to Gemma, feeling bad.

She smiled softly at me. "I got a call this morning and couldn't get back to sleep. I was sitting on the front porch with my coffee when they arrived. Figured I'd just escort them over here." I felt bad for her but nodded. "Looks like you were up early too."

My face flamed and I looked away from her as Chris came from the hallway. He smiled when he saw his mom and I immediately saw him sigh with whatever look she gave him.

I sat down on the couch beside the families and puppy pen. "These are the last two. We had five in total. These females are the sweetest and very playful," I shared.

"They are adorable! Where did you find them again? I was telling my husband about the post I saw," the mother said.

Her husband rolled his eyes with a smile on his face. Chris walked over and stood next to his mother by the kitchen counter.

"We got a call late one evening that they were at a shelter in Albany, so Chris and I jumped in the truck and went to get them. You already know the reputation of pit bulls, so we think someone just dropped them off with the intention of them being put down."

The mother had a hand to her heart and looked expectantly at her husband. The other man and woman just listened.

"See Roger, it's fate," she expressed while the kids giggled as the puppy nibbled playfully at their hands.

"Okay, fine. We'll get one," the husband gave up.

I grinned and Chris came over to stand beside me.

"Let the kids pick out their puppy and we'll take the last one," the other couple pitched in. "They are beautiful."

My heart soared with joy. I never thought helping to find homes for the puppies would bring me so much happiness. "That's great!"

"We can take you all back to the main house and get the paperwork started. I know we already did the home checks and everything was good," Chris said, his arm brushing mine.

"We got all the stuff we'd need before today, you know, just in case," the mother said with a wink, her husband glaring over at her. He obviously hadn't known.

We let the kids play with the puppies and they picked the female with the white spot on her chest. They wanted to name her Blue. The other couple picked up the last puppy and cradled her in their arms as she started to drift asleep.

The woman's eyes were teary as she looked up at Chris and me. "We just lost our pittie a few months ago and this is honestly the most joy we've felt in a while. So, thank you to you and your husband for rescuing them."

My mouth opened in surprise and not just from the sincere thank you but also from them calling Chris my husband. This was the second time someone assumed that. But this time, it felt different.

"Oh, we aren't–"

"Aww! Look at her!" the woman said as the puppy yawned big, looking adorable.

I didn't say anything more but glanced at Chris who leaned his shoulder into mine and smiled.

Chapter Eighteen

Yes, We're Together

Both families adopted the puppies, and we met Gemma at the main house after they left. Keith came down the steps just as Gemma put aside the checks and paperwork and lifted her glasses to look at me.

"I'm really impressed, Monica. This is the quickest we've ever adopted out puppies, and pit bulls at that."

I felt pride and my heart filled with joy. "I was glad I could help. I now know why you guys enjoy it."

She smiled at me. "It isn't always this wonderful, but I'll take it when it is." Keith leaned against the desk and looked between Chris and me. Chris had his hands in his pockets, his hat and work boots on.

It was silent for several seconds as his parents looked between us and I felt heat rising to my cheeks.

"So, what's going on with you two?" Keith asked.

"Dad," Chris snapped, and I saw Gemma's mouth twitch.

"Keith, honey, it's not our place," she said quietly to him.

He didn't seem to hear her. "You said to us last time that there wasn't anything going on, but you talked to her every night when we were away, and Gem said she spent the night. If you're together now, we want to make sure she's included in this family, Chris. You know how we feel about family."

My face was quickly turning bright red. Chris sighed and took off his hat to run a hand through his hair.

"I think this is my cue to leave," I said awkwardly.

"Yes, we're together," Chris announced.

All of us looked at him in shock. "That's great!" Gemma said and Keith just grinned.

When Chris met my gaze, I saw a light shining in his eyes that hadn't been there before.

"It's about time," Keith said. "Monica, we have family dinner Friday evenings, you're welcome to come."

"Alright, that's enough embarrassment for the day," Chris said, putting his arm around my waist and practically pushing me out the front door.

"See you later!" I yelled back to a grinning Keith and Gemma. We got onto the porch and Chris ran a hand over his face with a groan.

"I'm sorry about that."

I just laughed at the situation. His parents were good people, and they weren't being intrusive, well maybe a little but not in a bad way. "It's okay, Chris."

He paused to look me in the eyes and held me close to him. "Are we on the same page? About being together?"

Just the word *together* coming out of his mouth unleashed a rollercoaster within my chest. I cared about him a lot, and this was my chance to finally be with him like I'd wanted when we were young.

"Yes, we are on the same page." I ran my hand up his arm until it was on his neck.

His lips twitched into a dangerous smile as he leaned down to kiss me. It was a heated kiss filled with passion and memories from the night before. We were broken up by the sound of hooting and cat calls.

When we looked over, we saw Dale, Will, and several of the workers clapping and making sounds at us with grins on their faces.

"Stop sucking face and get to work, Rhodes!"

"Do you need some extra time in the tack room?" another roared and the rest laughed hard.

Chris sighed and dropped his hands. "Looks like I need to go fire a few horse handlers." He turned back to look at me, his eyes soft. "Are you staying with me tonight?"

My chest filled with warmth again. "If you want me to."

"I do."

He winced as he moved, and I looked down. "Are you okay? I saw you're limping?"

He clenched his jaw and looked away. "Yeah, I'm fine. I need to get going. I'll see you tonight."

He kissed me again but just quickly and we parted ways.

I spent the morning smiling stupidly to myself as I cleaned the kennels and spent time with Rex. When I finished up, I went to the stables where I saw everyone, including Chris, by the paddock where Will and the new horse were. The horse was shaking his head and scraping his hooves on the soft ground. His ears were back, and he seemed to be glaring at Will who had his hands on his knees.

"What's going on?" I came up beside Chris who was leaning on the fence with Dale on his other side.

Chris looked over, his sunglasses hiding his eyes from me. "Will keeps trying with this one."

"They've named him Lucifer," Dale said across Chris. "He's a beautiful horse but mean as a snake. He's been biting anyone who walks too close to him and even kicked Will a few times getting him out of the stall."

I frowned as I turned to look at the big brown horse. He was tall and broad and definitely reminded me a bit of a "Lucifer." But when my eyes connected to his, I saw something in him: *Fear*. He was afraid of everyone. No one had shown him he was safe here.

Will put his hands up in front of him and slowly walked over to the horse, but Lucifer stepped back and threw his head up when Will tried to reach for the lead rope.

Chris shook his head. "He's a lost cause I'm afraid."

"First one to fail here at Rhodes," Dale agreed.

Fail? "What does that mean?" I inquired.

"He doesn't have shoes, and it looks like his hooves haven't been taken care of either. We need to get him taken care of soon. But if we can't help him, we'll have to send him to someone who can."

I felt bad for the horse as I looked across the paddock at him. "Will he come back here then?"

"No, most likely not. He'll stay wherever they can take care of him," Chris explained.

"You gonna go fix that fence on the west field?" I heard Dale ask Chris.

"Yeah, I need to fix a few spots."

"Want me to ride along?" Dale suggested.

"I was going to take Monica with me," I heard Chris say and I looked over at him. He wasn't even looking at me, just Dale whose grin was knowing.

"Take me where?" I asked.

Chris pushed off the fence and nodded his head, so I followed him into the barn. "Want to go with me to fix the fence?"

It was a request this time, not a demand, so I agreed.

He let me ride Jasper and helped me tack him up. He saddled another horse then grabbed a few tools and put them in the saddle bag. The sun shone in my eyes as we trotted side by side along the trail. The path had been widened I noticed, and I wondered if Gemma had one of the volunteers mow it down after she and I talked about it.

I loved the feeling of sitting on a horse, the rhythmic movement as we rode, and the feeling of being high up. It was crazy that at the beginning of summer I was so fearful of horses, dogs, even Chris and commitment, and now…they'd become a big part of my life.

I looked over at him and he sat straight, looking like a cowboy from an old western. He met my gaze and smiled, then took off his hat and put it on my head. "You should've brought a hat."

"I don't own any hats. At least not ones I'd wear here," I said, adjusting it on my head.

He shook his head. "I should've known that."

"I think I've sold most of my expensive clothes anyhow, I could probably buy a few baseball caps now."

"Sold?"

I sighed sadly. “Well, I’m not making much money right now since I’ve been putting in my community service hours and I haven't had a lot of time to apply for jobs.” I sounded pathetic and I knew it. “I sold a few things to pay for my bills.”

“Oh,” Chris commented quietly. “Let’s stop here.”

I saw the downed fence. A post had fallen over, and the fence lay on the ground. He hopped off and before he could help me, I got down by myself. He looked impressed and I felt proud.

He reached into his saddle bag, pulled out a few tools, and went to the fence.

I helped him and we talked while we worked. It was…fun. I didn’t think I could say that about fixing a fence, but it was. I think it had to do with my work companion giving me bedroom eyes that made me swoon more than once.

We had it completed, and the wire stapled back onto the post within an hour. We got on the horses, moved further west, and fixed two more posts. This time when we were done, we didn’t head back to the house. Instead, he had me follow him further up the trail to the patch of woods. It was lush and cool underneath the canopy of leaves, and I sighed with relief. He got down and I followed suit, curious as to why we stopped here.

“Chris?”

He took my hand and pulled me towards an opening underneath the swaying trees and I saw headstones everywhere. I felt my throat get tight as I read some of them.

Petie.

Sprinkles.

Henry the Horse

Yeti.

"Is this an animal cemetery?" I whispered.

Chris turned to look at me sadly, his expression soft. "It is. My dad made this after we had to put down the first dog we rescued. He was a pit bull that had come to us because of his aggression. My dad trained him, and he ended up being his dog. He followed my dad everywhere, slept with him, and went on trips with him when he had to pick up animals."

"What happened to him?" I watched Chris's expression as it grew more remorseful.

"He got old. Lived to be fourteen and just couldn't see or walk much. We put him down and Dad didn't want to cremate him and put him on our mantel. So, he buried him out here. Then the next animal passed away and my dad dug another grave. It's a resting place for them. It keeps them here on the rescue."

I felt tears at the back of my eyes as I thought of Rex. Would he get the opportunity to be loved and cuddled before he was buried here?

I squeezed his hand. "Your family does an amazing job for these animals. You give them a second chance."

"Like my mom said today, it isn't always that way. God, this horse, Lucifer…I just don't know what to do about him," Chris muttered, running his free hand across his mouth.

"You said he could go someplace else to be trained?"

"He's already been traumatized coming here. I don't want to send him off to another place to make matters worse."

I felt bad for the horse and for the situation it put Chris in. I leaned my head against his arm and looked out across the mossy ground to the old worn stones scattered around.

We looked together until finally I spoke up. "Ever watch Pet Cemetery?"

"No."

"I wouldn't suggest it."

On our way back, I saw Chris rubbing his left knee and wincing. I wanted to ask about it, wanted to know if it was from his injury and why he didn't want to share it with me. He probably had a bad scar and was in a lot of pain.

"You okay?" I asked softly. His hat was loose on my head, but it shielded my eyes from the sun rays.

He quickly took his hand off his knee and straightened. "Yeah, I'm fine."

Ugh, men. "I'm going to run back to my apartment then go in to see Erin. I'll be back this evening. That is if you still want me to?"

His gaze snapped to mine. "Of course I do. I can cook something on the grill."

I grinned. "A girl could get used to a man cooking. Better not spoil me too much."

He just smiled back.

When we got close to the barn, he hopped off then helped me, making sure I slid along his entire body until my feet were on the ground. Even then he didn't let me go completely, just stared into my eyes as I threw my arms around his neck.

"I really like what you're saying with those eyes, Rhodes," I said quietly.

His full lips smirked. "You don't even know half of the dirty thoughts rolling around in my mind."

I leaned in until my lips were by his ear. "Show me."

"That's it! I'm done! He can be made into glue for all I care!" We both looked up in time to see Will strolling from the barn, his jaw set, his pants covered in dirt. He saw us and glared at Chris. "I won't be stepping foot back into that stall with Lucifer! He's all yours!" It was then I saw blood on his hand and realized he was probably going in to see Gemma to patch him up.

"Will, what the hell happened?" Chris said, letting me go.

"Damn thing bit me again! This is the second time!" he growled, walking briskly up to the house. Chris gave me an apologetic look as he walked his horse to a post and wrapped the reins around it, then followed after Will.

I took Jasper back into the barn and led him into the stall where I took off his bridle. When I shut the door, I heard neighing and stomping from a few stalls down. No other volunteers or horse handlers were in the barn. I looked at the brown horse. As he paced around the stall looking upset.

He seemed to pause as he saw me, his tail swishing back and forth, his eyes wide. I felt sad for him. He didn't know what was going on and probably had been abused. I walked up to the gate and leaned in, knowing I too could get bit by this fearful horse.

"Shhh, it's okay boy. I'm not going to hurt you," I said softly. He stayed towards the back of the stall, his front hoof hitting the ground, his head going up and down. I could see his hooves were caked with mud and who knew what else. Chris said an infection would start if they didn't get him cleaned up soon.

I stretched out my hand, wondering if I'd still have all five fingers when I pulled it back. The horse didn't move at first but eyed me carefully. I went still as he slowly walked toward me. He stretched his head down and came closer. My heart beat hard in my chest, wondering if he was going to bite me, but I kept my hand out. His velvety, soft nose ran along my palm. It almost tickled but I didn't dare move. He took another step forward but again, I stayed still. He snorted, snot coming out from his nose as he lifted his head to look at me again. He then moved to his water bowl and sloshed around, drinking.

I let out my breath and retracted my hand which was when I realized it was shaking.

"You're pretty good with horses. I thought you were more of a city girl," a voice said, shocking me. I squealed and jumped to see Dale behind me, leaning up against the tack room door.

"You scared the shit out of me!"

He just smiled and came over to stand next to me. "You know he's never come up to anyone like that before. Normally hands in the stall are when he starts biting," Dale explained.

"Wait, you watched me this whole time and let me put my hand in knowing I was most likely going to get bit?" I exclaimed.

He shrugged. "I wanted to see what he'd do. Didn't think you'd be that stupid to do it but look," he reached down and grabbed my hand. "You still got all five intact."

I snatched my hand away and glared. "Lucky for you."

He just chuckled and we went back to looking at the horse. “I think he was abused by a man.” Dale’s voice was softer, quieter.

I looked at him, his crow’s feet deep by his eyes as he frowned into the stall. “You think? Wasn’t he owned by one of Keith’s friends?”

He nodded. “Yes, but I think he got him from someone else. We’ve seen this type of thing with animals. I think that’s why he’s taken a liking to you.”

My eyes drifted back to the beautiful beast, and I smiled.

There was still hope for him then.

Chapter Nineteen

Satan Needs Some Earmuffs

Two weeks passed and Chris and I had become inseparable. I stayed at my apartment a few nights a week, but I spent a lot of my time with him. I walked Rex every day and hung around in the evenings with Chris and the horse handlers. On Friday evenings we'd eat dinner with his family, and I loved that time with them. Sometimes Gemma would make food, or Keith would stop and get takeout. It was always fun, and I enjoyed it. I especially loved going back to Chris's house and having our time alone.

One morning, after chatting with Gemma about a possible adopter, I left the house to find Keith and Dale. When I started walking to the barn, a truck pulled up to the house.

I swallowed as I recognized that truck.

My father.

I felt like a lamb frozen in her spot as the wolf approached. My father got out of his truck, his sunglasses on and his long black hair tied back.

"Dad," I said with surprise and most likely dread, which was hard to hide.

I could see his frown behind the glasses as he shut his door and walked over to me. "What are you doing here?" I asked.

Did Mom tell him to come check on me? To tell me to go home?

"I'm meeting with Keith about a tribal meeting coming up. What are you doing here?" His voice was deep and low.

"Oh. Um, I'm working for them right now. I can…I can take you to Keith," I offered.

He gave a tight nod and followed me into the barn. It was strange seeing my dad here. I felt like I was on the verge of getting yelled at and I was worried someone would spill the beans as to why I was actually here.

Dale and Keith were in the tack room when I stopped at the doorway. "Hey Keith, um, my dad is here for you."

Keith looked over and grinned when he saw my father. "Clayton! How are you?" He stood up and they gave a hearty handshake. My father actually cracked a smile, and I couldn't help but stare at that.

"I'm doing well. I came to discuss the horses for the tribal meeting in the fall," he said.

Dale looked at me and raised a brow as he saw me staring at the two. I gave a shrug and crossed my arms.

"I have a few things to finish up here with Dale, but Monica can show you the few we have," Keith responded. "Unfortunately, we don't have many that are good trail horses anymore. We're working with a few others, but they aren't quite ready yet,"

Wait, did he say Monica?

My dad looked at me and I swore I saw surprise on his stone face. "Um, sure. Which horses do you want him to see?"

"Cookie, Blaze, Ranger, Tex, and Honey. Clayton, have I told you how amazing your daughter is? She's been one of the best things to happen to this rescue," Keith mentioned.

I felt my breath leave me at his words. They made me fill with joy and a feeling I couldn't describe it even if I tried.

"Oh yeah?" Dad questioned, looking over Keith's shoulder at me. He had removed his glasses and now his dark eyes were boring into me.

I stood straighter, feeling empowered by what Keith said. "Most definitely. Listen, go on ahead, I'll meet up with you in a few minutes."

I went out the door first, not looking back to see if my dad was following. I felt lighter than I did earlier by Keith's sweet words. I owed that man a lot.

My dad's presence loomed behind me as I got to stalls in the middle of the large barn. I pointed to the left of me. "Here's Cookie and beside her is Tex. On your right is Ranger, Honey, and Blaze. If you need another, I'm sure I could ask Chris to let Jasper be utilized as well," I suggested.

Dad leaned on the stall door and Tex came over to sniff his hand and I watched him pet the horse. I leaned back against Ranger's gate, and he came up and nudged my back. I patted him and kissed his muzzle.

"These five should be fine," Dad finally answered.

He moved on to look at Cookie who was a beautiful brown and white mare, then he came over to inspect Honey, Blaze, and finally Ranger who I was standing next to. My father was starting to show a few gray wisps in his black hair, and it reminded me of how old even I was getting.

"Your grandma offered to buy me a horse when I was young," he said.

The fact that my father was having a conversation with me that didn't have to do with my accomplishments shocked me.

"Wh-what?"

He didn't look at me as he stroked Ranger's cheek, who was crunching on hay.

"I wasn't doing well in my English class in middle school. Her incentive was to buy me a horse if I passed that year," he said.

"Did you pass?" I wasn't sure if asking would prompt him not to tell me, but I still asked.

"No."

I frowned and finally my father stopped petting Ranger and looked over at me, his forearms resting on the stall door.

"It was the first time I saw disappointment in her eyes. I never wanted to see it again."

I didn't know if I was comprehending the conversation with my dad at this point, but I pretended that my fever dream was actually real.

"I doubt Grandma was that disappointed in you. She always saw the best in everyone," I said softly.

As if she was summoned, I saw a sparrow fly into the front of the barn and land on the stall door of the new horse. I heard him snort as if it scared him and when he rushed the gate it flew away.

"I know I haven't been easy on you, Monica."

I whipped my head towards my father so fast, I swore I heard my neck crack. My father's jaw was hard, and I thought for a moment I imagined what he'd just said.

"There are a lot of things in my life I've regretted. One of those is the night your grandma died." My father finally looked at me and I felt my nose burning. "I shouldn't have reacted the way I did about you wanting to stay. Your grandma was always proud of who you were. I am too, but I haven't told you enough."

Don't cry. Don't cry. Don't you dare cry, Monica!

"You're proud of me?"

"Yes, Monica. I am."

I hoped to god he never found out about the real reason I was here at the rescue. The proud comment may get revoked.

"Clayton, sorry about that. Dale and I had to run over a few things before he left for the day," Keith said, coming up to us. He saw my face and looked between us. "I'm sorry, am I interrupting something?"

My dad looked at Keith and shook his head. "No apologies necessary."

"I'll just go," I said, pointing to the opening of the barn as I headed towards it. I was in shock. I pinched my arm to make sure I wasn't sleeping but realized I wasn't. That really just happened. Dale met me as I was leaving the barn.

"I'm assuming that's your dad?"

"What gave it away?"

"His attitude for one. He definitely looks like he'd throw some shit when he gets mad," Dale jested.

I stopped walking and laughed. I smacked Dale's arm, but he cracked a smile too.

"Hey baby, what's so funny?" Chris asked, coming out of the main house and seeing Dale and I both laughing.

"Aww, now Chris, we really shouldn't use pet names. It makes the others jealous," Dale said with a hand going over his heart.

Chris just rolled his eyes. "You're hilarious. Whose truck is that?"

Before either of us could answer, my dad and Keith walked out of the barn towards us.

"I'll see you in a few weeks," my dad said to Keith as they shook hands again.

Instead of my dad getting in the truck right away he came over to give me a hug and kissed my head. "You're doing good here. Call your mom sometime. She misses you."

He waved to the others and got into his truck, and I watched as he drove down the gravel drive.

Keith and Dale were talking as I felt Chris come up beside me. "What was that about?"

"I don't know but I'm sure Satan is pretty cold right now. Might need to send him some earmuffs."

Later that day, I went to Spring Awake for my bi-weekly visit and found Erin behind the counter. I waved to her, and she enthusiastically waved back. I sat in my normal seat and pulled out my laptop to check social media and see what was next for Erin.

My whole mood was up since the conversation with my dad earlier in the day. I felt as if a burden had lifted from me. My dad, who had always been a hard man, had essentially apologized to me. It was something I never knew I needed until now.

My phone rang and I grabbed it quickly to answer.

"Hello?"

"Hi, is this Monica Locklear?"

I frowned at an unfamiliar female voice. "Yes, it is. Can I help you?"

"My name is Brenda Mulitch, with P&M Marketing Strategy. We saw you applied for our Content Manager position, and we'd like to bring you in for an interview next week. How's your schedule looking?"

P&M...? As in P&M in New York City? One of the biggest marketing companies in New York! This wasd a dream!

"Yes! I'd love to come in for an interview. I can make almost any day work." *Don't sound too desperate, Monica.* "Except Mondays," I added quickly. "I'd prefer to come earlier in the day since it's a bit of a drive."

"Of course!" Brenda said, sounding thrilled. "How about next Thursday at 11am? If we go past noon we can get lunch."

"That sounds amazing! Thank you, Brenda. I'll see you next week!"

I hung up and felt giddy. Then I looked up and saw Erin walking over to me and realized I'd have to give up doing marketing for her, for Emma, and even for Long Rhodes Ahead.

"I think showing the new smoothie for Labor Day will be a big hit," Erin explained, setting it down in front of me. “What do you think? Colorful and patriotic, like the one we did for the 4th.”

“Let’s add some fresh fruit for more color,” I suggested.

Erin’s untamed brown curly hair was pulled back into an elastic hair band. A few tendrils fell around her heart shaped face, highlighting her beautifully natural tan skin.

“That’s a good idea. Do you think we should post it a few days before?”

I nodded. “I’d say the Monday before is perfect.” I wrote down a few notes on my calendar to remind me while Erin watched.

She paused. “Do you have plans for the weekend?”

I put the drink down. “Not really. Just hanging out with Chris.”

It wasn’t unknown that Chris and I were together at this point. I’m sure Sam had found out already and my father probably put two and two together after this morning.

She bit her lip. “I was wondering if you maybe wanted to hang out? I haven’t really taken a day off and my part-time person offered to close Saturday night. I was thinking a movie night and some good wine.”

I was so shocked by her invitation that I choked on the drink. “Really? You actually want to hang out with me?” Granted it wasn’t in public, but I thought it was a win.

She smiled. "Yeah, I don't have a lot of girlfriends and…there's something different about you, Monica."

I couldn't help my smile. "I'll bring the nail polish."

A few days passed and I spent every night at Chris's. It was Friday and I was exhausted after a long day tending to the kennels, walking Rex, and running over to Spring Awake to do some work. When I got back to the rescue, Chris was at the house, his truck sitting in the driveway. I had stopped knocking on the door, knowing he left it open for me. A warmness seeped into my bones as I thought of that. What if we progressed along to the point that I moved in here with him? The house was plenty big enough and cozy. But what about the job in New York City? Did I even want it? Or was it stupid not to interview? I could ask about working remotely and even if I didn't take it, I could make connections. I hadn't told Chris about it because I just wasn't sure what to do.

I walked into the warm house and there was Chris lounging on the couch, his arm outstretched on the back as he looked at me over his shoulder.

He grinned and I took off my shoes and went to sit next to him. He wore his jeans still and a tight black t-shirt that showed off every muscle. I'd grown very used to seeing that chest.

I leaned into his side, and he kissed me. He wound a hand around my neck to cradle my head. The other gripped my waist and he suddenly pulled me onto his lap, so I was straddling him.

Breathless, he pulled away, leaving me dumb and mindlessly staring at him.

"You're supposed to say, 'Honey, I'm home'," he mused.

I smirked. "Do I look like Lucille Ball to you?"

"No, but you definitely act like her some days."

I laughed, putting my arms around his neck and shifting on his lap. His fingers went underneath my shirt and stroked my bare skin.

"Have you talked to Sam lately?" he asked before I could say something naughty.

I frowned. "No, not for a while." I didn't want to tell him we'd gotten into a fight because Sam had purposely not told me about the accident.

"He called my mom the other day wanting to know if you had your hours in yet. I guess he's planning to come do a check or something," Chris said.

I looked away from his eyes as I thought of my brother. He probably wanted to know exactly when I would be done and when I'd find a real job.

"Baby," Chris whispered, pulling my chin to point at him again. I melted at his soft expression. "It'll be fine. You're almost done."

I played with the collar of his shirt and touched the soft hair speckling his chest. "What will I do when I'm done?"

The question had been bugging me. I had no reason to stay any longer if my hours were complete.

His lips pressed together as he looked between my eyes. "You can stay, volunteer sometimes. Help my mom with marketing."

"Do you want that?" I asked.

The corner of his mouth turned up into a smile. "Yes. I want you to stay, Monica, if that's what you're asking."

I smiled back. "Good, because I want to be right here."

We didn't even eat dinner before we ended up in bed. By the time we did get to eat, I was almost falling asleep at the table. When I awoke sometime in the night, I was surprised to see the bed was empty. Under the door I saw light and I got up sluggishly. Maybe he got a call about a rescue? When I peeked my head out of the door, I saw the bathroom light was on and the door was slightly ajar. I glanced in and saw Chris standing in front of the mirror, face contorted in pain. His hand was reaching down grasping his left leg.

"Chris," I whispered, opening the door completely wearing only his shirt. He jumped, staring in surprise. "What's wrong?"

His expression hardened. “Nothing. Go back to bed.”

“I can help. Let me rub your leg or–”

“No,” he snapped, his voice rough. “Just go back to bed, Monica.”

I stepped closer, my hand outstretched. He didn't move away as I touched his arm.

“Please, Chris. Let me help.”

“I don't need your help!” he snapped, startling me.

I dropped my hand, feeling shaken. “Fine.”

I left the bathroom and went to bed where I sat thinking he may not return. I lay down and turned towards the wall. I don’t know how long it was until I heard the door open, but I felt the bed shift as he lay down. He didn’t reach over and neither did I.

Chapter Twenty

Girl's Night In

The next morning, I woke up to the smell of coffee. When I turned over, Chris was already out of bed. Things felt weird as I slipped on pants and went out into the kitchen. Chris had a mug of coffee in his hands. The TV was on, and they were talking about the weather forecast.

He was shirtless with his sweatpants hanging low on his hips. He looked at me and I saw regret staining his expression. Without a word he filled up another cup and walked over to where I stood leaning against the counter.

"Thanks," I mumbled awkwardly as I took a sip. It was a dark roast that Chris preferred so it was strong, black coffee. I made fun of him for it, but he never kept cream in the house, so I'd started drinking it black as well. As I looked over the rim of the cup at him, he watched me back. I kept seeing him in pain in the bathroom and his look of misery. For the last few weeks, I'd only ever seen him with boots or socks on. Maybe his foot was even messed up too.

"Last night–"

"I'm sorr–"

We both stopped as we realized the other had started to talk. Chris and I didn't laugh but he looked at me with a frown. I didn't say anything, just waited. He ran a hand over his face, looking away from me. "I'm sorry, Monica. About last night." His voice was rough and gravelly.

"Does it hurt a lot?"

He still wouldn't look at me, but he nodded. "Yeah, sometimes it comes on quickly and it's hard to work through it. I hate taking pain killers, so unless I have to, I don't. It normally hurts worse after physical therapy but last night was…bad."

I put a hand on his arm and ran it down to his hand so I could clasp it and squeeze. "What do you think set it off?"

He took a deep breath and exhaled. "I don't know."

"All the sex?" I questioned with a smirk.

He'd been amazing, but he'd been particular about which positions we were in, and he hadn't let me do anything to him. I just figured he wanted…things other than that.

He scoffed and finally looked me in the eyes. "Maybe, but that's not going to stop me."

I threw my arms around his neck and grinned. "Good. But you know, you could let me do some of the work… help you out a bit."

He pulled me as close as possible to him and caressed his lips against mine, teasing me. "I might be able to do that."

I kissed him then and his hands ran up and down my back until he pulled away. "I was thinking we could go riding Saturday evening, maybe have a picnic if the weather is nice."

I pouted. "I promised Erin a girls' night, but rain check?"

His brow raised. "Girls' night?"

I nodded eagerly. "She invited me over to hang out for the evening."

"Just..." he started but stopped.

"What?"

He looked conflicted about what he was going to say next. Finally, he continued, "If you want to drink, I'll come get you. Or stay at her house for the night."

The words hit my chest hard. I didn't know what to say other then, "Okay. I will."

He leaned in and kissed me quickly again, then brought me into his arms and I hugged him back. Whatever trauma he'd been through with his accident still stuck with him. I just wished he'd open up to me about it.

Saturday night came and I got Erin's address and met her at her apartment down the street from Spring Awake. It was within walking distance of her cafe, which I'm sure was convenient. She opened the door right after I knocked, and I smelled popcorn mixed with something fruity.

Erin looked comfortable in shorts and a big t-shirt. Her hair was in her signature tight corkscrew curls and was framed around her face.

“Hey! You came!” she said, sounding surprised.

I paused on the threshold with a bottle of wine. “Wait, you thought I wouldn’t?”

She laughed and pulled me in before shutting the door behind me. “I mean I figured you would but wasn’t sure if you’d change your mind,” she explained.

I followed her into her modern kitchen and put the wine on the counter. “Yeah no. I wasn’t going to pass up wine with a girlfriend!”

She grinned at that.

Erin had made a charcuterie board that was filled with cheeses, crackers, meats, and chocolates. We poured some wine and got comfortable on the couch in her quaint living room. We turned on the TV to a show we both liked but used it mainly as background noise while we talked.

“Do you remember when Phil asked out Renee in high school?” I asked, my cheeks hurting from smiling so hard.

“Yes! She shouted *no* so loudly everyone in gym class heard,” Erin said, starting to laugh.

“It was so embarrassing! Also, why would you ask a girl out after she ran two miles, and was sweaty and tired?”

“He was an idiot!” she agreed, then sighed. “Gosh, some days I look back and think of how much I hated that time and other days I think about how life was so…”

"Simple?" I finished for her.

Her brown eyes connected with mine and she nodded. "We were very conceited and thought life was only about high school and the people there, but it's so much more than that after you get out. Ugh, what I would give to go back where I had no responsibilities!"

"I couldn't agree with you more. Life is much more complicated and stupid and full of disappointments." I looked at her as she sipped her wine from her almost empty long-stemmed glass. "I'm sorry for making fun of you in high school, Erin."

She rolled her eyes and waved a hand. "It's fine. My dad always said, 'bullying builds character.' It definitely made me have thick skin, that's for sure."

I shook my head. "It wasn't right of me. I was just in a bad place. If I really dug deep, it was because I was so unhappy with my own life, I wanted to make others' lives just as miserable."

She tilted her head to the side and looked at me. "You were that miserable?"

I shifted on the couch, pulling my other leg up beside me. "I was until my senior year…but even then…it's complicated."

"Parents?" she guessed.

"Yeah, they've always had these high expectations, and I was never fulfilling them. However, my father just admitted to being a bit of dick during my childhood, but that's a story for another time when we have more wine," I joked.

We were quiet for a few moments as we both took another sip from our glasses. "You know, I forgive you for that, right?" she said quietly.

I looked up in surprise and smiled. "Thank you."

"I forgave you when I saw your half naked picture on social media. It definitely made up for the times you called me *brace face*."

We both erupted into laughter that almost resulted in wine being splashed across her couch and floor. By the end of the night, my stomach hurt from all the laughs, and I felt like I had made a true friend of Erin.

Maybe moving home and being stuck on the rescue wasn't all bad. It changed me in a lot of ways in the short time I'd been here. My life was starting to make a turn. No failure was in sight, and it felt good to finally have control of my own life.

When I got back to my apartment, I promptly texted Chris to let him know I was home and did not drive home drunk. Instead of texting back he called me, and it sounded like he was in the car.

"You're on your way to get a rescue?" I asked after he said hi.

"I am. Dad and I left a few hours ago. We're only going to Maryland so we should be back in a day or two."

I flopped down on my bed and already missed his bed and smelling his scent in the sheets. "Is it horses or dogs?"

"It's a few dogs and cats. It's a hoarder situation with a lot of animals involved. We've already gotten word that some had to be put down."

I felt a twinge of pain at the loss. "Do you need me to do anything?"

"Eh, maybe just check on my mom tomorrow? She's been stressed all day about this and she's worried about space right now. We only have four kennels available."

Already thinking of some ideas, I told him I would go in tomorrow to see how she's doing.

"And Monica," he said quietly, sounding like he was leaning into the window. "You can stay at my place if you want to."

I bit my lip. "You mean so you can fantasize about me taking baths in your tub or naked in your bed?"

He cleared his throat twice all the while I grinned like a fiend. "N-No, well yes, but just know it's there if you want to stay. There's a key under the floor mat out front."

I heard his dad chuckling in the background. "Goodnight Monica," Keith said loud enough for me to hear.

"Be careful you two," I said.

"We will. I'll call you later."

I stared at the phone after we hung up and realized I was so head over heels for this man.

The next day I looked at my community service hours and saw that I had four hours left. I'd been diligent about recording every hour I worked and helped out but recently, I'd stopped. I guess it didn't matter anymore because I wasn't done helping with the rescue and I didn't know if I ever would be. I thought of the upcoming interview with P&M Marketing on Thursday. It was only a few days away and I still hadn't said anything to Chris. I owed it to Brenda to go, just to see what it was about, even if I felt like I wouldn't actually take the job if it was offered.

I stopped in and saw Erin at Spring Awake. She grinned when she saw me. "It's not your normal day to work, what brought you in?"

"Chris and Keith are in Maryland doing a rescue, so Gemma needs some caffeine. I figured I'd grab something for her. Ooh, and two of those muffins. They look like heaven."

"They're fresh! Just made them this morning," Erin said, putting them into a bag and handing them over the counter, along with a to-go tray and two coffees.

"Thanks!" I paused and looked at her. "We should hang out again. It was a lot of fun."

"I think so too. Let's agree to do it once a month, a girls' night in. It gives me the chance to actually have a Saturday night off and not just sit around doing nothing."

"Maybe even hit up Sullivans so we can get you laid!" I joked.

Her face flamed and she shoved the bag into my hands as I laughed. "Monica Locklear!"

"I'm kidding! But you did tell me how long it's been and I think it'd be good for you."

She rolled her eyes with a smile. "You're getting plenty for the both of us. Now go look Gemma in the eyes and pretend you aren't screwing her son."

I just laughed again and waved as I headed out the door.

My phone beeped with a text and I quickly pulled it out of my purse to check.

Phoebe: *I was going to just show up in your hometown this week to give you a taste of your own medicine, however, I have no idea where the hell your hometown is and you know how I feel about anywhere but the city.*

Me: *Oh my gosh! You're coming to Cold Spring??*

Phoebe: *I'm flying into New York City for a fashion event and thought I'd come visit my little lying traitor friend. But yes, I want to see your beautiful face again!*

Me: *I'll send you my address! When??*

Phoebe said she had to look at the dates of her event and how long it'd be, but she'd get back to me about it. I was thrilled she decided to come out to the East Coast. She'd gone to New York City plenty of times, but she'd never really ventured anywhere else on this side of the country.

When I got to Long Rhodes Ahead, Gemma was flustered. She had piles of paperwork stacked around her and she was mumbling. The dogs came rushing towards me, but she didn't seem to notice. I patted their heads as Gemma finally glanced up.

"Monica, hi. Sorry, I can't find my glasses. They were here somewhere," she murmured looking all around. I set the coffee and the muffins on the desk where there was a free spot and came around to pull them off her head and hand them to her. She looked baffled by my discovery and thanked me.

"Listen, it's time for a break. I have coffee and a fresh muffin from Erin," I said nodding towards the stuff.

She rubbed a hand over her face and the gesture reminded me so much of Chris. "I can't, Monica. I have so much–"

"It can wait."

I convinced her to move to the kitchen where there was space, and we drank our coffee, and I made her eat. The dogs were smart enough to stay away right now as she shared some issues she was having.

"We need seven spaces, and we only have four," she expressed. "We can't double up dogs in kennels. It's not safe."

"What if they found foster homes? Are any adoptable?"

"We have a lot that are adoptable, they are just older or have a health issue, and no one seems to want them," she shared with sadness.

I bit my lip and tapped my finger on the to-go cup. "Let's post them out on social media and see if we can get homes or at least foster homes."

"Monica, that's…I don't know if we'll get someone in time." I could tell she hadn't slept much the last few days and I hated that she was doing this to herself.

I put my hand on hers and looked her in the eyes. "Let's try. There's no harm in that."

I took pictures with my cell phone of all the adoptable dogs and since I was familiar with them, I could give a short description of their personalities. Rex stood waiting for me, and I took his picture since he was so cute. I went back to the main house after waving to Dale and sat at Gemma's computer.

"You really think this could work?" she asked, biting at her nails.

"Maybe. We'll see what happens."

She watched as I posted each dog's picture and when it came to Rex's, I hesitated. He was sitting on his haunches, his tongue lolling out and it almost looked as if he was smiling at me. He was adorable and sweet and easy to train. He'd make a good family dog with the right people. But those people were not me. Right?

"You know you don't have to put Rex's name out there yet. We only need three spaces," Gemma said softly.

I swallowed but didn't turn to her. "He needs the opportunity to be in a family; I don't want to keep that from him."

I posted the pictures just as Gemma's phone rang. She answered it quickly. "Hey Honey, how's it going?"

I heard Keith on the other line and saw Gemma's eyebrows knit together. "Sure, hold on." She put Keith on speaker phone and sat it on the desk between us. "What's going on?"

"This hoarder situation is a lot worse than we anticipated, Gem. It's more dogs than we thought, a few goats, a pig, chickens, and a horse. There is probably about thirty or so animals," Keith explained with remorse. "I think we have room for the farm animals from what Chris is telling me, but we need at least eight kennels for the dogs."

"Monica just posted on social media some of the dogs to try to either get them adopted or fostered," Gemma said just as I got a message. It was a lady inquiring about the one dog, Hercules, a mid-age lab that was blind in one eye.

"Gemma, look!" I pointed to the computer, and she grinned widely.

"You're not going to believe this, Keith, we already have someone who wants to come see Hercules."

I heard Chris in the background laughing. "Leave it to Locklear."

"We should have an adoption event," I suggested. "Maybe even after we get a feel for the new dogs that are coming in. Get the whole town involved."

Gemma's eyes twinkled with hope, and for the first time in a long time I didn't feel like a failure; I felt successful.

"When do you think you'll be back? We can work on getting the kennels cleared if I have a timeline," Gemma asked. "I also need a rough count for the dogs."

There was shuffling on the phone as Chris spoke up. "We have to do some legal work first so I'm thinking at least two more days. We've got eight dogs as of now, but that number could grow."

"How long does it take to get adopters approved and the dog to go home with them?" I inquired.

"Maybe a day or two. If they are already in our system and we've done a home check, maybe same day," Gemma answered.

I turned back to the computer as another message came up about the Yorkie dog we had. "I think we might be able to get those spaces open."

By the end of the day, we had three possible adopters come to the farm to see the dogs. Two of the families went home with dogs and Gemma looked like she was about to cry. I sat down in the chair across from her desk and smiled.

"Where have you been my whole life? You realize that Hercules has been sitting in that kennel for three years? He's only been looked at twice!"

"The picture I took was a good angle for him."

She laughed, shaking her head. "Two kennels cleared; we just need two more, maybe three just for good measure."

"I think having a spare is a good idea. I did have a foster family come forward willing to take the puggle, Bigs. I sent them the application form."

She got up suddenly and left the room, disappearing into the kitchen. I frowned after her until she came back with a bottle of whisky and two glasses. She sat one down on the desk in front of me and filled a knuckles' length then did the same for her own. She looked at me as she perched on the edge of the desk and held her glass up.

"We're celebrating," she announced, and I picked up my whisky to tap hers. "Thank you,

Monica. This is the beginning of something good, I can feel it!"

We both took a long draw of the whisky, and she blew out a breath with a laugh. "I haven't had that in years. Not since Chris's accident."

"You don't drink around him?" I asked, curiously.

She filled her cup up again and offered to me, but I shook my head no.

"No, we don't. When he stopped, we stopped." She paused, swishing around the brown liquid. "Chris's accident didn't just affect him; it affected his dad and me too. To see our baby…" She stopped, eyes blinking. "Anyhow, it's something we just did."

We were quiet for a moment, and I wanted to ask more. Wanted to ask why he wouldn't talk to me about it. Why everyone in Cold Spring knew and didn't talk about it. It seemed very hush hush, which was abnormal for this nosy town.

"He still won't let me see it," I said softly. Gemma looked up at me with a frown. "His leg, I mean. I assume it's in rough shape and he's self-conscious about it. I just wish he'd share more of himself with me. He still has this wall up that I can't seem to break down." I hadn't realized I needed to talk about it until the words came out. Gemma was quiet. "He's everything I've wanted, and I want to be with him. I realize now that I should have never left."

Gemma was looking at me with a thoughtful expression. “I can’t read his mind, but I can guess why that wall is up.”

Hopeful, I asked, “Why?”

She took the last gulp of her whisky before answering. “He’s afraid you’re going to leave again.”

Chapter Twenty-One

I'm Not Wearing Panties

Gemma's words hung onto me all evening and the following morning. Could that be why Chris didn't break down all his walls? Is that why he hadn't shared more from that horrible night that changed his life? There were so many questions rolling around in my mind, it was hard to focus on the families that came in to see the animals. Gemma and I took two groups and introduced them to the dogs in separate yards. I took a medium size pit bull mix to the side yard to meet a husband and wife who wanted to foster him.

"He's very friendly. He likes walks and doesn't pull either. He's not great with cats but he gets along well with other dogs," I said to the couple as the husband sat on the ground and let the pit bull lick his face.

"He seems so sweet!" the wife exclaimed.

"He is," I agreed.

I felt someone behind me and looked to see Dale leaning against the chain link fence, watching me. I turned to the couple and smiled. "I'll be right back. He likes rope toys so feel free to play with him."

I walked over to meet Dale, and he was giving me a grin that I knew all too well. "You know, a month ago I knew a girl who was scared to death of dogs and horses. Now here she is adopting them out."

"Yeah, yeah. I guess Will went home for the day since you're here picking on me."

He chuckled. "Something like that. Boss lady wanted me to tell you Chris and Keith are renting another truck and trailer in Maryland because of all the animals. They're afraid we won't have enough volunteers for when they get back. It'll be all hands-on-deck."

"We don't have enough volunteers?" I asked with a frown.

"Not all can work all the time. Some are limited and can only do weekends or weeknights," Dale explained.

"But this is just one day, can't they make it work?"

Dale just shrugged.

Gemma walked over, her boots kicking up dust as she came to stand beside Dale. She was grinning widely.

"Just adopted out Bigs," Gemma said.

"I thought they were fostering?"

"They loved him so much they signed the paperwork already."

Dale whistled and patted me on the back. "This one is definitely good for the rescue."

Gemma whipped off her Long Rhodes Ahead baseball cap and stuck it on my head. "Welcome to the team officially, Monica."

That evening, I was so tired I decided to crash at Chris's house instead of driving back to my apartment. I took a quick shower, threw on one of Chris's t-shirts and slid in between the sheets. Before I could shut my eyes my phone rang and without even looking, I answered.

"Yes, I have no panties on, and no I'm not in your bathtub."

A female voice cleared her throat, and my eyes popped wide open as I realized it was not Chris. I glanced at the phone to see it was Emma.

"Emma," I said, my voice cracking with embarrassment.

"I'm assuming that conversation was meant for someone else and not your sister-in-law." Her words were tinged with amusement.

"Um, yeah. So, what's up?"

This was the first I'd talked to her since my blow up with Sam. Neither she nor Brynn had reached out and I figured it was because I had yelled at Cold Spring's "Golden Child", and everyone was pissed at me.

"I haven't heard from you…since the thing with Sam, and I wanted to check on you. Are you doing okay?" Emma sounded concerned.

I sat up in bed in surprise. "Yeah, Chris and I made up."

"Obviously, since you're not wearing panties."

We both laughed loudly about that. I told her about my dad's visit to the rescue and what he'd said. She was surprised just as much as I was. I talked to her about the rescue and where Chris was right now. I told her about how many dogs I'd helped get homes today and how Gemma had welcomed me to the team.

"Wow, Monica! This is amazing. I think you've found your calling. But how are they going to get the volunteers when they return? It sounds like there are a lot of animals coming," Emma said.

I bit my lip, wondering if my idea would do well. "Do you think if I post out on social media that we need volunteers, the people of Cold Spring would show up to help?"

Emma was quiet for a moment. "When Luke got shot, they made a ton of food for him and Brynn and really took care of them while he recovered. They may be nosy busy bodies, but they are decent humans, so I'd say yes, I think they would."

"I'll have to pitch it to Gemma, but I think I'm going to push for it. It'd be great for the rescue, and it would help Gemma maybe get a day off."

"I think it's great what you're doing, Monica," Emma explained. "Listen, I know your relationship with Sam is…"

"Shit?"

"I wasn't going to say that. It's strained right now, but I want you to know that I'm here for you if you ever want to talk. Whatever you say to me, stays between us."

I couldn't help my surprise. "You mean you're not going to tell Sam all my secrets?"

She laughed. "No. He doesn't know Brynn's secrets and Luke doesn't know mine. I just want you to know I'm here for you and a lot of times, I'm on your side. I just ask that you give Sam a chance to talk about this. I was here when Chris got into the accident and it really shook up the town, and especially Sam. It was hard for him to talk about it, even to me, which is why I think he never called you."

I hadn't thought about how it affected Sam. Maybe I really was selfish and should have listened to him, but part of me was still angry about it. He could have called or texted… or something.

"Thanks, Emma. I appreciate it."

"You're welcome. Anyhow, I'll let you call Chris and tell him about your idea and the panties. Goodnight!"

"Night."

As soon as I got off the phone, I called Chris.

"Hey, I thought you'd be in bed by now. Mom told Dad you looked exhausted," Chris said on the other end.

"Oh, I am but I have this idea and I want your opinion."

"If it's about taking three days off when I get home and never leaving my bedroom, yes."

I laughed and laid back against his pillows, enjoying the smell of him there. "No, it's better."

Chris loved the idea and the next morning I was rushing over to Gemma's house to pitch it to her. She hadn't gotten out of bed yet, so I'd made a pot of coffee and had a mug ready for her when she came downstairs. I'd put on my Long Rhodes Ahead baseball cap and wore jeans since the weather was getting chilly.

Gemma and I sat down at the table and discussed everything. She was thrilled and loved the idea.

"It'll be last minute…we may not get as much help as we need but I think it's worth a try," Gemma announced.

I grabbed her laptop and grinned. "Let's post now and see what we can do."

Two days passed and Chris called me to tell us they would be leaving early the next morning and should arrive by noon. Our posts on social media had gotten almost the entire town volunteering. Some came the day before to help ready stalls, kennels, and unload trucks of donations of foods and bedding. We had seven spots ready for the dogs but still needed one more open.

Phoebe had also reached out to say she would be arriving around noon. I had to give her the bad news that I'd be busy, so she offered to come and volunteer too. I didn't think she knew what she was getting in to, but she would as soon as she saw what was going on.

Gemma and I stood with the people and gave a job to everyone along with handing out name tags. Emma and Brynn were there, along with Luke and some men from the station who were off work.

"Emma, you and Brynn can come with me. I'll have you guys fill up the food for the dogs."

"I'm here!" I heard a voice yell, and we turned to see Mackayla running up wearing a cute dress and a denim shirt with cowgirl boots.

I smiled at the outfit. "You're going to get dirty, Mackayla."

She just gave me a wide smile. "But at least I'll look cute doing it!"

Brynn scoffed and put a hand to her head. "Mackayla."

Emma just giggled.

A car pulled up, the dust barely settling, before the door opened and Phoebe hoped out. She had on sunglasses and her blonde hair had bright purple highlights in it. She wore high waisted shorts with a babydoll white t-shirt underneath a furry sleeveless vest. Her sandals were brightly colored and covered with gems. It was very classic *Phoebe*.

"Phoebe!" I screeched and ran down the steps to barrel into her. She squealed and leaped towards me. I'd forgotten how small she really was compared to my tall frame. She'd always been jealous of my five-foot-nine frame and used me as a model sometimes for the different outfits she was working on.

"You have me in the middle of nowhere!" she said as we pulled back. Her lip curled up as she looked over my outfit. With one finger, she pushed her sunglasses down her nose to eye me up. "Girl, are you having a crisis? Because this outfit is screaming 'help me!'"

Instead of being completely insulted, I sighed. "I missed you."

She just smirked as she put her sunglasses back up.

"You're just in time to help with the dog kennels and meet my friends," I said as I looped my arm through hers and we walked towards the girls.

"I wore this vest specifically for today! It's faux fur because we don't harm animals! Well, hello," she said to them. She had beautiful tan skin which she spent thousands of dollars on and most of her outfit was her own creations.

"Guys, this is Phoebe. One of my best friends from San Diego," I introduced.

"This jerk didn't tell me she lived in the middle of nowhere."

I rolled my eyes as Mackayla agreed with her eagerly. "We need to get to work. Follow me."

I took them out to the kennels and showed them what to do. We unboxed new bowls then filled them up. Mackayla was attached to Phoebe as they worked together and she asked her tons of questions about being a designer, living in California, and which celebrities she'd met.

"Hi buddy," I said, going over to Rex's kennel to pet him. I'd been ignoring him for a while since I'd been so busy.

I got a call, and I quickly answered as Mackayla complained about the smell. "Hello?"

"Hi, Monica, it's Brenda with P&M. I'm just confirming our interview for Thursday."

Shit…that was in two days. I had totally forgotten about it. Was I really going to go? Things had changed so much but I still didn't have a full-time job. I should just go; they may not even offer the job.

"Yes, Brenda, I'll be there."

She gave me the address and other information about the building and what suite number and where to park. I hung up staring at the phone a minute longer. Rex whined and I looked up to see his snout shoved through one of the holes in the gate. I laughed and poked it.

"He's cute!" Emma said, coming up beside me to look at Rex.

"He is. We walk together in the evenings. We had a rough first few encounters, but now we're good."

“Monica,” Gemma said, coming into the kennel.

“Is that poop? Oh my god! There’s poop on my boots!” Mackayla screamed, her hands flailing in the air. Phoebe screeched too as the poop on her boots flew off and towards her.

Gemma just raised a brow as she walked past them but focused on me. “We still need one more kennel open. We don’t have any adopters as of now and we’re getting too close to the end of the day. Do we have any that get along with other dogs? I can keep one in the house.”

I looked at Rex and his tail wagged expectantly. “I can keep Rex at Chris’s until we have an open kennel.”

She looked surprised and so did Emma. “Really?”

I nodded. “I’m sure Chris doesn’t care. And maybe it’ll help domesticate him a bit more, make him more adoptable.”

Gemma just gave me a knowing smile. “Okay then. Grab a leash and take him out. We need to clean his kennel and get it prepped.”

“You got it!” I said, saluting. She waved a hand at me and walked out. Emma turned to me, arms crossed and eyed me. “What?” I asked.

“You’re different, Monica.”

I’d been hearing that a lot lately. I grabbed a harness from the wall behind and opened the gate.

Rex was quick to rush forward and let me buckle him in.

"A lot has happened I guess," I finally replied.

"Your parents would be proud of what you're doing, so would Sam."

I snorted and straightened. "I'm not making money so none of them would be. Speaking of the *One Who Does No Wrong*, where is my brother?"

She sighed and pushed a lock of her blonde hair out of her eyes. "He's working today but he said he'll try to be here tomorrow."

Rex panted and whined, thinking we were going on a walk. "I'm going to take him to Chris's. Phoebe, are you okay to hang out here until I get him settled?"

Phoebe had gloves on and seemed disgusted by them but looked up at me. "Of course! You go do you, I can hang out with these ladies in the meantime."

I steered Rex out of the barn and heard Mackayla squeal again. "It touched me!"

Brynn, Emma, and Phoebe's laughter floated after me.

I got Rex settled into the house and he wanted to sniff everything. I hoped he wouldn't pee on anything. I went back and got everything squared away with Gemma and the volunteers. She instructed all of them to come back the next morning at nine to get ready for the arrival of the group. I said goodbye to Brynn, Emma, and Mackayla.

Phoebe and I stood in the driveway next to her little rental car. "You sure you don't want to come back to Chris's house? He has a spare room."

"My boss is paying for a nice hotel in New York City so I'm going to take advantage of that. I'll be back in the morning though, promise," Phoebe said with a hand to her heart. "Unlike you, I tell people when I don't plan on coming back."

"Ouch," I muttered with a guilty smile. "I deserved that."

"You do, but I love you. You look like you could use a face mask and a bottle of wine. Go do that."

I laughed and hugged her tightly. "Text me in the morning."

She got into her car and waved as she drove off down the long driveway.

When I got some food in my stomach, I flopped down on Chris's bed. Rex jumped up and made himself comfortable by my side. He looked at me with large, brown, adoring eyes and stretched out his paw to me. I brushed his ears, and he rolled onto his side to show his stomach, his tongue lolling out.

It felt nice to come home and have someone waiting for you. He might not be human, but having Rex was close enough.

I giggled as he rolled around, his head landing on Chris's pillow.

My phone rang and this time I made sure it was him before answering.

"I've got another man in your bed; I hope you don't mind."

He laughed, knowing I was kidding. "Oh yeah?"

"He's a bit hairy and smells like kibbles and bits but he's a great cuddler."

"He better not get used to it because tomorrow night you're mine," Chris said, his voice sending a shiver down my spine.

"He said that's fine, he doesn't want to hear any of that anyhow." Chris's chuckle was manly and made me sigh. "I miss you, Chris."

"I miss you too, baby."

The longing in both of our voices made my heart ache. I hated that he had to leave so much but I knew I had to get used to it if we were doing this.

"What is Rex doing in my bed, by the way?" Chris inquired.

"We needed one more space for the dogs tomorrow and it wasn't looking like that was going to happen, so I told your mom I'd take Rex. Is it okay that he's in your house?" I belatedly asked.

"Yes, that's fine. I'd rather you have him there than with Mom. She's got enough dogs that sleep in her bed," he said with amusement.

I laughed. "She has to since your dad is barely there! She needs something to cuddle," I said, nuzzling into Rex's furry back.

"Yeah, he needs to start slowing down soon," he said quietly.

"Does that mean you'll do more?" I could hear even in my own voice the worry of not seeing him much.

He sighed. "I don't know. I guess it'll depend."

"Oh what?"

"On you and me." Hearing him say that made my blood warm.

"How so?"

"I don't like being away from you. I don't like not being able to touch you whenever I want. I don't like the idea of you being naked in my bed without me. I'd rather have you go with me on these trips because missing you is hard on me."

His confession made me ache to have him here. "I want to be with you too, Chris. Every second if I could."

"Then it's settled. Next trip Dad will stay back, and you and I will go."

It felt like more than that. It was his declaration that our relationship was going to last, that this wasn't temporary. It was going to be forever.

"I think I can do that."

"Good. Now, did your brother and Emma come today? You haven't seen them much."

I sighed, petting down Rex's back. I could hear his faint snores. He seemed so happy here and so at ease.

"Emma did but Sam didn't. She said he was working. We haven't... we haven't talked in a while, so I'm not surprised he wasn't here. Emma said he'll be here tomorrow, but I won't hold my breath."

"Why haven't you been talking?"

I bit my lip, wondering if I should tell him. "Because after our first date I went over and yelled at him for not telling me about your accident. It was a rough conversation and the worst argument we've had."

"Oh."

We were quiet for a few seconds. "Will you tell me more about that night some day? I know it's hard to relive some of those memories, but I just feel like you're keeping a lot from me. I want you to share that burden."

"I will. It's just... it's a lot and it's too hard to explain over the phone." It sounded like he was running a hand over his face again.

"That's fine," I encouraged, finally feeling as if we'd broken ground. "Now, onto better news."

"Oh yeah? What's that?"
"The panty-less in your bed part."
He groaned as I smiled devilishly.

Chapter Twenty-Two

Homecoming

The next day was a whirlwind of excitement, nervousness, and chaos. All the volunteers showed up first thing in the morning. Erin came with boxes of hot coffee, muffins, donuts, and other pastries to share. I hugged her so tightly she almost couldn't breathe. Phoebe showed up last, looking tired and acting a little grumpy. Everyone got their job assignments, and we had the morning chores done before 11 a.m.

When lunch came, a volunteer brought in enough food for everyone to have seconds and thirds. Gemma and I looked at each other and I saw tears blur her eyes. She came over and hugged me as everyone sat around eating and chatting.

"This wouldn't be possible without you, Monica."

I shrugged, feeling embarrassed. "It wasn't just me; you helped too."

"Nah, it was definitely you," Will said, shoving half of his sub into his mouth as he winked and walked down the steps, passing Emma, Brynn, Luke, Phoebe, and Mackayla. I watched Mackayla's eyes track him.

She kicked Brynn and whispered, "I told you there'd be hot guys here! I knew I should have worn something cute!"

Brynn and Emma just snickered and shook their heads. I caught Will looking over his shoulder at Mackayla and giving a smirk before heading into the barn.

Then I saw two familiar people walking up to join the others and my mouth dropped.

"Mom...Dad?" I walked down the steps to them and my father still had that same intimidating look on his face while my mother wore a small smile.

"We thought we'd stop in to help for a bit. We have a meeting going on today, but we wanted to come support the Rhodes," my mother said.

I grinned. "That's great! It means a lot to them."

I couldn't believe my eyes as they moved over to a couple they knew from the tribe and started talking. I went back to stand beside Gemma, and she smiled at me, bumping her shoulder into mine. As if to say, *see, they aren't that bad.* And honestly, maybe they weren't.

Skyler McCauslin walked up the steps, gloves on, wearing farm clothing. "All the meds are ready. I brought a few vet techs to help check each animal and administer medicine."

"Perfect! Thank you, Doc! I know it wasn't easy to find a babysitter so I'm grateful for you working on your day off," Gemma said. Skyler smiled, her beauty showing brightly.

"Gracie loves spending time with my parents, and you know I don't mind giving back to you guys."

Gemma nodded, looking a little misty-eyed.

Skyler walked back down the steps and started talking with Brynn as I felt Gemma's hand on my shoulder.

"You know, one of the volunteers is adopting Fluffy, so we have room to put Rex back in the kennels."

I knew she was trying to hint at me adopting him but instead I just nodded. "We should say something to everyone before Keith and Chris get here."

She smiled and patted me on the shoulder. "That's all you, I'll collect everyone." Her phone rang and she answered it. "Great! We'll see you in 10 minutes!" I knew what that meant; Keith and Chris were almost here.

"Everyone, gather around. We'd like to chat before the animals arrive!" Gemma called out after hanging up her phone.

Everyone moved out below the steps of the house, and it was then I saw how many people had truly showed up. It seemed like half the town.

Gemma and Dale stood on either side of me as I took a breath. My parents stood in the crowd listening and I felt even more of my nerves prickling me.

"Thank you everyone for coming to help us today." I straightened my hat and cleared my throat, a little nervous that everyone was watching. Especially when I saw Sam get out of his car and come stand at the back of the crowd. *Show him that this wasn't just a community service job, that you're different now and you've forgiven him.* "Showing up here today isn't just about the animals that we're rescuing, but about community and loyalty. Gemma, Keith, and Chris have been a huge part of Cold Spring over the years. Long Rhodes Ahead has been the place we go when we want to adopt a pet, the place that will try to rehome a pet when someone can no longer take care of them, or the place where we know that lonely animal we found wandering the roads will get a fresh start and find their forever home. Helping today is helping our community. So, thank you for being here."

The group cheered and clapped; Emma whistled loudly, scaring Mackayla. Phoebe yelled out a "you go girl!"

Just as I finished, we all saw the first trailer pulling into the driveway. Everyone quickly started moving and getting into their places to prepare. When Keith jumped out of the first truck, he looked dumbstruck as people came to ask him for the key to unlock the trailer and another person brought him a sandwich. Gemma put her arm around me as she smiled at Keith.

Then Chris got out of the second truck and his eyes connected with mine right away.

"Go get him," Gemma said with a slight push to my arm.

I smiled and walked down to meet him. People buzzed around us, but we only had eyes for one another. He scooped me up in his arms as soon as I was close enough and put his face in the crook of my neck.

"It's about time you got back home," I said, breathing in his hair, his scent, everything.

He pulled back and cupped my cheek, his nose almost brushing mine. "You amaze me every day, Locklear."

"Good. Someone has to be the amazing one."

He shook his head, turned my hat backwards and kissed me. People hooted and hollered around us, but we didn't care. He tipped me back, his arms holding me tightly as he deepened our kiss.

My mind and thoughts scattered, and my heart was beating at an abnormal pace by the time he stood me upright and steadied me.

"I love you, Monica."

My heart jumped as his hand slipped to my neck, and he looked deeply into my eyes. This man…he had stolen my soul years ago and never gave it back. Maybe that's why I'd never felt fulfilled by anyone. It was almost as if I was a shell of a person. But being back here, with Chris, made me feel complete.

If Grandma was here, she would say we were soul mates and when one was gone the other was broken. Not now though— we were finally whole again.

I ran my hand on the back of his neck. "I love you too."

"Alright, enough of the declarations of love, we got some animals to take care of on these trailers!" Dale said loud enough for everyone to hear.

I bit my lip, still not taking my eyes off Chris, whose matching smile told me everything. We would never leave each other again.

Chris looked over my shoulder. "Are your parents both here?"

I turned just as my parents walked up to us. "Chris, it's been a while since we've seen you," my mother said politely.

Something seemed to flash across his eyes before it disappeared quickly. "Nice to see you both again. Thank you for coming out today to help," Chris answered.

"We actually have to go but I'm sure we'll see you around soon, right Monica?" my mother asked, insinuating that I bring him around. I couldn't even stop my stupid smile because that's exactly what I planned to do. My dad had waved that white flag and if that meant making things better between us, I wanted that.

"Yes, you'll see him soon."

We waved goodbye to them both then I squeezed his hand. "You owe me a very awkward Locklear family dinner."

He just shook his head at me.

Goats, sheep, horses, chickens, dogs, all were brought off the trailers one by one. Everyone was careful handling them as they put them into their new homes. I worked with Brynn, Emma, Phoebe, and Mackayla as we cared for the dogs.

"This one is sooo sweet! I want to take her home! I bet she'd fit into my purse," Mackayla said, holding a small Pomeranian. The dog licked her face and Mackayla laughed.

Phoebe held a French bulldog who was black-and-gray spotted that only had three legs. "This one is already my favorite. How much work goes into having a dog? Is it like a relationship? I have commitment issues, so I want to make sure I know what I'm getting into."

I laughed and shook my head. "You would love having a dog. Both should be ready for adoption after Doc looks at them and sees what type of treatment they need."

Emma laughed. "Listen to you being all 'sales lady.' You should come work at the store."

I smiled at that.

"Whew, I'm tired. I don't know how you do this every day, Monica," Brynn said, wiping her brow.

"I could get used to this," Mackayla said, petting the fluffy dog in her lap.

"It was hard at first, but I started to really like it," I said honestly. It was true. The work was hard, but I enjoyed it after a while. It gave me something purposeful to do.

"If I had to look at that hot piece of cowboy pie every day, I'd love this job too," Phoebe muttered.

It was early evening, and we'd gotten all the animals examined by Skyler and her team, given them their meds, baths, and food before settling them into their beds for the night. Most of the volunteers had left and I could feel my exhaustion rolling in. Mackayla was almost in tears having to leave the little dog behind in the kennel as we headed back to the house. Phoebe sighed and brushed her hand across her forehead.

"I cannot wait to go back to my hotel and take a long ass shower," she said.

"Do you want to come back to Chris's and hang out?" I asked, hopeful that I could spend a bit more time with her.

She put her hands on her hips, "And listen to you guys make kissy noises all evening? No, thank you. I'd rather put my face through a woodchipper, and you know how I feel about my beautiful face. Besides, I have an early day tomorrow anyhow."

I snorted. "Alright, I get it. But you promise to come see me again?"

"Of course!" She hugged me then she and Mackayla walked to their cars, exchanging numbers.

Emma was about to say something to me when Sam appeared in front of us, and I could see he wanted to talk.

I stopped and stared at him. *How would this go? Would he talk to me like an adult and not like his troubled young sister?*

"Go," Emma encouraged me. There were still a few people standing around the house getting water and chatting, so Sam and I walked over to the barn. We were quiet as our boots echoed off the cement floors.

He sighed. "What are you doing here, Monica?"

I stopped walking, the sound of a record screeching in my ear. "What?"

"This isn't a job. This is your community service. Does this pay?" Sam asked, turning to look at me.

I blinked, not comprehending what he was saying. "Gemma is going to pay me, yes."

He shook his head. "I'm supposed to come check on you, as a member of the Police Department, to make sure you're doing your hours. I still haven't told Mom and Dad why you're here because I'm trying to let you get your shit together."

"Get my shit together? You are the only person in my life who thinks I don't," I scoffed, my hands curling into fists by my sides. I thought he'd be proud of me, not acting like this.

"This isn't a job, Monica. You can't live off what they'd pay you, not by yourself."

I couldn't believe what I was hearing. "You realize Mom and Dad were here today and are supporting not just this rescue, but me? You are the only one right now who is concerned about my 'failure of a life' as you call it."

"Monica, stop. You're being childish."

"No, I'm not. You came here to tell me I need to find a real job instead of being happy for me that I'm helping one of the best families in Cold Spring."

"I think it's nice what you're doing but it isn't supporting you. You still have bills to pay for, a house–"

"Which is none of your business! I pay my bills and I'm not asking for help, so what is it to you?" I snapped.

"You're making this out to be more than what it is," he said, raising his hands. "You're my little sister and I care about you."

My anger simmered. I was so sick of being treated this way by him. Even my parents had eased up after Dad and I talked. They seemed actually happy for me today. But not Sam. I'd heard this from him my whole life and I'd had enough.

"I have an interview tomorrow with P&M Marketing Strategies in New York City. I applied for jobs and I'm trying! And you know what? Maybe I'll leave this stupid town again like I did before just to get away from you!" I yelled.

Sam frowned at me, about to say something, when he looked over my shoulder. I whipped around and saw Chris standing at the entrance of the barn, looking shocked.

"No...wait," I said helplessly. "Chris, that isn't–" I stopped. What had he heard? That I was leaving? That I hated this town? But it wasn't true...I was angry at Sam.

He didn't say anything to me; he just walked off. I turned back to Sam, my hands going to my head.

No, no, no. This wasn't how today was supposed to go! I didn't want to leave, why would I say that?

It was my fight or flight response. And it had always been flight. I had to talk to Chris; I had to tell him I was just mad at Sam. I wasn't leaving.

I ran out of the barn hearing Sam call after me.

"Screw off, Sam!" I snapped. I looked all around but didn't see Chris. I barged into the front door of Gemma and Keith's house and saw Chris bent over the desk writing on something.

"Chris, that isn't what I meant. Sam was–"

He turned and handed me a piece of paper. I frowned at it as he looked at me. His expression was cold and unyielding.

It took me a second but finally I looked down and saw the last four hours were filled in and he'd signed his name at the bottom. He checked the box that said the hours were completed and the community service was fulfilled.

"You're done." His words were cool.

I looked at him and pleaded. "Chris, I am staying here. I don't want that job in New York City."

"Then why didn't you tell me about it?" he demanded.

I flinched. "I don't know. I just…"

"You were always planning to leave, weren't you? Stay long enough to make me fall for you again and then just leave."

"No, that's not it at all! Chris," I reached for him, but he pulled away which broke my heart. "I love you. I'm not leaving."

"Go home, Monica," he said and walked out of Gemma's house. I stood there, staring at the paper, angry at Sam, angry at Chris, and angry at myself.

I growled as I pushed open the screen door and let it bang behind me.

I failed at everything! Relationships, my job, my life.

Sam was gone, along with the last of the volunteers. I shoved the paper into my pocket and looked up at the sky, tears filling my eyes. Dust floated in the evening air as my gaze drifted to the barn. The paper in my back pocket seemed to burn a reminder that it had changed my life completely.

I heard a loud neigh and went over to the barn again. Inside I found Lucifer pacing in his stall, looking upset and frazzled. It was probably from all the people in and out today that was making him like this.

I leaned over the stall door and stared at him. He moved towards me, sniffing. A thought crept into my mind. "You know what, we stop failing today. And that means you too."

Chapter Twenty-Three

Once a Failure, Always a Failure

Getting the saddle on him was tricky, especially because he kept shifting and eyeing me up like he was going to kick me. I tightened the cinch, watching him to make sure he wasn't going to bite. After the saddle was on, he pretty much stopped moving. He seemed still as I put the bridle on him then grabbed the reins and guided him out to the round pen.

He was hesitant but followed me. I shut the gate and turned to look at him, my hands on my hips. "Listen Luce, I'm going to climb on your back and we're going to walk around this ring and then we're going to celebrate. Deal?"

He shook his head, his brown mane swishing. I threw the reins over the horn of the saddle and walked to his side. His brown eyes stared back at me as I put one foot in the stirrup. I paused, waiting to see what would happen. When I felt good, I lifted myself but before I could even throw my other leg over, he took off and I fell back onto my butt.

Luckily it didn't hurt that bad, so I got up, brushed my pants off and went to get him again. I tried it slower, but as soon as my leg went over him, he freaked, but this time I jumped off before he could take me on a wild ride. I landed on my ankle and winced.

I stood up and put weight on it and it seemed okay, just a little painful. I breathed a few breaths in and out. I was determined. This was going to work, one way or another.

I walked across the pen and got the reins again, but I looked him in the eyes this time.

"I thought we had an agreement, you and me. You don't buck me off and I give you whatever treat your horsey heart desires. We're going to do this again, okay?"

I put my foot in the stirrup, and he moved away, my foot falling out, so I tried it again and then, I lifted myself up, pausing to watch him. Nothing happened. Slowly, I put my other foot in the stirrup and that's when it happened again, but this time, I wasn't prepared for it. He kicked and I fell. My hair was coming out of my ponytail, so I angrily stood up, ripped off the hat and threw it across the dirt.

"That's it, this is war now."

You know that saying, if you keep falling, get back on that horse? Or maybe if you fall seven times, get up eight? Yeah, the people who said that were the biggest assholes. No one said I'd *actually* be falling off a horse. I thought it would be a metaphorical horse, not a real one.

My body slammed to the ground, dust floating around me. I puffed out a breath I didn't even know I had left in my body. I think at some point I'd popped a lung.

Was that possible? It felt like it.

I groaned as I sat up on my elbows just in time to see the brown horse galloping off towards the edge of the pen, his ears back. I slowly stood up and glared at him as I brushed the dust off my already raggedy clothes. My black jeans officially had rips in the knees, and though I didn't spend hundreds of dollars on them, twenty dollars at a country store was still twenty dollars.

"Chicken shit!" I yelled towards the horse in the late evening light.

Just like everything else in my life, I was failing. To Sam, that wasn't a big surprise and to the people of Cold Spring, it was normal. To me, I was pissed. I failed at my relationships, my job, my family…even at horse training, which I shouldn't have been doing in the first place. Had Grandma still been around, she would have been standing beside me and encouraging me to not give up.

"Stop your complaining. No one is going to help you back up when you fall. You have to do it yourself. So do it."

Grandma was right, no one had ever helped me up when I fell, and no one was about to now. It was my job to do it.

Monica Locklear stops failing as of today.

I walked over and grabbed the reins of the devil horse. "We are going to work together if it's the last thing I do. You will not be another failure for me, got it? You and I are going to be successful."

He shook his head and neighed. I took that as a good sign as I put my hands onto the horn of the saddle and pulled myself up. He paused, as if we had a breakthrough. As if this was finally him realizing I wasn't here to hurt him but to help him.

Yes! This was it. I did it!

Before I could celebrate any more, I felt him buck and of course I went flying.

My back hit the ground again but this time I lay there and stared up at the fading blue sky in the evening light.

Okay, so maybe today is another failure day. There's always tomorrow.

A bird flew in front of me, and I watched it land on a fence post. The sparrow watched me and tilted its head from side to side.

I laughed with no humor. "Not funny, Grandma!" I said hoarsely. Of course she was here, just to make a point. I hadn't seen much of that stupid bird lately but now seemed like the perfect time for her to show up.

I closed my eyes and willed myself to move but I was sore, sorer than I'd ever been in my life. Then I felt something tickling my nose and I opened my eyes to see Lucifer nuzzling me.

I shoved his head away, but he came back to nibble more. "You're an asshole."

He snorted as I pushed him back to sit up. I was covered in dust, and I could feel myself sweating through my black t-shirt.

Lucifer neighed again and I put my head on my knees. I was done. I failed this stupid horse just like everyone else. "You'll be glue next time I see you," I muttered angrily. The sparrow was still on the post watching us. "I don't know what you're waiting for!" I said to the bird. "Nothing is going to happen." When it still didn't move, I ran towards it, and it flew off. Immediately I felt guilty as I leaned against the fence. I took a breath then climbed up onto it and turned to sit down and stare towards Lucifer. He watched me then and slowly he made his way towards me. I almost tipped back when his body nudged up against me, his side pushing into my legs. I frowned at the action, unsure why he was doing it this. He shook his head and looked back at me as I stared at the saddle in front of me.

Did he want me to mount from the fence? No…that couldn't be.

"If you buck me off one more time, I swear to god I'm feeding you to the wolves," I muttered as I grabbed the horn. I slipped my leg over cautiously without putting my feet in the stirrups and settled on top. He didn't move, didn't budge, just stood still.

I swallowed, my nerves shot as I felt how sore my legs were. I went to put my feet in the stirrups but felt him tense. I slipped my feet back out of the stirrups and didn't move. Then I nudged my heel against his side and he slowly started walking.

"No freaking way," I exclaimed.

Was that all it was? He didn't like the stirrups? Or was it mounting from the ground he didn't like?

I took the reins in my hands and steered him to the right, and he followed, then to the left. Lucifer's ears were straight forward, and his tail swished happily behind him. I clicked my tongue, and he walked a little faster, I guided him with the reins in a wide circle, around the pen. My heart burst with joy and excitement.

I was doing it! We were doing it!

I tapped him a little with my foot and his pace picked up until we were trotting. I bounced in the saddle and held on as tightly as I could. Without the stirrups, I felt more unbalanced. But this was working…not putting my feet in the stirrups seemed to help him feel more secure for some reason.

"We did it!" I yelled, laughing. "We aren't failures!" I announced. I looked for the sparrow, but it was gone. I smiled, knowing what that bird had meant. Grandma had once again been there for me when I needed her.

I slowed the horse down and he listened as I pulled the reins back. I leaned forward and hugged his thick neck. "You are officially named Lucy!"

My heart filled with hope and I knew I had to tell Chris. This was my sign that I wouldn't give up on our relationship.

After putting Lucy back in his stall, I ran across the rescue to Chris's house. I knew he was still going to be mad at me, but I didn't care. I also didn't care that it was almost 9 p.m. and he might even be asleep after the long day we had.

I knocked hard at the door, but he didn't answer. "Chris! Please, I need to talk to you!" I said from the other side. I knocked again.

Screw it, I wasn't taking no for an answer. I turned the doorknob, and it opened, and I walked in. "Chris, I'm sor–" I stopped as I saw Chris sitting on the couch, his hand rubbing his knee and his leg...his *artificial* leg was propped by the coffee table.

Chris's face looked white as paper, then it transformed into anger. "What are you doing here?"

Chapter Twenty-Four

Past Secrets

It suddenly struck me what was going on. Chris…he didn't have part of his leg; he had a prosthetic leg. His accident…he hadn't just injured his leg—he'd *lost* it. It all started to make sense: the occasional limp, him only wearing jeans and boots, the reason he always wore pants when we were intimate.

"Chris…" I whispered, my eyes filling with tears as I moved over to him. He grabbed the prosthetic and slipped it on under his knee and shoved his pant leg down. "You…you lost it in the accident, didn't you?"

He wouldn't look at me, his hands curling into fists by his side as he sat on the couch. "Just go home, Monica."

I moved closer to him. "Why did you keep this from me?" I sat down on the couch, and he still refused to look at me. "Chris, I didn't know… I didn't know about this."

His hand rested on his left knee, but he didn't move. "This isn't your concern anymore."

I felt my heart ache for him. Not only had he been in a bad accident, but he'd lost so much that night. Not just his leg but his freedom. That's why his parents helped him build a house close to them without stairs. It was why the town was so shaken up about it. And I…I had been in San Diego getting drunk at college and living my life while he suffered.

“Why didn't you tell me?” I whispered again, tears falling from my eyes.

He finally looked at me, his eyes cold and devoid of any emotion, which hurt even worse. “There’s nothing to tell. I lost my leg that night and my life has never been the same.”

I felt broken for him and mad at myself for never reaching out, for never trying to talk to him through the last eight years. “Chris, I wish you would have shared this with me—"

“And why would I? I knew I would never be the reason you would stay. Not only am I not one of your dumb California men, but I'm a college dropout that lost his leg.”

“Chris! Stop. You were always the one I was supposed to be with. I never should have left but I did, and I can’t change that, even if I wanted to. I can promise you now that I’m not leaving.”

He scoffed. “Right, and one day I’ll go to your house, and you’ll be gone. Just like you did before.”

“I won’t do that again!” I said strongly.

“Then why didn’t you tell me about the damn job interview?” he demanded.

I opened my mouth, but nothing came out. He had a right not to trust me. I had kept that information from him, and I wasn’t sure why.

“Because I wasn't even sure if I was going.”

"Don't give me that bullshit, Monica. Was this your plan all along? As soon as you got the right opportunity, you'd leave?" he snapped.

I ground my teeth. "I will admit, yes, I thought of moving if I get this job but after my time here, with *you*, I don't want to. I want to be with you, Chris." I reached for him, but he stood unsteadily.

"Go to your interview and when they offer it to you, take it. You hated it here from the beginning. Why did I think that was ever going to change?"

I stood up too. "I'm a hell of a lot different than I was eight years ago."

He scoffed. "No, you aren't."

I felt that anger stirring again. "You're such a hypocrite, Chris Rhodes."

"Me?" he demanded.

"Yes! You kept this a secret from me, and you think I'm terrible for not telling you about a stupid interview? I shared everything with you except that." I took a breath, trying to curb my anger. "You have kept your accident and injury from me since the beginning. I had to find out about it from Erin, and even since we've been together you have kept the biggest secret from me." I felt my tears drying up as my anger took over. "When you finally get your head out of your ass and realize I'm not leaving, come find me."

As I ripped open his door to leave, I looked over my shoulder and added, "Oh, and by the way, Lucy doesn't like using stirrups. That's why no one has been able to ride him."

Shock spread across Chris's face as I slammed the door behind me. When I walked down the steps away from the house, I didn't feel any better, but I was different. I was done letting everyone give their opinion about me or try to tell me how to live my life. Monica Locklear isn't a failure and she's done with people thinking she is.

A week went by and even though I was miserable not being at the rescue and not seeing Chris, I felt more myself than ever before. I didn't go to the interview; instead, I called that morning and canceled, saying that I didn't want to move. Brenda was understanding and said she'd share my resume with some other businesses that offer remote positions. The following day I got a call from one of them and after a virtual interview, I was offered the job. It was bittersweet accepting it, knowing that my dream of helping the rescue was squashed.

When I sat on my couch alone one evening, I realized how empty it was. I hadn't seen Rex in a week, and I longed to visit him. I even missed Lucy. Before I could stop myself, I got up, grabbed my keys and went downstairs to the bagel shop. Billy, my landlord, was prepping for the next morning when I knocked on the glass door. He waved me in, and I greeted him with a friendly smile.

"Monica, how's the apartment?"

"It's good. I have a question. Would you allow a dog?" I asked, surprising even myself.

He pressed his lips together. "What type? My insurance is particular about certain breeds. German shepherds, pit bulls, and rottweilers aren't allowed."

I flinched. "He's a German Shepherd but he's a really good dog and I've trained him a little!"

He eyed me speculatively. "Is he one of Gemma and Keith's rescues?"

"Yes." I held my breath.

"I guess the insurance company can think he's a Yorkie. What they don't know won't hurt them."

"You are the best landlord!" I reached across and hugged the old man, and he let out a surprised laugh.

I left the bagel shop and got into my rental car and drove to Long Rhodes Ahead. My hands felt sweaty as I thought about possibly seeing Chris.

It still hurt me to think of what he lost that night. *Why had he kept that from me? Was he worried I wouldn't like him because of that? How conceited did he think I was?*

I put the thoughts out of my head as I pulled up in front of Keith and Gemma's house. Chris's truck wasn't around, and I felt a wave of relief.

I knocked on the screen door and saw Gemma behind her desk looking over papers. She glanced up and her eyes widened. "Monica, come in."

I did and I petted the dogs that rushed up to greet me and quickly removed my foot before Wheely could run it over. "Do you have a few minutes?"

She took her glasses off and nodded towards the chair in front of her desk. I could tell by her expression she knew what happened or at least knew that we weren't…that Chris and I weren't together anymore. Even the thought made me feel pain.

"I'd like to adopt Rex."

She raised a brow. "Really?"

"Yes. Am I too late?" I asked, concerned.

"Oh no, we haven't had any applications. I'm just…surprised."

I swallowed and looked towards the screen door. "Since I finished my hours, I realized how much I missed him."

Her smile was sad. "You aren't going to be working with us anymore, are you?"

I clasped my hands together on my lap. "I don't think that would be healthy for me or him."

She knew which *him* I meant and slowly nodded. "He's still keeping Rex at his place. I'll start the paperwork if you want to go get him."

I frowned. "He's at Chris's? I thought we had an open kennel?"

"We do; he just never put him back in."

"Is he adopting him?" I questioned. The last thing I wanted to do was take Rex from Chris. That would cause way more issues than I'd like.

"No, he's not." She started filling out a paper as I stood up hesitating to leave. "He's out with Keith and won't be back for a few hours," Gemma said, reassuring me

I left the house and paused on the steps as I looked at the barn. It wouldn't hurt to see Lucy quickly. Who knows if I ever would again?

I walked into the barn and saw a few of the handlers talking and working with a horse in the round pen but none paid any mind to me. I went to Lucy's stall, and he seemed more at ease than ever before.

"Hi Luce," I said softly, and he leaned out to me, head down. He nuzzled my head, and I petted his nose. He'd changed a lot, I realized, since our last run in. He seemed calmer.

"Chris has worked with him this week and he's made a breakthrough," a voice said, startling me. I clutched my chest and turned around to see Dale walking into the barn.

"That's good, I'm glad to hear that."

I'm sure Chris told him what happened or maybe he didn't, but everyone could assume what happened since I wasn't around anymore.

"I'm wondering if Lucy here had someone else training him before Chris got to him." Dale's tone told me he knew that someone was me.

"It wasn't training. I just didn't want to give up on him," I said, stroking Lucy's cheek.

"Good thing you didn't. He's been great and easy to train."

Did Dale know about Chris's leg? Did he open up to him? Or was he quiet about it, even with all of them? I didn't dare ask since that was Chris' story to tell and explain. Hell, even I didn't know all of what happened.

"I need to go get Rex. It was good to see you, Dale," I said, smiling sadly at him. His hands were in his pockets as he looked at me.

"We'll see you around soon, right, Monica?"

I swallowed the lump in my throat. "Sure, Dale. I'll see you soon."

I walked to Chris' door and wasn't surprised to find it unlocked. The smell of his home brought back thoughts of us eating dinner together, relaxing on the couch, and falling asleep together in his bed. It hurt even more than I thought it would.

Rex barked until he saw me then he raced over to jump and lick my face. There was a dog bed in the living room that Rex had been on, and my heart hurt a little. Why had Chris kept him here? Would he be mad that I was taking him? I wasn't going to feel guilty about taking my dog. I worked with him, I helped him with his aggression. Chris could shove it. I grabbed the harness by the front door, put it on Rex, and left.

Chapter Twenty-Five

Is Hell a Dry or Humid Heat?

Rex and I fell into our own routine and even though my heart broke for the failed relationship with Chris, Rex was helping me heal. I hadn't heard from Sam or even Emma, but Erin and I hung out several times during the week and Phoebe started to call me after I told her about Chris and I breaking up. Even Mackayla had come over to visit me and we'd drank wine and talked.

I started my new job, and I was starting to feel good about my life other than being sexless and Chris-less. I felt as if I was finally where I needed to be mentally to go talk to Sam. Emma's car wasn't in their driveway, but Sam's cruiser was, so I knew I came at a good time.

I knocked on the door and Sam opened it in civilian clothing. I could see right away the guilt that marred his expression.

"Mon, I…I was going to call you."

"I want to talk."

He waved me into their living room, and I sat down on their comfy couch while Sam took the armchair across from me. There were pictures of Savannah plastered everywhere in the room, which made me smile.

"God, Mon, I don't know where to start. I heard about you and Chris–"

"I'm not here to talk about that. Well, not yet anyway," I started. "I've always been jealous of you. You have your life together. Mom and Dad look at you as if the sun rises and falls on you. You've never failed, and it shows. You have an amazing wife and baby, a home, and a great job. But there are some of us who haven't had that and it's okay. Yes, my life has been chaotic and crazy at times but it's *my* life and I chose it. Failing is a part of learning and growing and if I don't fail, then I'll never get anywhere." I felt myself take a breath. "I want you to be a part of my life. Actually, I'd trade you in for Emma any day but since you're family, I want you here. However, I'm done with you treating me like a child. I'm twenty-six years old and even though I'm not where you were when you were my age, that doesn't mean it's the wrong place. If you can't keep your opinions to yourself, you can stay out of my life."

Sam was quiet as I ended, and I watched him assess the situation. "I can do that."

I paused because I'd been ready for a fight. "Really?"

"I respect that."

I stared at him in silence. "Emma really put you in your place, didn't she?"

My brother scratched the back of his neck with his head down. "Yeah, we won't talk about that night."

I smiled wistfully. "I want to be her one day."

"I am sorry for how I acted, Monica. I see your potential and I know you can do great things."

"Those great things can be here in Cold Spring, Sam. They can be helping Brynn and Emma with their store or Erin with hers, or someplace where I make minimum wage. I've been on my own since I was eighteen, I'll be fine without my big brother trying to run my life. I have Mom and Dad doing that," I said the last part quietly.

He sighed. "You know you remind me a lot of Grandma. She would have ripped me a new one for what I said to you."

I laughed, my thoughts going to the frown she made when someone upset her. "Yeah, she would have. I miss her every day."

Sam's eyes saddened. "I do too."

We talked for over an hour and by the end of the conversation, we steered back to Chris. I had a soda in my hands while Sam had a beer as we sat back more comfortably on our seats.

It'd been a long time since I'd really talked to my big brother. We even discussed our mom and dad, and I told him what Dad had said to me. He'd been surprised to hear that but happy that our relationship wasn't as strained. Maybe this was what we were missing all along: communication.

"So, what's going on with you guys?" Sam asked, taking a sip from his beer.

I leaned my head back against the couch. "We broke up. Well, he broke it off with me after he heard what I said to you in the barn." He flinched. "I went to try to explain things and…he has a prosthetic leg."

Sam didn't say anything, so I raised my head up quickly to see his expression. It was mournful. "You knew?"

He sighed, a deep one, and I saw the scars in his eyes from that night. "I didn't know for sure, but I held Chris's hand when they extracted him from the truck. I knew it wasn't good just looking at it."

I felt my heart cave at his words. The trauma for both of them must have been hard. "Tell me what happened that night, please."

Sam played with the label on the beer bottle and looked at it. "We got the call from a neighbor that they heard the tires squealing and the loud impact. When we got there, Chris was unconscious. He smelled of alcohol and as we got the jaws of life on the truck, he woke up." I saw him swallow at the memories and I felt like shit for making him talk about it. "I took Chris's hand and talked him through it, asked him about his favorite things…" Sam looked up at me and I knew what he was going to say next. "He told me about a girl named Monica who he thought he was going to marry one day, and still hoped she'd come back so he could. He even bought a plane ticket to go after her. He was leaving in two days."

I couldn't breathe, couldn't think clearly as he spoke the words. I felt it again...the tears that threatened to spill from my eyes. He bought a plane ticket? He was coming out to see me, to say goodbye? Tell me he cared for me?

"He told me about football and college and then when the medics got him out, they flew him to the hospital," Sam continued. "My boss made me see a therapist after that for a few months. I didn't see Chris for a while and when I did, we didn't discuss it."

I reached across and took Sam's hand and squeezed. "Thank you for sharing that with me."

He squeezed back, his eyes looking less sad. "Chris is a good guy."

"I know. He's just stubborn and stupid right now."

He laughed softly. "Only you would say that."

After we were done talking, I went to Spring Awake to work and see Erin. She waved at me behind the counter as I walked up

"Still on for girls' night tomorrow?" she asked.

"Wouldn't miss it! My place again?"

"Of course! I need to see Rexy. I bought him a new toy," Erin said with a grin.

"You know–"

"Yeah, yeah, I know Gemma has tons of dogs that need homes. I can't have an animal right now. And by the way, who are you? The poster child for Long Rhodes Ahead?"

I sighed. "Something like that."

She took my order and I went to sit down at my regular spot. It was then Sophie came in and walked over. She looked annoyed as she stared down her nose at me. She had tagged me in that stupid half naked picture the teens had posted on social media. I still hadn't quite forgiven her for it.

"Monica."

"Hi Sophie."

"I heard you finished your community service finally," she said.

"I did. Oh, and thanks for tagging me in that horrendous picture. It really made it easy for the kid's mom to find me."

She ignored that. "I heard you and Chris didn't work out. Sad too, but it's not like you've been great at keeping relationships. It's probably for the best."

I tried not to let it bother me, but this new and improved Monica wasn't taking it anymore.

"How would you know?"

"No offense but even on social media I haven't seen you really keep a guy around long. Maybe you should see someone for that?"

"Maybe you should keep your nose out of other people's business," I finally snapped. "But then again, you've never been good at that, have you? Didn't you tell Brandon when Natalie cheated on him with Ryan?"

She gasped in outrage. So maybe the old Monica was still there and was too willing to take the bait. I swallowed it whole.

"You're a bitch, Monica Locklear!"

"At least I'm not a snitch," I retorted back as she left Spring Awake in a huff. A few customers stared at the interaction, but I just shrugged at them.

I turned back to my computer as Erin came over with my cup of coffee.

"Do you think hell is a humid heat or a dry heat?" I asked her.

She set down the warm, steaming pastry. "Mm, I'd think a humid heat. Why do you ask?"

"I figure since I'm going there in a nice handbasket, I should probably prepare."

"Good idea. Send me a postcard when you get there and let me know," Erin chirped as she turned on her heel and went back to the counter.

My phone rang and I looked at the number. "Hi Mom," I answered.

"Your dad and I heard that you got a job," she said right away. *Getting right to the point, I can appreciate that.*

"Yep, sure did." I took a sip of my coffee, drowning in the warm sweetness of it. Too bad I couldn't fully submerge myself in it.

"Does this mean you're staying here or moving?"

"No, the job is remote, so I'll only have to go into the office maybe twice a month. It's based out of Albany so it's not far," I responded.

"Good. Anything else you want to tell us?" she asked, her tone a little different than it had been. My parents had been much better with me, and I'd even went over for dinner one night.

"I don't think so."

"Maybe the fact that you got community service?"

I flinched. I flinched so hard that the lady across from me flinched too. She must have heard the sharp words from my mother. "Oh, um, you heard about that?"

"Yes, your father heard from his barber. I'm wondering now why you or Sam didn't tell us."

"It happened so quickly, then I got busy, it just kind of slipped my mind," I said quickly.

"Slipped your mind?" Her voice went higher than I'd ever heard it. "We've seen you three times already! Also, is this why you were 'helping' Gemma and Keith? Your dad's barber said you were doing community service there."

"Yes, but listen, I'll come over this weekend and explain it all."

"You better, Monica Claire Locklear."

I flinched again at the middle name. "If I say I love you, does that make things better?"

She paused. "Well…maybe. I love you too, Mon. But seriously, we know you get into things you shouldn't, but give us a heads up so we don't find out this way?"

I laughed; I couldn't help it. "I will, Mom."

We talked a little bit more about Rex and the rescue and then I got off the phone feeling better than I ever had. Then my thoughts saddened again as I thought of Chris. I made up with Sam and my parents, I just wanted things to be better with him. I wanted him more than I wanted anything in my life, but he had to come to terms with that.

After finishing my coffee and food, I said goodbye to Erin and headed back to my apartment. It was getting cool now with autumn heading into Cold Spring. When I opened my door, Rex greeted me right away.

"Hi buddy!" I said scratching behind his ears.

I slipped off my jacket just as there was a knock on the door.

Must be Billy, the landlord. He said he was going to come visit Rex just to say hi. When I opened the door, my breath was almost knocked out of me.

"Chris?"

Chapter Twenty-Six

The Make Up

He stood in my hallway wearing a long sleeve t-shirt, jeans, and his boots. His hair was messy, and he wasn't wearing a hat. In his arms were paperwork and a dog bed.

Seeing him again rekindled all sorts of emotions and memories. There was a deep longing for him, his touch, our conversations. God, I missed his scent and the feeling of his strong arms around me. I fought the urge to push all the things from his hands and force him to hold me.

His expression was odd as he looked me over from head to my feet. He seemed worn and tired but...did I see longing too? Hope soared in me as I thought maybe he was here for another reason.

"I brought this over," he finally announced, looking down at the papers.

"Oh," I said in disappointment. "What is it?" I took the papers he handed me, making sure not to touch him.

"It's the official adoption papers for Rex," he said, his voice grave. At his name, Rex trotted over to see Chris. He couldn't seem to take his eyes off me as I looked over the papers and he petted Rex's head.

"Okay, thank you. And what's that?" I pointed to the bed.

"Oh, uh, this is his. I bought it for him, and I don't need it anymore." He didn't hand it over to me as we stood in the hallway just looking at each other.

I cleared my throat. "You can come in."

He did and put the bed in the living room then straightened, running his hand through his hair. My stomach whirled as I saw his arms flex with muscles, and I remembered them wrapped around me.

I put the adoption papers on the kitchen counter then crossed my arms. "You didn't have to bring this stuff over. I could have stopped by the rescue."

"Would you have actually come?" he asked, softly.

I shrugged, looking down at my feet. "What are you doing here, Chris?"

I felt him move closer to me and my heart beat heavily against my chest as I looked up to find him within a foot of me.

"I took my head out of my ass."

It took me a moment to understand what he was saying as his lips crashed into mine, taking all my thoughts away. He caged me against the counter, and in seconds, I wrapped my arms around his neck and pulled him to me as tightly as I could.

Yes! I had him back. He was mine and there was no way I'd ever let him get away again.

He pulled back and I complained, which made him laugh. He brushed my hair behind my ear as he peppered my cheek and neck with kisses.

"I'm sorry, Monica."

"That's such a turn on, say it again," I whispered with a smile.

He chuckled, his hands tightening around my hips. "I heard you took a remote job and turned down the one in New York City."

"I did. I'm not leaving again Chris. I'm here to stay."

His thumb brushed my cheek as I saw the vulnerability in those brown eyes that made me melt. "I wasn't wrong when I said you were the same," he started, making me frown. "You are the same beautiful woman that you were before with me. I saw the side of you that you never showed anyone else." I softened, realizing what he meant. "I know that if you'd heard I was hurt, you would have come."

"Yes, I would have taken the first redeye home just to make sure you were okay." I pressed my lips together. "Sam told me about that night."

He took a breath then exhaled. "I didn't realize who he was until later on, but he helped me through some of the worst of it." He rubbed the side of his face. "Hell, I barely remember some of it, but I do remember him talking to me."

"Did you really buy a plane ticket to come see me?" I asked, twining my fingers through the hair at the nape of his neck.

He smiled shyly, which was adorably handsome. "Yeah, I did. When I went to meet you for our date and I talked to your parents, they said you left suddenly. Then I heard the news about your grandma. I thought you'd come home but after a few months, I realized you weren't, so I bought a ticket."

"But never got to use it."

"No, I was ready to but…the accident was my own stupid fault. I should have never been drinking and driving. I have no one to blame but myself for my leg," he said remorsefully. "I was just glad no one else was involved."

I looked down at his clothed leg. "Does it hurt like it did that night?"

"I get phantom pains a lot and if I leave the prosthetic on too long, it can make it sore," he said.

"I don't know how I didn't notice it." I felt stupid for not having seen it.

He laughed without humor. "I hide it well. The only people who know about it are my parents and Dale."

I frowned. "Why only them?"

"I don't want anyone to think I can't do something just because I'm an amputee."

I tilted my head sideways, feeling his sadness into my bones. "You know the wounded guy thing is kind of a turn on for me."

His laugh met his eyes and lit up his features, reminding me of the happy boy I knew in high school.

"Good, because I have a thing for girls who fail and move home," he joked.

I joined in his laughter and leaned my forehead against his. "I love you, Chris Rhodes."

Had I not lost my job in San Diego and moved back here, showed my boobs to some minors and did my community service at the rescue, I wouldn't be where I am now. In Chris' arms.

I kissed him then and the whole world tilted and fell away until it was just us, two souls who were always meant to be together again.

If this is what failure feels like, I don't mind it one bit.

Epilogue

9 months later

"Baby, come on, we got to go," Chris said, pulling me away from the puppies in their pen in the living room. Rex was already outside waiting for us, looking excited.

"But wait! The girl is doing something really cute, and I have to get a picture!"

He chuckled, grabbing me around the waist. "No way, let's go. We have a sunset to catch."

"Ugh! Fine!" I relented as I let him pull me out of our house.

We had been together nine months, and it was nothing but perfect. I moved in with him shortly after we made up, Rex too, and started helping with the rescue again. Within two months, I quit my remote job and went full-time helping Gemma and Ketih. I still worked for Erin and Brynn and Emma on the side though. I thought working with Chris every day and living with him would be too much, but it wasn't. I loved it.

Keith stopped going on rescue trips so just Chris, me, and Rex went instead. We'd traveled all across the country together. When we got new adoptable animals, I did our marketing to find them fosters or forever homes. Our volunteer numbers were up along with our donations and our animals were getting homes quickly. We had become a good team. It took a little bit of time for my parents to see that, but after Gemma and Keith invited them to the rescue to see what I did, they loosened up a bit.

Somehow Emma had convinced Sam to adopt a cat. She told him it was for Savannah who was easily the star of the show and who had turned one in March. Sam couldn't say no to her and Emma took full advantage. Not that I could blame her.

We walked to the barn to saddle our horses to go for a ride. Lucy became my horse since I'd tamed him and worked with him once I got back to the rescue. It shocked the horse handlers when Chris told them what to do to get Lucy to cooperate. They couldn't believe I'd been bucked off ten times and still got back on, then figured out exactly what Lucy needed.

We took the horses out of the barn and started on our trail. Keith had worked on widening the trails around the rescue and our volunteers walked the dogs around in the morning and evenings. Tonight though, no one was around.

Chris and I frequently went on rides after chores were done to spend time together and enjoy the warm weather that was approaching. It was early June, and the fields and woods were getting greener, and the birds were singing.

“I can’t wait for summer,” I said out loud after we’d been silent for a while. Chris wore his signature hat while I wore my Long Rhodes Ahead t-shirt. I’d swapped out my designer brands for rescue branded clothes.

It was a beautiful evening with the sky turning shades of pink, purple, and blue as the sun set in the west. The stomp of the hooves against the soft earth was rhythmic to my ears. Chris was still quiet, and I looked over but couldn’t see his expression. Rex walked along side us without a leash. He’d become an amazing farm dog and didn’t leave our side. He sniffed at everything as we went.

We got to the highest part of the property where the cows were fenced, and I saw there was a picnic set up.

“Aw, Chris, this is so sweet. I didn’t realize you were doing this!”

He looked over and smiled shyly at me as he got down from Jasper then came to assist me. He didn’t need to help me since I’d become a pro at it, but I let him. We sat down on the red and white checkered tablecloth, and he opened the brown wicker basket. From it he pulled sandwiches, chips, and root beer.

After we finished eating, I leaned back into Chris’s arms, and he drew circles on my thighs. Rex finally settled at our feet while the horses grazed. The wind picked up and it was a warmer breeze.

"You've been quiet," I said softly, not wanting to disturb too much.

I felt his lips press into my neck making me shiver. "Just a lot on my mind."

I turned my head to look up at him and finally could see his eyes behind the brim of his hat. "What is it?"

He looked back to the picnic basket. "Open it."

I frowned as I leaned forward to do just that. There in the bottom of the basket was a box. A *ring* box.

My heart thudded hard in my chest as I reached for it then turned to fully look at him, holding the box in my hands. "Chris…what's this?"

He sat up and turned to look at me seriously. "I've loved you for a long time, Monica. I thought from the moment I met you when we were in high school that I would marry you one day. And I keep my promises."

I felt my heart leaping now, wanting to burst through my chest to be next to his.

"Will you marry me, Monica Locklear?"

"Yes." I didn't hesitate as I kissed him, the ring box in my shaky hands. When we both pulled back breathless, he took the box from me and opened it, displaying a beautiful silver ring with a big diamond in the center.

Old fancy Monica was drooling inside.

He slipped the ring on my finger, and I swooned at it there.

"You know, I never did get car insurance," I said, looking at him.

He laughed loudly, startling Rex. "Don't worry, I'll have you make it up to me one day." He pulled me back into his arms. I leaned in and put my hand up to stare at the ring. It looked amazing and as my eyes adjusted beyond my hand, I saw a sparrow sitting on a fence post, looking at us.

"Thanks, Grandma," I whispered.

"What was that?"

"Oh, nothing. Just thinking about the future."

He nuzzled my neck again and wrapped his arms tighter around me. "Good, because you're my future."

Trigger Warning List

- Underage drinking (on paper)
- Drunk driving that results in car accident (on paper and talked about)
- Amputation of leg
- Animal abuse and hoarding situation (talked about)
- Animal death (talked about)

Author's Note

Wow! This was a long time coming. Ever since Monica walked into Emma and Sam's engagement dinner, I knew she was going to have her own story. She has been one of my favorite characters since the beginning. I hope you've enjoyed reading their book as much as I did writing it!

Towards the end of completing WTDTYAF, it was harder for me to continue because we were seeing a slow decline of our dog, Tango. If you read my young adult dragon books, you may have seen an actual picture of our Pitbull pup. I always called him our "first baby" because he was the center of our life until our baby girl was born. Tango was a rescue from an amazing place called Speranza. My husband volunteered there for a little while and fell in love with Tango. He was the best dog we could have ever asked for. Except we thought we'd have more years with him. It was disappointing knowing that our daughter wouldn't get to grow up with such an amazing dog. We laid him to rest on November 20th, 2024. It was one of the hardest days of our life, but we knew it was time. Having an animal is the best thing but it is heartbreaking when it ends. They are a part of your soul, your life. They leave a mark on you forever. Even when you get another dog, you never truly forgot the ones who came before.

There are so many animal rescues that deserve attention for what they do. All the hard work and energy and money that goes into it. I hope that I reflected some of what they do in this book.

Your author friend,
JK Weyant

Acknowledgements

First and foremost, thank you to my mom for ALWAYS helping me, supporting me, and editing. I wouldn't have been able to get as far as I have without you.

Thank you to my husband, Dan, for dealing with my late-night writing and for always supporting my dream of being an author. Your comment "is this about dogs? I may read it" definitely made me chuckle. Also, thank you for letting me bounce ideas off you and answering all my weird questions. Thank you to my mother-in-law, Jeanne, for helping me with amputation questions that were probably a little odd until I explained why!

Thank you to my beta readers: Lynzie, Kristin, Emma, Sarah, and Sharon. Your input was greatly appreciated!

A big shout out to Rachel who was my horse girl and gave me lots of great feedback and made sure I was using the right terminology! Thank you for responding to all my annoying messages asking you about certain things and making sure everything sounded right.

Again, thank you to everyone who has supported me through the last few years with my writing. Your kind words and encouragement help push me to continue to write. I hope you've enjoyed WTDTYAF and look out for some more books from me soon!

About the Author

J.K.Weyant is an independent author who has been writing since she was thirteen years old. With encouragement from family, friends, and her husband, she made the jump to self-publish. J.K. Weyant has a love for fantasy and romance novels and a way to travel wherever she wants with just reading words from a book. She hopes she can bring laughter, joy and adventure to all who reads her stories.

If you enjoyed my book, please share with friends and family to get the word out! You can also follow me on Instagram and Facebook for updates on book releases and other news. Or you can join my newsletter chain!
https://www.facebook.comJK-Weyant-104865088842555
https://www.instagram.com/jkweyantauthor82/
jkweyantauthor@gmail.com

www.ingramcontent.com/pod-product-compliance
Lightning Source LLC
LaVergne TN
LVHW020520100826
845148LV00010B/1299